'An encounter that will take readers into the darkest recesses of the human psyche' – *Crime Time*

'Well written and chock full of surprises, this hard-hitting, edge-of-the-seat instalment is yet another treat… Geraldine Steel looks set to become a household name. Highly recommended' – *Euro Crime*

'Good, old-fashioned, heart-hammering police thriller… a no-frills delivery of pure excitement' – *SAGA Magazine*

'*Cut Short* is not a comfortable read, but it is a compelling and important one. Highly recommended' – *Mystery Women*

'A gritty and totally addictive novel' – *New York Journal of Books*

D0321261

Also by Leigh Russell

Geraldine Steel Mysteries
Cut Short
Road Closed
Dead End
Death Bed
Stop Dead
Fatal Act
Killer Plan
Murder Ring
Deadly Alibi
Class Murder
Death Rope

Ian Peterson Murder Investigations
Cold Sacrifice
Race to Death
Blood Axe

Lucy Hall Mystery
Journey to Death
Girl in Danger
The Wrong Suspect

LEIGH RUSSELL

ROGUE KILLER

A GERALDINE STEEL MYSTERY

NO EXIT PRESS

First published in 2019 by No Exit Press,
an imprint of Oldcastle Books Ltd,
PO Box 394, Harpenden,
Herts, AL5 1XJ, UK
noexit.co.uk
@noexitpress

ISBN
978-1-84344-938-6 (Print)
978-1-84344-939-3 (Epub)

2 4 6 8 10 9 7 5 3 1

Typeset in 11.25pt Times New Roman
by Avocet Typeset, Somerton, Somerset, TA11 6RT
Printed and bound by Clays Ltd, Elcograf S.p.A.

To
Michael, Jo, Phillipa, Phil, Rian, and Kezia
With my love

Prologue

There was so much blood. The dead man's clothes were saturated, his hands sticky. Blood lodged under his fingernails and fixed in the creases of his skin. By contrast, the gloves absorbed nothing, allowing the blood to slide around easily with a satisfying oily smoothness.

Not far away a car horn beeped.

With a sudden sense of urgency, hands that had moved with such assurance a moment ago now fumbled to remove gloves slippery with blood, peeling them delicately across palms and down the fingers to avoid the wet surfaces touching any skin. Stepping carefully across an inert trickle of blood, the killer strode away from the alley, leaving behind a heap of flesh and sodden fabric.

A solitary car disappeared round a corner, leaving the street deserted.

1

STRIDING HOME THROUGH THE dark streets of York with a bloody plastic cape and rubber gloves concealed inside a polythene bag in his rucksack, he congratulated himself on a successful outing. He had come a long way since leaving the house where he had spent his unhappy childhood. He had done his best, but even then he had known that the cats he killed had been paving the way for other victims. At that time he had been forced to suffocate his victims, as he couldn't return home covered in blood. Because the most annoying aspect of his life back then was that whenever he flung himself through the front door, bag on his back and blond fringe flopping over his forehead, his parents would be there, waiting…

He turned away from his parents, refusing to look at them, certain they would crush his excitement. Glancing up, he gave a defiant smile at his father's reflection frowning at him in the mirror. If they persisted in worrying about him when he stayed out late, that was their problem. It wasn't fair of them to spoil his fun.

He had given up insisting that it was his life to live as he pleased. Instead he had resolved to ignore them. In any case, they didn't know the half of it. He took risks they knew nothing about. But the pay-off was worth all the preparation. His parents would never understand. No one would. In their small-minded way, people like them would assume he was driven by a sordid sexual urge, but nothing could be further from the truth. More intense than anything they could imagine, his pleasure was momentous; he had learned to exercise power over life itself. Compared to the triumph of a kill, all other experiences were petty.

Despite all their questions, he never told them where he was going or who he was seeing. For a long time he had simply told them he was meeting his 'mates'. They didn't need to know more than that.

'Have you any idea what time it is?' his father asked severely.

When he didn't answer, his mother spoke, her voice shrill with anxiety.

'You know it's nearly two o'clock. Where have you been? One night you're going to get yourself in trouble. You could be attacked, and left for dead in a gutter, and we'd know nothing about it until the police knocked on the door to tell us you'd been killed. You have to come home at a sensible time. You'll be the death of us with all this staying out late. We need to get to bed –'

'Oh, give it a rest, will you? If you want to go to bed, who's stopping you? Did I ask you to wait up for me? What's your problem? Nothing's going to happen to me.'

Even though he was not quite sixteen, he hated the way they made him sound like a petulant teenager. He was so much more than that: a master of life and death.

'You can't say that,' she replied.

'Well, I just did.'

'Don't be flippant with us, son,' his father snapped. 'The point is, however independent you think you are, you don't know what might happen to you. No one does. A youngster like you, out on the streets on your own, you've no idea who might be out there, and what they might be after. People get assaulted, and young boys are especially vulnerable.'

They had been through the argument many times without reaching a resolution, but his parents refused to give up.

Forcing a smile, his father said, 'Why don't you at least let me come and pick you up, when you want to stay out late?'

'You're having a laugh. You? Come and pick me up? Not bloody likely. You'd spoil everything.'

'Well, I could come and meet you somewhere then, if you like. Jesus, you must know you're putting yourself at risk going out on your own at night. You're only fifteen, and you don't know anything of the world yet. Why don't you at least tell me where you are, so I can come and give you a lift home? For your mother's sake, if nothing else. You know she worries about you being mugged.'

'What if one of these muggers you're so worried about attacked *you*?' He spat the words out. He wasn't laughing now. 'You're just as likely to be mugged as me, you know. Now, stop pestering me, because I told you nothing's going to happen. Not to me, anyway.' He turned away to hang up his coat. 'I know what you're trying to do,' he resumed, turning back to face them. 'It's not going to work. You don't own me. I'm not a child. You can't control me anymore.'

Seeing his father cower backwards when he lifted his hand to pull off his scarf, he grinned, his good humour restored.

'You thought I was going to hit you just then! You did, didn't you? And you think *you* can scare *me*! Ha!'

He snapped his fingers in the air with a faint click. His mother stepped forward, one hand raised, but he stood his ground, taunting her.

'What are you going to do? Hit me? That's why you go on and on and on about something happening to me, because that's what you want, to see me punished. You'd like me to suffer, just to prove you were right.'

'Don't talk such nonsense. You know that's not true.'

'Isn't it?' He held out his arm to display a series of scratches. 'What's this then?'

His father shook his head in disgust. 'You know perfectly well you told us a cat scratched you. Now, I'll ask you again, where have you been all this time?'

'Oh, give it a rest, old man. Have you got any idea how stupid you sound, asking the same questions, over and over again?'

With a flick of his head he tossed their sour protests aside, and his long fringe spun around his head. He stroked it into place with the flat of his hand, enjoying the feel of its sleek softness. Until he was old enough to do as he pleased, his parents had never allowed him to grow his hair long enough to cover his ears. That was just one of many reasons why he hated them. As though it should be up to them to control his appearance! Now they had lost their authority over him, they were nothing in his eyes. Less than nothing.

He understood their efforts to confine him were driven by anxiety, but he was different from them. He was fearless. Ordinary people like his parents could have no idea what he was capable of achieving. They didn't know him at all. No one did. They were never going to understand that there was no need to be concerned on his account. They should be worrying about their own safety while he was living under their roof.

2

'IT'S SO DULL AROUND here,' Ariadne grumbled. 'Not that I'm complaining,' she added with a slightly embarrassed laugh, 'but you know what I mean.' She lowered eyes as dark and impenetrable as Geraldine's.

'I know *exactly* what you mean,' Geraldine said.

Neither of them admitted out loud that they had chosen to work in serious crime to avoid sitting behind a desk. Of course no one was pleased to hear that an innocent victim had been killed, but the job could be tedious when they weren't working on a murder case. What made the time pass even more slowly for Geraldine was that she didn't know anyone in York outside of her work colleagues. Her lifestyle had changed significantly over the course of the past year. Demoted from the rank of detective inspector in the London Metropolitan Police force, she had relocated to York where she now worked as a detective sergeant. Only her unswerving commitment to her work had sustained her throughout what had been a very difficult year. Now, for a change, her work life had been quiet for a couple of months, allowing her to relax and enjoy exploring the city of York, and get to know her colleagues.

To some extent, she and Ariadne had been thrown together as their desks stood opposite one another. Whenever Geraldine glanced up, she saw her colleague's dark head lowered over her desk. Sometimes they both looked up at the same time, and exchanged smiles. Geraldine was pleased to have made a new friend at work. In her mid-thirties, Ariadne was only a few years younger than Geraldine, and they were both single. They even looked vaguely similar, with dark hair and eyes, although Geraldine wore her hair short while Ariadne's glossy curls touched her shoulders. Sometimes they went out together for an evening, but when they weren't occupied with an investigation, Geraldine's weekends were usually spent visiting family. Although these were social calls, she spent more time on the road than anywhere else, driving all the way to London to see her identical twin, and even further to Kent to visit her adopted sister.

Geraldine was used to batting away antagonism. With years of experience, it wasn't difficult to distance herself from extreme animosity, which she understood was directed against her office as a detective sergeant working in a serious crime unit, and not personal. Yet somehow, where her twin sister was concerned, she struggled to keep her emotions under control. It disturbed her to know how easily Helena could upset her. Apart from their physical similarity, they couldn't have been less alike. Geraldine had spent her adult life in the service of justice. The identical twin she had only recently met was a recovering heroin addict, involved in petty crime of one kind or another for longer than Geraldine had been a police officer.

Geraldine was startled when Ariadne interrupted her musings to ask whether she wanted to take a break and go for a coffee.

'Sorry if I disturbed you, but you can't think about work all the time,' Ariadne added, laughing, and Geraldine gave a guilty smile because she hadn't been thinking about work, but about her twin sister.

They were sipping coffee and Geraldine was listening to Ariadne describe the Greek island where her mother had grown up, when they were summoned to the major incident room. They glanced wordlessly at one another, aware that so peremptory a summons most likely signified a murder on their patch. Moments after they arrived, the detective chief inspector strode in. Eileen Duncan was a broad-shouldered, forceful woman. Sharp features in her square face were framed by dark hair that was turning grey. She gazed around at the assembled team with a faintly aggressive expression that Geraldine suspected masked an underlying anxiety. The mood in the room was sombre, and everyone fell silent as Eileen spoke.

'A body was discovered early this morning in Pope's Head Alley, one of the snickelways.'

'Snickelways are narrow alleyways,' Ariadne whispered. 'You'll find them all over town.'

Geraldine grunted in response. Having lived in York for nearly six months, she had studied the local area and its history, and was familiar with the network of narrow passageways that criss-crossed the city streets.

'It's one of the oldest snickelways in the city,' another sergeant murmured, as though that somehow made the murder more heinous.

'We've closed it off at both ends, but there's not much room to manoeuvre along there. It's less than a metre wide.'

They all listened intently as the detective chief inspector went on to give details of the site where the body had been found, in a passageway running between Peter Lane and High Ousegate.

'Check your tasks with the duty sergeant and keep everyone updated with anything you discover. We need to find out what happened, and quickly.' With that exhortation, the detective chief inspector swept out of the room.

'Let's hope this one's over and done with soon,' Geraldine muttered. 'I've got a holiday booked next month.'

'You can still go away if you've booked the time off,' Ariadne said.

Geraldine didn't answer but she knew that once she was involved in a murder investigation she could never walk away, not even for a day, let alone two weeks.

She had mixed feelings when she saw that she would be

working with her ex-colleague, Ian Peterson. They knew one another well, having worked together in the past when she had been an inspector and Ian had been her sergeant. Now their roles had been reversed, thanks to his advancement and her own demotion. At times she struggled to remember that he was her senior officer. She wasn't sure whether he sometimes came across as bombastic because he also found the situation awkward, and felt the need to assert his authority over her. It was equally possible that he had become more authoritarian with everyone as he moved up the career ladder.

Whatever the reason for the change in his attitude towards her, she had come to terms with her disappointment at the reception he had given her on her arrival in York, and the realisation that she had evidently valued their friendship more than he did. While not unfriendly, he had hardly greeted her arrival with the enthusiasm she had been foolish enough to anticipate. She told herself that beyond her hurt ego she didn't really care. But however hard she tried to suppress her feelings, she knew that Ian mattered to her, perhaps more than any other man she had ever met.

Pulling on protective shoes, she passed through the cordon at the end of Pope's Head Alley and entered the narrow passageway behind Ian. It was enclosed on both sides by high brick walls, almost like a tunnel, except that it was open to the sky. As they turned a corner, a couple of uniformed officers stood aside to let them through. There was barely enough room to squeeze past them.

'It's just up there, towards High Ousegate,' one of the constables said.

Geraldine followed Ian across the plastic stepping plates of the common approach path lining the passageway, until they reached the site.

She noticed the blood first. Camouflaged on red-brick walls enclosing the snickelway, the scarlet runnels were startlingly brilliant against grey paving stones on the ground. As she looked down at the dead man, the high walls seemed to close in on her and the scene took on a dreamlike quality. A dark puddle had pooled beside the dead man's head. Nothing about the shape or colouring of the body looked even vaguely human. Only the short mousy hair, crusty with dried blood, indicated that the hump of clothes at her feet had once been a person.

For a few seconds she stood perfectly still, taking in every detail of the scene. The crime team who were on their way would struggle to work in such a confined space, photographing the body and searching every centimetre of the passageway for evidence, but for now the time was hers. High Ousegate was closer than Peter Lane, and from the position of the body she thought the dead man had probably entered the alleyway from the Peter Lane end. The cause of death wasn't immediately obvious, although the blood indicated he had been stabbed.

The silence was disturbed by a faint cacophony that grew in volume behind her. Two white-coated scene of crime officers appeared around the bend in the snickelway.

'Let's get out of here,' Ian said.

Geraldine nodded. There was barely room for her and Ian to stand side by side against the wall. Two more white-coated officers appeared in front of them, on the far side of the body. They manoeuvred their way past the officers waiting behind them and returned to Peter Lane.

'Phew,' Geraldine said as they emerged back on to the street. 'That was tight.'

'And bloody,' Ian muttered.

Peter Lane was busier than it had been when they arrived. People were hurrying past on their way to work, most of them barely glancing at the cordon across the lane. As she entered the bustling street, Geraldine felt as though she was waking from a nightmare.

They drove back to the police station in silence. Without evidence there was nothing useful to discuss, only speculation. Once they knew the identity of the victim, and the details of his violent death, they would be in a position to consider what had happened. If they had witnessed the victim of a mugging, as seemed probable, they could only hope the killer had left clear traces of DNA behind, enabling them to find a match straightaway.

'That was a vicious attack,' Ian said as they drew up in the police station car park. He shuddered. 'Let's hope we get him quickly.'

'Or her,' Geraldine replied.

Ian frowned. 'That seems unlikely but, either way, we don't want a violent psychopath loose in the city.'

Geraldine didn't say what she suspected they were both thinking. They were responsible for protecting the innocent, and if this was not a one-off crime of passion but a random assault, other innocent lives might be at risk. The many alleyways that criss-crossed the city of York were quaint and historically interesting. She hoped they had not become a hunting ground for a dangerous killer.

3

AFTER A HURRIED LUNCH in the canteen, Geraldine attended a briefing. Not all of her colleagues were there when she reached the incident room, and the detective chief inspector, Eileen Duncan, had not yet arrived. A young constable, Naomi, was whispering to Ian, so Geraldine walked past them to join Ariadne who was standing by herself at the side of the room. They had barely had time to exchange a greeting when Eileen entered. Striding past them all, she made her way to the front of the room where she stood looking around at the assembled team.

'It seems we're looking at a street crime that went too far,' she said. 'We all know about the spate of attacks that have been happening recently. There have been several accounts of victims being threatened with a knife in the course of a mugging and there's nothing to suggest this was anything other than an unfortunate victim who tried to resist an approach from this criminal gang. With the increase in violent assaults on the streets, this was a fatality waiting to happen. We need to find this gang of muggers and put a stop to them before things escalate any further.'

Geraldine wasn't sure how much further the situation could escalate, considering the latest stabbing had been fatal, but she understood what the detective chief inspector meant. The past few months had seen a series of muggings in York. Witness reports suggested that a gang of youths armed with knives was responsible, but so far no one had been apprehended. The police hadn't even identified any suspects. But then, none of the victims had been murdered until now. This death catapulted the situation from an investigation into street muggings into a completely different league. The Major Crimes Unit was involved, with access to vastly enhanced resources.

'We're not going to let the grass grow under our feet,' Eileen said, as though the team previously investigating the muggings had been idle. 'It looks as though the mugger was disturbed, because the victim wasn't robbed this time. He still had his phone and his wallet on him, and they were easy to find in the pockets of his jeans. So at least we know who *he* is.'

The victim was a thirty-two-year-old history teacher who had lived in York with his wife. Nothing in his life so far had linked him to any criminal activity. Everything about him indicated that he had been an innocent victim. But of course they all knew that appearances could mask a very different reality.

'So are you saying you don't think the attacker intended to kill his victim, and ran off in a panic when he realised what he had done?' Ariadne suggested.

There was a general murmur of agreement.

'Or perhaps this wasn't a mugging at all,' Geraldine added softly.

'There's nothing so far to suggest this was anything other than a mugging gone wrong,' Eileen replied, a little too firmly.

Geraldine hesitated to challenge her superior officer, but the absence of footprints leading away from the scene bothered her.

'The ground around the body was so bloody,' she said. 'I just don't see how someone running off in a panic could have quit the scene without leaving a single footprint.' She frowned. 'He must have – oh, I don't know – changed his shoes before he left the scene? And that doesn't sound like someone in a panic to get away.'

'It's hardly likely he would have stopped to change his shoes,' Eileen agreed.

'Not if it was a mugger,' Geraldine said. 'But what if that wasn't what happened? What if this victim was deliberately targeted in a carefully planned attack?'

'You're suggesting this was murder?' Eileen asked, her tone tinged with hostility.

Geraldine shrugged. 'I'm raising the possibility because it just doesn't look like an opportunistic mugging.'

Eileen didn't disagree but merely concluded that they needed more information. In the meantime, knowing the victim's identity gave them plenty to do.

'And there's the knife to follow up. We know a great deal about it already.'

The assembled officers nodded at one another. A couple of constables muttered under their breath. All of them had read the report. Microscopic fragments of metal had been detected in the victim's throat, indicating that the blade had been recently sharpened.

'And we have a DNA sample on the victim's sleeve where it might have brushed against the killer. So let's get going. We have a lot to do,' Eileen said. 'We need to put an end to all this.'

Eileen was clinging to the theory that they were investigating a mugging that had got out of hand, but Geraldine couldn't help thinking the killer's departure from the scene had been too slick for an accidental killing. There was nothing to be gained by challenging the detective chief inspector's opinion again without further grounds so, for the time being, Geraldine decided to wait and see how the evidence panned out.

The duty sergeant allocated tasks and Geraldine set off to speak to the pathologist who was conducting the post mortem. Had her long-standing friend and colleague, Ian, not been squeamish at post mortems, he might have accompanied her. As it was, she didn't mind going to view the body alone. She sometimes wondered at her own indifference to corpses, but it was the living who disturbed her, not the dead who were past suffering and pain. Besides, there was a practical reason for attending post mortems since murder victims could provide crucial evidence about their killers.

'One stab wound,' the pathologist, Jonah Hetherington, said without pausing to greet her as she entered the room.

His calm fascination with cadavers made her feel less uncomfortable with her own dispassionate response to the dead.

'It's a neat job,' he went on, almost as though he admired the killer's handiwork. 'The killer appears to be skilled at using a knife. Someone who doesn't know what they're doing is more likely to end up with a gory mess.'

'There was a lot of blood at the scene.'

'Even so, the wound is quite neat.'

'Are you saying you think the killer was a professional?'

'You mean, a hired killer?'

'Well, no. I meant, do you think he was killed by someone used to wielding a knife? A butcher, or a surgeon perhaps?'

Jonah chuckled. 'Or a pathologist?'

She returned his smile.

'No,' he shook his head, serious once more. 'All I can say is that this was a deft incision, but I don't think we can draw any useful conclusions from the nature of the wound. It could have been luck that the first strike proved fatal.'

'Not very lucky for him,' Geraldine muttered, nodding at the body.

'Well, no. Not lucky for him, except that he probably wouldn't have known much about it. Bleeding profusely and unable to breathe, he would have lost consciousness fairly quickly. The neck was sliced through, severing the carotid artery and the windpipe with one slash of a sharp blade.'

'Like I said, there was a lot of blood.'

Jonah grunted. 'Yes, I saw the pictures.'

'Which surely makes it unlikely an opportunistic assailant would have left the scene without a trace.'

Jonah raised his eyebrows. 'Do you mean to say there wasn't

a trail of bloody footprints leading to the villain's hideout?'

Geraldine laughed. 'What else can you tell us about the killer?'

'You want a description?'

'That would be good for starters. And how about his name and address while we're at it?' She laughed again. 'But seriously, is there anything you can tell us? Anything definite? Anything likely? Anything even vaguely possible…' She stared gloomily at the body. 'There don't seem to be any defence wounds.'

'No, you're right. Just the one wound that killed him pretty quickly.'

'Isn't that unusual in a mugging? Wouldn't you expect him to have tried to fight back?'

'If the victim had been sober the absence of defence wounds would suggest he was taken by surprise, but our man here had been drinking so heavily it's hard to say whether he knew what was happening or not. The killer could have taken his time over it, his victim was so pissed. He was killed around midnight, and my guess is he'd been drinking all evening, on an otherwise fairly empty stomach. The killer attacked suddenly, with one lunge, and I'd say the poor bloke was dead before he even realised what had hit him.'

Geraldine frowned, picturing the white lump of flesh on the table clothed and making his way along the snickelway, so drunk he was barely able to put one foot in front of the other. Staggering and swaying, maybe whistling as he made his way unsteadily along the lane, he encountered a shadowy figure. As the two of them attempted to manoeuvre their way past one another in the narrow space, the stranger whipped out a knife, took aim and slashed. It would have been over in seconds.

'Do you think it was a man? A woman?'

Again Jonah shook his head. 'Nothing about the attack to suggest the gender of the assailant.'

'Forensics have come up with DNA that might be helpful,' she said.

Jonah looked up and smiled. 'Now she tells me.' But of course he already knew about the DNA. 'So what else have you been hiding from me?'

'Other than that we're looking for a Caucasian male, we're still working in the dark. The killer seems to have vanished without leaving a trace.'

'Isn't that unusual?'

She drew in a deep breath. 'It might suggest that this wasn't just a stray strike in a mugging, but the result of a more carefully planned attack.'

'That sounds like bad news.'

'It's just my opinion. A hunch, if you like. Don't quote me on it. The boss is convinced this was a mugging that went badly wrong. Don't let on that I have a different theory.'

Jonah nodded. 'Silent as the grave.'

'Is there anything else you've noticed that might be at all helpful?'

He sighed. 'I'm not a wizard, Geraldine. You know all about the fragments of metal we found embedded in his throat?'

'Yes. Meaning the knife had recently been sharpened.'

'It was certainly sharp. The blade sliced very neatly through his windpipe. But I'm not telling you anything new.'

'Well, if you come across anything else, just call me.'

Returning to her desk she wrote up her report as factually as possible, saying nothing about her disappointment with Jonah's inconclusive findings, then went to find Ian to express her frustration aloud.

'I don't see why you're so bugged. The post mortem has confirmed what we already knew,' Ian said. 'The victim was drunk as a lord, and killed with one slash of his throat. Tolerate street muggings, and sooner or later something like this is bound to happen. That's why we have to redouble our efforts to put a stop to it.'

Like Eileen, he believed this death had been the result of a mugging that had gone too far.

'There are things about this incident that just don't add up,' Geraldine insisted. 'This wasn't a mugging gone wrong. There's something else going on here.'

'Why? Because the victim wasn't robbed?'

'Yes, that's part of it. But there's more to it than that. Why did the mugger disappear without leaving a trace? How come there wasn't a single bloody footprint leaving the scene?'

'He could have taken his shoes off when he realised he'd stepped in blood and was going to leave a trail of footprints leading back to his house. All that tells us is that he wasn't a complete idiot, more's the pity. It makes life more difficult for us, but there's nothing more to it than that.'

'It could mean this attack was deliberate.'

'I think you're reading more into it than the evidence warrants.'

There was no point in continuing the discussion. Only hard proof could establish what had really occurred that night, but so far all the evidence was inconclusive. They would have to wait for the results of the forensic examination of the scene and hope it could provide them with some helpful information.

4

'THE POINT IS, THE fucking point is –' Daryl broke off to take a swig of tepid beer.

He tipped his head right back and light from the naked bulb shone on his pale forehead as he straightened up. He was clutching the bottle so tightly the dints in his knuckle bones were visible.

'The point is?' Carver repeated, fingers tapping impatiently on his thigh while his face grew taut with unspoken menace.

At nineteen, and the oldest of the three boys, he was sprawled in the only comfortable seat in the garage, an armchair upholstered in faded red velvet, threadbare yet retaining a vestige of past opulence. As though to remind the others of the reason for his nickname, he took out the knife that was said to have killed a man. Daryl made a show of studying the label on his beer bottle, but Carver knew the younger boy was watching the blade as it flicked in and out, in and out, with a barely audible clicking.

Daryl's hand shook as he leaned forward to set his bottle down on the floor. A solitary bead of sweat trickled down his forehead. His eyes darted around the sparsely furnished garage, seeking inspiration. His gaze lingered for a second or two on the dirty boards nailed over the window, before it alighted on the third boy in the room. Squatting on the floor, Nelson turned away and spat, refusing to answer Daryl's mute plea.

'The point?' Carver prompted him again, holding up his knife and touching the tip of the sharpened blade with one finger. 'What is your point, Daryl?' He leaned forward. 'What is the point of *you*, Daryl?' Proud of his pun, he repeated it, his teeth bared in a grin.

'The point is, they're gonna think it was us shivved that dude.'

Carver laid his knife down on his leg, the blade pointing towards Daryl. The handle gleamed darkly.

'What you talking about? You off your face? Who's gonna think it was us?'

'The pigs, man.' Daryl glared, giving up the attempt to conceal his agitation. 'They been looking for us. I seen it on the news, man. A gang of muggers they called us. I heard it with my own ears, man. They're out there looking for us.'

'They haven't found us yet,' Nelson pointed out complacently, without turning round.

Carver paid no attention to the interruption. This was between him and Daryl.

'And now some dude's been shivved,' Daryl went on, his terror of Carver momentarily overtaken by fear of the police. 'They're gonna think it was us done it. A street mugging gone wrong is what they said. I'm telling you, if we get nicked, they're gonna do us for killing that stiff.'

'They can't pin it on us without any evidence,' Nelson said, drawing out the final sound in a hiss.

Daryl shook his head, while a snarl of laughter rumbled up from somewhere deep in his guts.

'They can pin anything they want on guys like us,' he said. 'And I'm telling you, they're gonna be like dogs on heat trying to pin that murder on someone. You think we can slug it out with the pigs? We're the obvious scapegoats. They've got to nail this crime on someone and who's gonna leap to defend us? Think about it. The dude croaked. They don't give a shit that it wasn't one of us done for him.'

'Who says it wasn't one of us?' Carver said.

He picked up his knife and began flicking the blade again, in and out, in and out, a slick well-oiled weapon. Three pairs of eyes stared at the moving sliver of metal.

'The dude's dead,' Daryl persisted. 'I seen it –'

'Yeah, yeah, you seen it on the news. And they're saying it was us done for him.' Carver grinned. 'That means we're big news, man. Everyone's gonna know about us.'

'That means they're gonna be hunting for us, man,' Daryl cried out, losing his grip on the last vestiges of his self-control.

'Don't talk shit,' Carver growled. 'You'd best shut your face unless you wanna seriously piss me off.'

Daryl subsided, grumbling under his breath.

Without stirring from his seat or raising his voice, Carver seemed to swell to fill the space between them. 'What's that you say, boy? If you lost your nerve, you just come out with it right now.'

'Nothing,' Daryl mumbled. 'I didn't say nothing.'

Nelson flapped his elbows, clucking and sniggering.

Lifting his bottle to his lips, Daryl watched Carver through narrowed eyelids.

Nelson rose to his feet in one lithe movement. 'We run out of booze.' The other two boys ignored him. 'And we run out of fags.' He stretched his skinny legs.

'Where do you think you're going?' Carver asked, his eyes still fixed on Daryl.

'I told you, bro. We run out of fags.'

Carver's eyes didn't move. 'Sit down.'

'I'm dying for a smoke, man.'

For a moment Nelson held his ground. He knew he was useful, because he could fix almost anything. It was Nelson who had tapped into the electricity supply of a neighbouring property to give them a light overhead.

'I said, sit down.'

Nelson hesitated, nearly said something, then glanced at the switchblade in Carver's hand and complied. He crouched down, eyes on the floor, hands dangling between his skinny knees, eyebrows lowered in a scowl.

From outside came the noise of a car engine that revved and roared off down the road, while in the room the air grew heavy with silence. Somewhere far away a siren wailed. The three boys stiffened almost imperceptibly. For a few minutes no one stirred, then the faint clicking resumed, the blade slipping in and out, in and out. Daryl began to fidget, his gaze shifting from the stain on the carpet to the blade in Carver's hand, and back again.

At last Carver spoke. 'What now?'

Daryl shrugged without looking up. 'We wait till they pin that murder on some other fucker and we're cool.'

'I'm cool,' Carver turned to Nelson. 'You cool, blad?'

'I'm cool.'

'So what we gonna do, genius?' Carver asked.

'If you're asking me,' Daryl replied, with a burst of frantic animation, 'I'd say the best thing we can do is lay low for a while. No one's come after us yet. They don't know who we are. We just stay out of trouble until the heat dies down. It always does. So we only need to be patient and stay off the streets, out of sight, and as long as we hold our nerve –'

'I mean who's gonna get in the booze and fags.' Carver cut him off with a sneer. 'You're full of shit, man. Why don't you shut the fuck up? Lay low, stay off the streets, hold our nerve? What the fuck are you talking about? I swear you flap like a gash. Now, what I want to know is, who's gonna get me some fags? I could do with a smoke.'

He leaned back comfortably in his chair and closed his eyes, while a smile spread slowly across his broad face. The knife resumed flicking, in and out, in and out, clicking faintly in the silence, regular as a ticking bomb.

5

THE VICTIM HAD LIVED in a two-bedroomed terraced house just a short walk from the train station but, for the moment, it was understandable that his widow had chosen to go and stay with a sister in Heslington, a few miles away from the centre of town. Geraldine and Ian drew up outside an old house with a rambling rose growing up one brick wall. In the front garden the leaves of a gnarled tree bent almost double with age were dotted with waxy magnolia blooms. The idyllic setting was poor recompense for the morbid reason for their visit. They walked carefully along an uneven path to the front door which was opened almost at once by a harassed-looking woman. Still holding the edge of the door, she brushed an untidy strand of hair off her face with the back of her free hand.

'Mrs Jamieson?'

The woman frowned. 'What is it you want? Only I'm sorry, I'm very busy right now –'

For answer they displayed their identity cards, and she screwed up her eyes to scrutinise them, her face twisting in a frown at the sound of a small child wailing in the house behind her.

'This really isn't a good time –' she began again.

'Please, Mrs Jamieson,' Geraldine said gently, 'we really do need to speak to your sister, if she's here. We won't keep her long.'

The woman drew in a deep shuddering breath and shook her head. 'Well, you'd best come in then. You can speak to her, but I doubt you'll get much sense out of her. She's in a real state, which is hardly surprising. And I don't suppose you pestering her is going to help any.'

She led them into a front room where a dining table was littered with torn wrapping paper and toys, birthday cards and cake crumbs, and half eaten chocolate fingers.

'It was my youngest son's birthday yesterday,' she said apologetically. 'We decided to go ahead, even though... The children don't understand what's happened, and anyway it was too late to cancel everyone.'

She shrugged, embarrassed at having held a party on the day her brother-in-law's body had been discovered. Somewhere in the house a child could be heard whining.

'I'll go and find Ellie now. Please, sit down.'

She left the room and returned a few moments later with another woman trailing behind her.

'Ellie, these are the police officers I just told you about. I'm sorry,' she added, with an anxious glance at Geraldine, 'but I'd better go and see to my daughter before she gets hysterical.'

She withdrew, leaving her sister standing in the doorway. Slim and fair-haired, she would have been pretty had her face not been blotchy, her pale blue eyes swollen from crying.

'Come and sit down, Ellie.'

When the young widow didn't respond, Geraldine repeated her invitation, doing her best to speak firmly yet kindly.

'Ellie, we need to ask you a few questions,' Ian said.

'It's about Grant,' Geraldine added gently.

At her husband's name, the widow started and her eyes travelled uneasily from Geraldine to Ian and back again.

'You can't speak to Grant,' she said, her voice barely louder than a whisper. 'Grant is dead.' She began to shake, and tears slid down her cheeks. 'He's dead,' she repeated in a shaky voice.

'We're so sorry,' Geraldine said. 'We're sure you'd like to do whatever you can to help us find out who did this terrible thing.'

Ellie shuffled forwards into the room. Taking a seat, she stared at the table.

'I can't help you,' she said in a flat voice. 'I wasn't there. No one was there.' She raised one hand to her lips, stifling a sob. 'He was all by himself when...' Unable to control herself any longer, she broke down in tears, covering her face in her hands. 'He was a good man,' she mumbled through her fingers. 'What kind of monster would do something like that?' Lowering her hands, she glared at Geraldine, her eyes hardening with anger. 'Find out who did it. I want to look Grant's killer in the eye and – and –' Her emotions overwhelmed her again and she put her head in her hands and sobbed, rocking backwards and forwards on her chair.

Ian glanced helplessly at Geraldine, and they waited until the widow's crying fit subsided.

'Ellie,' Geraldine said, 'can you think of anyone who might have wanted to harm your husband?'

'No,' came the muffled response.

'Had he fallen out with anyone?'

Ellie's head jerked up and her red-rimmed eyes widened in surprise. 'What are you talking about?' She hiccupped. 'I thought – that is, they said – they told me he was mugged.'

Geraldine gave a cautious nod.

'So why are you asking about people arguing with him, wanting to harm him? I don't understand. Are you saying... What *are* you saying, exactly?' Her expression of surprise switched to anger, and her voice hardened with suspicion. 'Tell me what you mean.'

Geraldine spoke slowly. 'We're exploring the possibility that your husband's death may have been the result of a deliberate attempt on his life.'

'Deliberate? I don't know what you mean. Are you telling me Grant was murdered?'

'At this stage in our investigation we have to pursue every line of enquiry.'

Geraldine was aware that she was being evasive, but she was reluctant to say anything that might start the widow crying again. She didn't want to cause her any unnecessary distress, but they couldn't shy away from the truth indefinitely.

'We believe there's a chance your husband may have been murdered,' she said gently.

Ellie looked agitated. 'No, that's not true!' she burst out. 'No one would want to hurt Grant. You didn't know him, but he was a lovely man. A wonderful, kind man. No, what you're suggesting, it's just not possible. Everyone liked Grant.'

Clearly nothing Geraldine could say was going to persuade her to alter her opinion that her husband had been popular with everyone who had known him. Grant's wife had loved him, and if he had made any enemies she had been ignorant of their existence.

'Unless she was covering up something she knew,' Ian suggested as they walked away from the picturesque house. 'Maybe she was protecting someone?'

Geraldine shook her head. 'I don't think so. No, I believed her.'

Ian nodded. 'I'm sure you're right.'

Her face impassive, she was nevertheless pleased by his ready acquiescence. They had worked on many cases together and she was gratified to know he trusted her opinion.

Their next visit was to the school where the victim had taught history. It was closed for the weekend but the senior management, along with the members of the history department, had all agreed to attend a meeting with Ian and Geraldine. The head teacher had assured Ian that supporting the police in their investigation into Grant's murder would take priority over everything else for himself and his staff. As they drew into the car park, the head teacher himself emerged to greet them. A tall robust man in middle age, he led them into a staff room where half a dozen people were waiting for them. After they had introduced themselves, the two detectives set to work.

Dividing the victim's colleagues into two groups, they questioned the staff individually. It took a while, but no one raised any objections. On the contrary, everyone seemed keen to do whatever they could to help. The same picture emerged, regardless of who was being questioned. Grant Marcus had been an easy-going member of the history department, friendly and committed to his job. There was no sense that anyone was holding back out of reluctance to speak ill of the dead. All his colleagues had genuinely liked him, and enjoyed working with him. What was more, they all reported that he had been popular with the pupils as well.

'A little too popular,' the Head of History added, when Geraldine was questioning her about Grant.

'What do you mean?'

'Oh, never anything untoward. Grant wasn't like that.'

'Like what?'

The teacher looked flustered. 'I mean, he wouldn't have done anything inappropriate. He was happily married.'

'Was there any accusation of wrongdoing?'

'No, not really. It was just a silly fourth former who had a crush on him and pestered him for a while. We moved her to my set and she was peeved. She got her parents to kick up a fuss about it at first, but it all died down when they heard why we had moved her. It was no reflection on him.'

'When was that?'

'Last year.'

'Is she still in the school?'

'Yes, but nothing happened. I probably shouldn't have mentioned it.'

'Do you think she, or her parents, might have held a grudge against him?'

'I doubt it very much. Her parents were involved in all the discussions, and very supportive of our actions. In fact, they were both mortified by the girl's behaviour. And her history grades improved when she moved to my set – only because she was focusing on her work, not on her teacher,' she added quickly. 'There was never any hint that Grant hadn't acted properly or done a good job. He was an excellent teacher.' She sighed. 'We'll all miss him.'

'All the same, I'd like to see records of the incident.'

The headmaster handed over the pupil's file readily, reiterating the departmental head's assurances that nothing inappropriate had taken place, and summing up the general consensus, that the dead man had been conscientious and personable.

Ellie's assurance that Grant had no enemies was echoed by everyone who had known him. Not only that but, according to his sister-in-law, he had been in a steady relationship with his wife since they had met in their first year at university, and it had been the first serious romance for them both. There was little chance either of them had a jealous ex. It was looking as though their initial theory was correct after all, that Grant had unfortunately walked along Pope's Head Alley at the wrong time.

On the night Grant had been killed, he had gone out for a curry with the other members of the history department, one of whom was retiring at the end of the term. Other than one woman who been driving, they all admitted to having drunk quite a lot that evening. 'Rather too much, in fact,' one of them confessed. That explained why Grant had drunk so much on the night he was killed. After thanking the assembled staff for their time, Geraldine and Ian left. They had learned a lot about Grant, but were no nearer to discovering the identity of his killer.

6

A STUDY OF THE file the headmaster had given to Geraldine made the situation very clear. The basis of the pupil's complaint was that her history teacher had refused to give her individual coaching. He had agreed to see her with two other pupils for extra lessons at lunchtime, but she had wanted his undivided attention. When the girl's parents had complained he wasn't giving her the support she needed, he had passed the issue to his head of department who had promptly moved the girl out of his set and offered her a few individual sessions that the girl had failed to attend.

Facing Geraldine on Monday morning, the girl looked excited.

'Is this about Mr Marcus?' she asked.

'Yes. You liked him, didn't you?'

'Everyone liked him.'

'Why were you moved out of his history set?'

'What?' The girl blushed. 'Oh that. Yes, we had a bit of a thing.'

'Can you explain what you mean by that?'

The girl's eyes rolled and she began to fidget with her cuff. 'We liked each other, you know.' She giggled suddenly. 'Oh, all right, I'll tell you. I fancied the pants off him, and of course he fancied me too. But then Mrs Beer decided to split us up so she made me change set, and my parents backed her, so there was nothing Mr Marcus – Grant – and I could do about it. We were heartbroken, of course, and the other girls were really bitchy about it, but they were just jealous because of me and Mr – Grant, and then Freddy came along.'

'Freddy?'

'Yes, my boyfriend. And before you ask to see him, he's not here. He's left school. He's twenty. Well, nearly twenty.'

Her boyfriend's age was clearly something she liked to boast about. Taking the way the girl spoke about Grant, together with the absence of any evidence of wrongdoing, Geraldine was sure the school had been right to dismiss the girl's complaint against her teacher. Thanking the headmaster, she returned the file.

'Of course, if there's any possibility of any inappropriate conduct we would suspend a member of staff immediately pending investigation, but all we could discover here was that the teacher in question was, quite rightly, refusing to be alone with this girl.' He sighed. 'Teenage girls can be tricky around the young male teachers.'

Following that dead end, there was a surge of excitement at the police station when a familial match was reported for the DNA sample found at the crime scene. The connection led to Peter Drury, a convicted criminal who had died in prison three years before. Peter Drury had a brother called Jamie, and it seemed that he could be the killer they were looking for. Jamie had never been arrested, but they knew his identity. Finding him was now only a matter of time.

Peter and Jamie's mother was also dead. When Geraldine volunteered to question their father, who lived near Oxford, Eileen told her a local constable had already been despatched to question him discreetly, without revealing the reason for the police interest in his family. The team all felt as though they were holding their breath until the disappointing message reached them that both Mr Drury's sons were dead. His only daughter had drowned as a child over twenty years earlier, one of his sons had died in prison, and his other son had died in Australia or Thailand two years before. It was a severe blow to the morale of the team, who had all been quietly confident the killer had been found, but they had to accept that DNA matches weren't always completely reliable, and move on with the investigation.

Geraldine checked with the team of officers who had been searching CCTV footage for images of the victim approaching Pope's Head Alley, to see if anyone had been nearby when he had entered the passageway. One camera had recorded a figure walking along Peter Lane travelling in the direction of the snickelway at eleven forty on the night Grant was killed. Geraldine studied the grainy image of a man, staggering slightly as he made his way along the pavement. His face wasn't easy to distinguish, and forensic image enhancement had only enabled them to make a positive identification because the time he appeared fitted in with the time of the attack, so they concluded it must have been Grant.

'If this was TV, not only would the victim's identity have been obvious straightaway, but all the other images would have been magically enhanced to give us a clear view of a manageable pool of potential suspects to find and interview,' Ian grumbled.

'If only,' Geraldine agreed.

In real life, the film was of little use. There was no sign of anyone following the victim, which suggested the killer had entered Pope's Head Alley from the opposite end. High Ousegate had been busier than Peter Lane at that time of night, and several pedestrians had been caught on film passing along the street in the direction of Pope's Head Alley, but there was no camera directly facing the entrance to the snickelway so once again the footage was of limited use. Several indistinct figures who passed by one camera and didn't reappear later could have turned into the passageway but they might just as easily have entered a side street, a building, or a car, or even turned around and walked back in the opposite direction, away from Pope's Head Alley. Technical officers were working on different sections of film trying to isolate images and improve them, but they remained blurred. In the absence of any other evidence, this was a potentially crucial line of enquiry since any one of the passersby might have seen something helpful, if they could only be identified and tracked down for questioning. And one of them must be the killer.

With that in mind, Eileen was preparing an item to be broadcast on the local news, asking anyone who had been in the vicinity around the time of the attack to come forward. It was hard to believe, but the forensic team had come up with no evidence whatsoever, and it actually seemed that finding a chance eye witness was the best they could hope for.

'Do you still think this was a random unplanned attack?' Geraldine asked Ian. 'Even now we know the killer left nothing behind?'

He glanced up from his desk and sighed. 'It's our worst nightmare,' he replied. 'A lucky criminal.'

'Luck can only get you so far,' she replied. 'It can't hold out against tenacity and hard graft.'

She hoped she was right, but they both knew her words were empty rhetoric. The fact was they had no suspect, and no leads. The killer had struck and vanished without a trace.

'This doesn't seem unplanned to me,' she insisted.

Geraldine had arranged to see her twin sister in London that evening, but called to postpone her visit. Helena didn't work, so Geraldine could go and see her later in the week. Right now she wanted to speak to the woman who had discovered the body in the snickelway. Her twin remonstrated, but caved in readily enough when Geraldine promised to make it up to her. Geraldine knew there was need for her to do that, but she lived in fear of Helena reverting to her former drug habit and, well aware of that, Helena did what she could to make Geraldine feel guilty.

'I hate to let you down at the last minute like this,' Geraldine said, wary of succumbing to Helena's habitual moral blackmail, 'it's just that something's come up at work.'

'And of course that's got to be more important than seeing me.'

'You know I'd rather see you, but things are time sensitive in a murder investigation. The longer we leave it, the colder the trace becomes.'

'Oh yes, your all-important work. And the all-important investigation that would grind to a halt if you weren't there for one afternoon.'

Although Geraldine tried not to feel crushed, Helena had a knack of penetrating her defences. Of course Geraldine knew the police investigation would continue unhindered whether she was working on it or not, but she was stung by Helena's readiness to assume it was her ego that fuelled her desire to succeed. In fact her dedication to her work wasn't driven by vanity, but by the need to feel that what she did actually mattered.

'You know it's not that I don't want to see you,' Geraldine said, trying to conceal her annoyance. 'You must know by now that I care about you. I'm here for you, and I'm going to go on doing everything in my power to support you. I'll never let you down. But I have to show my commitment at work and make sure I keep my job.'

She stopped short of saying what they both knew, that she was paying Helena's bills in addition to her own, and living in London wasn't cheap. If she lost her job, it would affect them both. Eventually Helena tired of baiting her and ended the conversation, confident she had gained the moral advantage by excusing her sister for letting her down. Geraldine did her best to overlook Helena's machinations. Her twin had struggled to survive, growing up in poverty and succumbing early to drug addiction. In some ways she had proved stronger than Geraldine, the successful career woman. Certainly she had faced greater hardship in her life, and had done well to overcome her habit. But it was hard to forgive her efforts to take advantage of Geraldine, who was already unnecessarily generous towards her.

Banishing her family problems to the back of her mind, Geraldine turned her attention to her next task, which was to question the young woman who had stumbled on Grant's body. Still upset by her discovery, she had taken a few days off work to recover from her experience. A police officer had spoken to her shortly after she had found the body, but Geraldine was keen to find out whether she could add anything to her original statement. Witnesses were not always coherent immediately after so shocking a discovery and it was possible she might recall some detail that she had failed to mention the previous day.

A middle-aged woman opened the door to the house in Driffield where the girl lived with her parents.

'You've come to see Chrissie?' she asked.

Geraldine nodded, holding up her identity card.

The witness was in her early twenties, although she looked about thirteen. Wearing no make-up and dressed in jeans and a loose T-shirt, she smiled miserably as Geraldine joined her in a small living room.

'I know you've given us your statement,' Geraldine said as she sat down, 'and we're very grateful to you for your help. I just wanted to ask if you can remember anything else from yesterday morning? Anything at all?'

The girl shrugged her narrow shoulders. 'Do you know who did it?'

Geraldine didn't hesitate. 'We're following up several leads,' she fibbed, 'and we hope to make an arrest very soon.' That much, at least, was true. 'But anything you can tell us would be helpful. The slightest detail could be significant, however unimportant it may seem.'

'What else do you want to know?'

Gently, Geraldine prompted her to go over her statement once again, but the girl could add nothing to what she had already told them. As soon as she had seen the body, she had turned away and called the emergency services. She retained only a hazy memory of seeing blood everywhere, up the walls and pooled on the ground around a heap of blood-drenched clothes that blocked the walkway.

'I didn't even see his face,' she added. 'But the thought of it... that it was a dead body...' She broke off with a shudder.

Geraldine couldn't recall ever experiencing a similar reaction on seeing a corpse. Not for the first time, she wondered whether she was missing some common characteristic of humanity, because for her the dead prompted only a fierce longing to discover the truth, as though each corpse was a voice crying out for justice.

'It was horrible,' the girl resumed. 'It really grossed me out. I mean, like I said, I didn't actually see who it was, but just the idea that it was a dead body... I couldn't go near it...'

As she walked back to her car, Geraldine wondered what path her own life might have taken had she shared that girl's revulsion for the dead. If it had been less frustrating, it would probably also have been less challenging. Refusing to be downhearted at her lack of progress so far, she set off to visit Grant's neighbours and find out whether any of them could add to what the police knew about the dead man. But as before, she learned nothing useful. The neighbours on both sides of Grant's house, and over the road, reiterated what she had already heard. Grant and his wife had impressed everyone as a pleasant young couple, polite and friendly, and they had appeared very happy together.

'That poor young woman,' was a refrain Geraldine heard several times, along with assurances that Grant had been 'really nice'. The question, 'Who would do such a thing?' was repeated, in one form or another, by everyone she met.

Having spent the best part of the afternoon knocking on doors and talking to people living in the same street as the victim, Geraldine went home to her empty flat to write up her notes. With a glass of wine in her hand, she pored over all the documentation pertaining to the case, but it was pointless. The depressing truth was that there was no obvious suspect, and the killer had left no trace. Geraldine had no compelling reason to challenge the theory that Grant had chanced upon a mugger or, if not a mugger, an opportunistic psychopath seizing on a random victim. But she remained convinced that his death had been deliberately planned and executed by a killer who was all the more dangerous because he was cunning enough to evade detection.

7

THE MOOD AT THE police station was lively on Tuesday morning. Reasonably even-tempered as a rule, Geraldine had arrived feeling unusually despondent, but the cheerful banter among her colleagues soon dispelled her bad mood.

'Blinking muggers,' Ariadne complained as she sat down.

'Don't you worry, we'll sort them out,' a constable told her.

'They're just a bunch of kids,' someone else agreed. 'It won't take long to find them, not now we're on the case.'

'Brought your crystal ball to work then, have you?' someone called out.

'And when we get our hands on them, we ought to tan their backsides,' a sergeant close to retirement chipped in.

'You going to do it, grandad?' someone called out. 'Mind you don't strain yourself.'

'Kids these days, they're a bloody nightmare,' the sergeant said.

'Let's not tar all young people with the same brush –' Geraldine began.

'They're a spoiled generation,' her older colleague interrupted her. 'And God help anyone who says anything to upset them. We mustn't hurt their tender feelings. What about other people's feelings, that's what I want to know. Aren't we entitled to a little consideration for *our* tender feelings in our old age?'

'Nothing tender about you,' one of his colleagues replied. 'Tough as old boots, you are.'

'No one worries about having a go at *us*,' the sergeant

continued, ignoring the interruptions, 'or whether any criticism of us is justified or not. And most of the time it's a load of bull.'

'Fake news, fake news,' someone called out.

'Oh, stop complaining and get on with some work,' Ariadne said, giving the speaker a good-natured tap on the arm with a rolled-up paper.

'Just as well I'm not sixteen or I'd have had you for assault,' the sergeant laughed. 'Ow, ow! I think you've broken my arm.'

'Now you're confusing teenagers with footballers,' someone else said.

'Hey, less of that,' protested a constable whose son was a footballer.

'Let's get going on those muggers,' Geraldine said.

In a way she was relieved to abandon her own theory about the murder in favour of the consensus that he had inadvertently come across one of the muggers currently plaguing the city streets. The local intelligence team who had earlier been tasked with tracking down the gang of muggers were now working alongside the serious crime unit. By combining their expertise and manpower, even Eileen was confident they would soon find the muggers.

'Let's hope her confidence doesn't prove to be misplaced,' a local intelligence officer murmured to Geraldine. 'We've been looking for this gang for months, and we're no closer to finding them now than we were when we first started the search. And believe me, it's not for want of trying that we've drawn a blank. It's an impossible task. We're like a foreign army fighting guerilla warfare in the mountains against an indigenous army who know the terrain.'

'They're kids,' she replied. 'They can't hide from us forever.'

'That's what we said when we started looking for them. They're just kids. We're the fucking police, goddammit. They can't stay hidden from us. But it's been nearly four months, and we haven't found them yet. Not even a sniff of them.'

'We'll just have to keep looking. It's only a matter of time.'

'Easy to say,' she heard him mutter as she walked away.

In the light of what she had heard from several of her colleagues, Geraldine began to revise her opinion of Eileen. It couldn't be easy to remain upbeat in the face of a constant barrage of negativity. For a long time the police had been under attack from the media and some sectors of the public, but now the rot seemed to be spreading. Not only had public distrust of the police grown, but many of her colleagues seemed to be affected by it. The change had come about quite rapidly, due in part to the government constantly chipping away at recruitment until the police were running almost a skeleton service. But corruption within the force itself had done more to wreck the image of the police than anything else and, as was so often the case in life, a corrosive minority threatened to undermine the whole system. The media were quick to pick up on rumours of thugs in uniform bullying and intimidating members of the public. A small fraction of the reported abuse of authority was undoubtedly true, which wasn't helpful.

Geraldine had noticed a change in the way people reacted to her identity card, which was treated with increasing suspicion and even hostility. The days of the friendly local bobby were over, and society was the poorer for it. She was afraid the police had only themselves to blame for their diminishing popularity. Her fleeting good mood gone, she returned to her desk and spent the rest of the morning organising a team to gather details of anyone convicted or accused of a knife crime in the locality over the past twenty years, cross checking their details on the National DNA Database. If they failed to find what they were looking for, she would extend their search further back in time, and over a wider area.

It was a huge job that would have taken the team at her disposal years to complete without the technology now available to them. But, of course, before everything was digitised the task couldn't have been attempted at all. An initial search of the national database for a match for their sample from the murder victim's sleeve had yielded no results. Meanwhile, a search of the crime scene was still ongoing. With her team set up, Geraldine joined Ian who was studying reports from victims of recent muggings. There were around two dozen of them in total.

'It all happened so quickly,' was a common refrain to explain why none of the witnesses was able to give a detailed description of their attackers. All the victims had been alone when they were attacked. A few were women whose bags had been snatched; most were men who had been forced at knife point to hand over their wallets and phones. A couple of men had lost a few hundred pounds each, but mostly the pickings were small. While the effort and risk for so insignificant a return suggested the muggers were young, the speed and efficiency of the attacks indicated an intelligence directing their activity. They had certainly been successful in avoiding any serious police attention. Until now.

'They must realise the murder was a game changer,' Ian said.

'Hardly a game,' Geraldine muttered.

'You know very well what I mean. They must know we'll be throwing everything we have at finding them after this. They've put themselves in the firing line in a way that simply wasn't the case before. The chances are the killer's a rogue psychopath in a gang of kids who were happy just nicking phones and wallets, and the rest of the gang are going to be running scared now. Why should they cover up for him? There's a good chance one of them will come forward, as long as we pitch this right in the media and frighten the rest of them enough. They're only kids. At least one of them's bound to respond to the threat of being treated as an accessory to murder.'

Geraldine shook her head. 'More likely they'll be terrified of the killer in their midst and, worse, they'll look up to him. After something like this, he'll be the leader of the pack. They won't betray him. They'll revere him.'

'He killed someone,' Ian protested.

They exchanged a miserable glance. He knew she was right. In silence they continued reading witness statements. A picture emerged of three or possibly four caucasian youths, probably not yet out of their teens. They wore hooded jackets, jeans and trainers, a description that fitted most of the youngsters in the area. Short of questioning every teenager in the region, they had no way of narrowing down the search. And even if they did set up a search on a large enough scale, there was no guarantee they would find the youngsters they were looking for. The muggers had managed to escape the police so far. It was likely local officers had already spoken to them without identifying them as the wanted gang. Tracking them down was an almost insurmountable task.

Geraldine recalled the words of a local intelligence officer: 'We're like a foreign army fighting guerilla warfare in the mountains against an indigenous army who know the terrain.' With a sigh, she turned to the next witness statement and read depressingly familiar words. 'It all happened so fast…'

8

ONE OF THE VISUAL image detection officers reported seeing a woman walking quickly along High Ousegate away from Pope's Head Alley shortly after midnight on the night of the murder. Geraldine went straight along the corridor to watch the footage. It wasn't absolutely clear the woman had come out of Pope's Head Alley but it was possible, in which case she might have caught sight of the killer just before the attack. She might even have witnessed the murder and been too frightened to come forward. Geraldine asked her colleague to replay the film and they watched it carefully together. Recorded after night had fallen, the image was indistinct, but they could see the woman had long dark hair, and she was in a hurry. Something about her rapid stride drew Geraldine's attention. There could have been any number of reasons why she was walking so fast, not least of which was that it was late and she was out on the streets alone. All the same, Geraldine asked the visual image detection officer to try and trace where the woman went.

'She could be a vital witness in our murder enquiry,' she said. 'Good work spotting her.'

The constable nodded and turned back to her screen, smiling.

When Geraldine reported the discovery to the detective chief inspector, Eileen was sceptical about how useful the sighting might be.

'Just because someone was walking along the street nearby doesn't mean they witnessed the murder. We don't even know who this woman is. As evidence, it's pretty flimsy, but follow it up, Geraldine. Let's see what we can find out.'

The visual image detection officer called Geraldine to say she had followed the woman as far as she could. After leaving the western end of High Ousegate, the woman had turned right into Coney Street, then right again along St Helens Square, doubling back on herself to pass the Minster and along Petergate to Gillygate where she had disappeared into a side street. The whole journey had only been just over a mile, although she could have taken a shorter route along Pope's Head Alley into Peter Lane.

'Can you identify the point where she had turned off Gillygate, before she disappeared from view?' Geraldine asked.

'Yes. We can pinpoint that exactly.'

'Good work.'

What was even more encouraging was that the street the woman had turned into was a dead end. Geraldine thought she might drive there after work and look for the woman, but as she was packing up to leave, Ian stopped by her desk and asked her whether she would like to go for a drink on her way home. His fair hair was neatly combed, but there was an unfamiliar stubble on his chin and he looked tired. She had the impression he was more troubled than usual, and wondered whether he was focusing on the case or thinking about his estranged wife. Thinking he might want to talk about his marital problems, she postponed her planned trip to Gillygate and nodded.

'That would be nice.'

They walked together along the street to the nearby pub and Geraldine took a seat while Ian fetched a couple of beers.

'How's things with you?' Geraldine asked as he sat down opposite her in a brooding silence. 'Have you heard from Bev at all? Or would you rather not talk about it?'

'It?' he replied, raising his eyebrows.

'You know what I mean. Your marriage. And the baby.'

'The marriage is over, and the baby's not mine,' he replied shortly. 'She ran off with her former boss, and they're having a baby. What more is there to say?'

Before she could respond, Geraldine was vexed to see their young colleague, Naomi, approaching.

'Can I join you?'

Geraldine would have liked to continue her conversation with Ian in private but she could hardly object, so she smiled up at her young colleague as Ian grunted his assent.

'So, what are we talking about?' Naomi asked as she sat down. 'I take it you're discussing the case?'

Geraldine smiled to hide her resentment at the intrusion, and Ian grunted again.

Oblivious to the fact that she had interrupted a completely different conversation, Naomi went on.

'Eileen's idea is probably right.'

'What? That it was a mugging gone wrong?' Geraldine asked. 'I don't see why this murder would be anything to do with the muggers. Firstly, the victim wasn't robbed, so it actually makes no sense to assume this was a mugging.'

'Perhaps they were disturbed?'

'There was no evidence of that, and nothing to connect the muggers to the murder,' Geraldine replied, doing her best to hide her annoyance. 'I mean, the two might be linked but it's no more than a stab in the dark to think that, if you'll pardon the pun. I just think it's early days to begin indulging in unsubstantiated speculation.'

'So what are your thoughts on the murder?' Ian asked.

Geraldine told them about the woman who had been spotted on CCTV.

'She just appeared out of nowhere, so she could have come from Pope's Head Alley.'

'Isn't *that* just speculation?' Naomi muttered.

'No, it's something to regard as a possible lead,' Geraldine snapped. Aware that she was allowing her irritation to show, she went on in a more measured tone. 'If she *did* come from Pope's Head Alley, I just wonder whether she might have seen the killer. The thing is, she could have taken a short cut along there but she chose to walk the long way round along Coney Street. Maybe she didn't want to walk past something she'd seen?'

'Or perhaps she didn't want to walk along a snickelway late at night,' Naomi replied. 'Anyway, if she'd seen anything, she would have spoken to us. This is a murder investigation. People can't choose not to tell us anything they know.'

'She wouldn't necessarily have come forward,' Geraldine replied.

'It's naive to think everyone is public spirited and wants to help us,' Ian agreed.

Finishing her drink, Geraldine stood up. 'I think it's time I went home,' she said. 'I don't know about you two, but I'm worn out.'

Naomi turned to Ian. 'Are you hungry?'

Without waiting to hear his reply, Geraldine left. At the door she glanced back. Naomi was still sitting beside Ian, talking to him, and he was leaning forward in his chair, nodding and smiling. With a sigh, Geraldine walked back to her car alone. Almost without thinking she drove to Gillygate. Parking her car at the end of the side road where the woman with long dark hair had vanished, she walked along the pavement, wondering where the woman lived. Seeing a man manoeuvring his bicycle through a gate, she hailed him as she passed.

'I'm looking for a friend of mine,' she said. 'She's got long dark hair.'

She hoped he wouldn't ask her for her friend's name. If he did, she would have to make something up, which might render her question pointless. But he shook his head.

'Sorry, I've only recently moved in. I don't know anyone around here.'

Geraldine hung around for a while, walking slowly along the pavement. At the end of the street she saw a B & B sign in one of the windows, and rang the bell. A portly woman answered the door.

'Excuse me, I'm not looking for a room.'

The landlady's expression altered subtly but she asked Geraldine politely enough what she wanted. Geraldine trotted out the same story: that she was looking for a friend. She held back from showing her identity card. If the woman she was looking for *had* seen anything at the crime scene, she was clearly in no hurry to share her information with the police. That being the case, Geraldine thought it best not to alert her to the fact that they were looking for her.

'There are a few women along here who might fit that description,' the woman replied.

Geraldine waited, wary of appearing too keen.

'But I'm not sure I should tell you,' the landlady added. 'I mean, I don't suppose it's any great secret, or anything. You could have seen her walking by. But it's really none of my business. I think I'd rather not say.'

Reluctantly, Geraldine took out her identity card. 'I'd like you to be discreet about this, please. I'm investigating a crime.'

The landlady's eyes widened in alarm.

'The woman who lives along here isn't suspected of any criminal activity, but we think she might have witnessed something that could help us in our enquiry, and she might not be aware that she could help us. So it's vital I speak to her. But we don't want to worry her by letting her think we're looking for her. It's nothing like that.' She laughed. 'We'd normally just put out a request for her to come forward via the media, and hope for a response, but as we happen to have stumbled on the fact that she lives somewhere along this road, we thought we'd come and look for her.'

It sounded slightly odd, but it was the truth. The landlady studied the card and nodded.

'It could be the woman who lives three doors down,' she said. 'She's the only one I can think of with very long hair. But that's all I can tell you about her. We've never spoken. I've just seen her going by, usually late at night.'

Geraldine thanked her and went to the house the landlady had pointed out, but there was no answer when she rang the bell. Concealing her own identity, she checked with the neighbours on either side of the house, both of whom confirmed what the landlady had said. There was little point in hanging around, so having identified a house where the potential witness might live she left, intending to return the following day. If this woman could tell her anything that might help the police to track down the killer, Geraldine wanted to hear about it. Thoughtfully she wrote up her notes that evening, hoping she was wrong. A gang of muggers would be much easier to track down than an intelligent solitary killer.

9

THE DAY AFTER THE body was discovered, a short article appeared in the local papers about his recent victim. Frowning with concentration, he read that a local school teacher had received a fatal stab wound in Pope's Head Alley. The article went on to give details of the location, which ran between Peter Lane and High Ousegate. The street names made him smile. They had a magical ring to them, an other-worldly resonance, reminding him of the Narnia books he used to read as a child. There was a photograph of the alleyway – without a body – an image pulled off the internet.

He stared at the small black and white picture, remembering how he had followed his victim. The man had made it easy for him, stumbling along the narrow passage without once looking round. He had even been singing under his breath, preventing any possibility that he might hear footsteps behind him. He had been too drunk to resist the attack, too drunk even to understand what was happening to him. By the time he grasped what was going on, it was too late. Not until blood spurted from his throat had his eyes widened in understanding, but by then his eyes were already glazing over and he was sinking to the ground.

'You... you...' he had stammered, his voice slurred with drink, and gurgling as the blood reached his throat.

The dying man had lifted his arms, reaching out for help. Their eyes met above the bloody hands raised in supplication, and then the arms fell back and he lay still. Once his victim was dead, the killer had slipped away. No one saw him leave the lane, his bloody accoutrements concealed in the rucksack he had carefully placed out of range of the gushing blood.

The paper gave the victim's age as thirty-two, and said he had lived and worked in York, but there was no mention of his name. That was a pity. It somehow added to his satisfaction to be able to think of his victims by name. But that would no doubt be forthcoming in time. He had learned to be patient. The rest of the article comprised comments from the headmaster of the school where he had taught, and a brief reference to a wife left behind, grieving and in shock. According to the head, the victim had been 'a gifted teacher who will be sorely missed by his pupils and colleagues'.

He laughed out loud at that. The head would never have said, 'He was a boring teacher whose loss will give his pupils a welcome break from lessons,' even though that was far more likely to be true.

The article went on to say the police were following several leads, and a senior investigating officer was quoted as saying they were expecting to make an arrest soon. As if!

'In your dreams, Detective Chief Inspector Eileen Duncan,' he muttered.

But he wasn't angry. On the contrary, their lies made him smile.

After that he kept a careful eye on the papers and watched the local news on the television, and was pleased when interest in the case quickly died down. Within a few days it was no longer mentioned at all, as though it had never happened. He smiled. He liked to keep things strictly between himself and the people he killed. Discretion was vital; the less fuss his murders provoked, the less likely he was to be caught. And he had no intention of being caught. Not now. Not ever.

10

GERALDINE HAD SEEN THE papers, and now the item had attracted attention from the local television news, where a self-appointed community spokesperson was accusing the police of negligence in allowing a gang of muggers free rein to run amok on the streets of the city. Geraldine listened to a few minutes of a discussion where a relatively mild-mannered police representative was struggling to counter the opinionated campaigner's arguments.

'So what you're telling us is that the police are powerless to protect us?'

'No, that's not what I'm saying at all. Please don't twist my words –'

'You told us the police have been unable to stop these muggings, so the criminals responsible – and let's not mince words, these are dangerous criminals we're talking about here – have been allowed to continue roaming the streets unhindered, terrorising their victims, and now they've murdered an innocent man, which was a tragedy waiting to happen. So I repeat my question: what's the point of paying the police if they can't protect our citizens?'

'What I said was –'

'We all heard what you said. It's a matter of public record now.'

'If you'd let me finish my point –'

'Answer my question. What is being done to stop this danger threatening the safety of everyone walking on the streets of York? Or are we all to stay indoors for fear of being murdered?'

'The police are following several leads –'

'Everyone knows those are empty words. The police still don't know who's responsible for killing Grant Marcus, do they?'

Geraldine muted the television in disgust. The media had allowed them only four days to investigate before leaping in with their scaremongering, with the result that the police spokesperson was forced to deal with a verbal lashing live on air. Even allowing for the fact that it was always easier to attack than defend, the police came across as feeble. She doubted the discussion would be allowed to develop into a justified complaint about limited police resources. A fatal assault on an innocent man was far more sensational than the problem of reduced budgets and insufficient manpower. Angrily, she flicked through the channels until she found an old black and white war film. Life had seemed so much simpler then, when everyone could identify a common enemy.

She and Ariadne commiserated over the appalling television debate as they sat drinking coffee in the canteen the following morning.

'The trouble is, these days moral lines are increasingly blurred,' Ariadne complained. 'Before long television presenters are going to be giving air time to some campaigner who's demanding to know what's being done to help the poor youths abandoned by society, left to walk the streets mugging and killing people. They'll no longer be treated as criminals but unfortunate victims of the system, and we'll be the bad guys.'

'I think we already are,' Geraldine replied.

She wondered how things had gone so badly wrong as they sat swapping horror stories about how the police were disrespected, until it was time for the early morning briefing.

Eileen looked around, one foot tapping impatiently on the floor.

'Grant's widow is agitating to know when she can arrange

the funeral, and of course that won't be for a while, and in the meantime she's been speaking to some bloody journalist, and there's a huge palaver blowing up about it in the media. Why the hell can't they back off and leave us to get on with the job?' It was a rhetorical question.

Eileen looked around the incident room with a glare that Geraldine had come to recognise as typical of her when a case was proceeding slowly, as if she thought there was more the assembled officers could be doing to track down the culprit. Geraldine looked over at Ian who was on the other side of the room. When she first arrived in York, they had shared a mutual impatience with the detective chief inspector's hectoring. But Ian was standing beside Naomi and now, instead of catching Geraldine's eye, he turned his head to exchange a glance with Naomi. Geraldine suppressed an irrational flush of jealousy. Ian was entitled to stand next to Naomi, and to look at her. At last Eileen drew the meeting to a close and they dispersed to continue with their work.

Geraldine and Ian had been studying statements given by the victims of recent muggings, listing common features that appeared in the descriptions of the muggers themselves. They were fairly diverse, and most of them were uselessly vague, but some similar details cropped up in several of the accounts. A number of the witnesses were so hysterical that, for the most part, their exaggerated claims had to be discounted. The lucid ones reported seeing three youths, the first one stocky, the second tall and skinny, and the third member of the gang small and, according to one witness, quite possibly the youngest of the three.

'He looked nervous,' the witness added.

All the attacks followed a similar pattern. Standing in front of the victim to block his or her path, the sturdy youth pulled out a flick knife. As he did so, his accomplices positioned themselves around the victim who was thus hemmed in by a triangle of thieves. No one reported seeing the other two boys holding weapons. The boy brandishing a blade would bark at the victim to drop his or her possessions on the pavement. As soon as the two boys flanking the victim had darted forward to retrieve the stolen items, the three boys scuttled away.

'So it looks as though we've got a ringleader,' Geraldine said. 'Maybe we can persuade one of his henchmen to talk.'

'If we can find them,' Ian replied grimly.

The gang didn't appear to frequent a particular part of town but had struck in different areas and at different times of day. It seemed they wandered around searching for suitable victims out alone on quiet streets. Watching her colleague's familiar features contorted in frustration, Geraldine swallowed a sigh.

'Don't look so down in the dumps,' Ian said, glancing up and catching her expression. 'We'll get them in the end.'

Geraldine nodded, but she didn't respond straightaway. She could hardly explain that she was feeling sad on his account, knowing that his wife would soon be giving birth to another man's baby.

'We always find our man,' he added.

She did her best not to wince at the cliché. They both knew that even when they tracked down the muggers, they still might not find Grant's killer.

'My money's on the thickset youth, the one wielding a knife,' Ian went on, his craggy features creased in a smile that failed to light up his eyes. 'When we get him, we'll not only have the ringleader of the gang and stop the muggings, but with any luck we'll have our killer nailed into the bargain.'

Once again Geraldine nodded in silence. Since his promotion to inspector, Ian seemed to be increasingly glib. More and more he sounded as though he was concerned with encouraging the sergeants and constables under him at the expense of focusing on the pursuit of hard evidence. She wondered if he was trying to counterbalance Eileen's negativity, but she didn't dare challenge him. Somehow, he intimidated her in a way that none of her other senior officers could.

'Right,' Ian said, 'you share these descriptions with the VIIDO team, and I'll get an e-fit officer on to them, and let's see if we can get a visual the muggers' victims can agree on.'

Geraldine was on her way to speak to the VIIDO team watching CCTV of the areas where victims had encountered the muggers when Eileen summoned everyone again. Hopeful that there had been a positive development in the investigation, Geraldine joined the small throng of officers heading for the major incident room. The mood of subdued optimism faded at the sight of Eileen's face. She looked drained. Seeming to force her lips to frame the words, she said only, 'There's been another one.'

11

LESS THAN A WEEK after Grant had been stabbed to death, a second body was discovered, this time along the edge of the river beneath Lendal Bridge, near the centre of the city. Initially the emergency team that had been summoned assumed the victim had suffered a fatal accident, as the dead woman was found face down, caught in weeds growing by the tow path. Several cyclists, joggers, and pedestrians hurrying to work must have passed by without noticing the body trapped at the water's edge. Only a retired postman taking a morning stroll had seen the body and raised the alarm. But not long after the body was hauled out of the water, it became apparent that the woman hadn't drowned.

Geraldine and Ian arrived at the scene as quickly as they could. Already a forensic tent had been erected and a group of scene of crime officers were busy in the cordoned off area of the river bank, examining the ground for evidence. Geraldine gazed along the stretch of water, peaceful in the morning sunshine. A few fluffy white clouds floated lazily across a bright blue backdrop high above the trees, dwarfing the officers far below. In their protective white suits they resembled fat white slugs. It was hard to believe a murder had been committed in such an idyllic scene. She felt a sudden yearning to walk away from all the activity and follow the path that led alongside the river until she could breathe in peace.

With a sigh, she turned her attention back to her work. Ian was deep in conversation with a SOCO and didn't see her glance at him. Instead of waiting for him, she decided to go ahead and check out the scene for herself. Pulling on protective clothing, she entered the tent where a team of white-coated officers were examining the ground, picking at the grass and poking around in the mud. No one seemed to be paying attention to the dead woman who was the catalyst for all their activity.

Lying rigid on its back, the body lay where it had been placed after being dragged from the water, the face slightly bloated and glistening. Assuming one of the rescuers had closed the eyes, Geraldine was pleased to see the dead woman had been accorded that much respect, at least. Not that it made any difference to her. She had evidently not been in the water for very long, because she was still reasonably intact, although her face and her positioning were too rigid to give an impression of someone sleeping.

Beneath an unbuttoned black coat she was wearing a yellow dress with a flared skirt that reached just below her knees. The coat and dress were both drenched and discoloured with mud and grass stains. Her shoes were missing, presumably lost in the water.

'You can see where she was stabbed, right through the heart,' a SOCO told Geraldine.

'Stabbed?' she repeated, staring down at the body.

The message had been passed on to them only that the victim had been murdered. Now, looking closely in the bright lighting that had been rigged up, she saw a dark stain on the muddy fabric of the dead woman's dress.

'Yes,' the SOCO said. 'She was stabbed before she was thrown, or perhaps fell, in the water. We thought as much when we first pulled her out, but we couldn't be sure until the medical examiner arrived to take a look and confirm what we suspected. The blood on her dress was the clue. Bit of a giveaway, really.'

His eyes crinkled, and behind his mask Geraldine thought he was smiling. She didn't smile back. Instead she turned back to look at the body.

'So she was stabbed?' she repeated, speaking more to herself than her colleague.

'Yes,' he agreed cheerfully. 'So it looks like this is one for you.'

'We're already on a case.' She sighed before adding pensively, 'Another stabbing.' Suddenly brisk, she turned to the scene of crime officer. 'When was she killed?'

'Assuming she was killed by the knife wound, she died before she entered the water sometime last night. The medical officer judged she was in the water for about twelve hours, but I think that was more of a guess than anything definite. He seemed to be in a hurry to get away.'

Geraldine nodded. The precise cause of death wouldn't be established until the post mortem, but it seemed fairly safe to attribute her death to the stab wound to her chest, even if she had managed to stagger and slip into the water while injured but still living.

'Do we know who she was?'

The other officer shook his head. 'She had no means of identification on her and we haven't managed to find any belongings round about.'

'No handbag?'

He shook his head. 'Nothing at all. No bag, no keys, no purse, no phone, nothing.'

Geraldine studied the dead woman's face. She could have been about thirty. Long blond hair hung around her face in straggly wet strands, and her face bore smudged vestiges of scarlet lipstick and heavy mascara that streaked her cheeks like black tears. A woman wearing make-up was unlikely to go out without a handbag. It was likely the killer had taken it, but they would still have to dredge the river to look for it. But first they would search all along the river bank in case she had dropped it before entering the water.

With a final glance around, Geraldine thanked the scene of crime officer and left the tent. There was nothing more to learn there as the body had been brought to the river bank by the rescue team. The stabbing might not even have occurred close to the site where the body currently lay. Finding the killer was their priority, but they also needed to find out the victim's identity.

'This was a stabbing,' she told Ian.

He nodded, frowning, having heard the details from another officer at the scene.

'No bag, no money,' Ian replied.

Geraldine nodded. 'You think this was a mugging?'

It was Ian's turn to nod. 'Stands to reason, wouldn't you say? Given that she was robbed.'

Geraldine didn't argue. But the fact that this victim had also been stabbed raised a disturbing possibility. They could only hope that the post mortem examination and subsequent forensic analysis didn't find evidence to link the two murders to the same killer. Two accidental fatalities would be terrible enough. To learn that they were hunting for a multiple murderer would be far worse, as there was no reason to suppose he might stop at two victims.

That lunchtime Geraldine had arranged to go out for a Chinese meal with her colleague, Ariadne. Both frustrated by the stalling investigation into Grant's death, they tried to chat about other matters, but the conversation kept drifting back to their current case.

'I can't believe we haven't found a match yet,' Ariadne said as they finished a bowl of prawn crackers which had arrived while they were waiting for their order. 'We've checked the DNA of everyone we could find who knew Grant, and we've eliminated just about all his friends, as well as his family and his colleagues. So unless we come up with a match, it seems to confirm he was killed by a stranger. My guess is it was one of those blasted muggers who've been a thorn in our side for months.'

'That's what Ian thinks, and so does Eileen.'

Ariadne gave Geraldine a searching look. 'You sound as though you don't agree with them?'

Geraldine shrugged. Privately she suspected the murder was unrelated to the muggings. The crimes felt different. As a detective inspector working in London she had always been ready to voice her opinion, but since her demotion she was less forthcoming about her views. In retrospect she realised that even at her most confident, she had never really known whether her hunches would turn out to be correct. Occasionally she had been proved wrong. Perhaps it had just been luck that her instincts had mostly been spot on in the past.

'I don't know,' she admitted. 'I've absolutely no idea whether the murderer was involved in those muggings or not.'

Relieved to change the subject, she watched a sizzling plate as it was placed on the table in front of her.

'This looks good,' she smiled.

They spent the next few minutes tasting the different dishes and commenting on them, and the conversation moved on from the murder enquiry. Ariadne's company offered a brief respite from her worries, but when Geraldine returned to her desk that afternoon, her disquiet came flooding back. It was important to stop the gang of muggers, who were a group of callous thugs, but until now they hadn't physically injured anyone. On the contrary, they had been scrupulously careful to avoid any physical contact with their victims. Grant's murder marked a complete departure from their previous operations, which suggested it might have been carried out by someone else altogether. By focusing the search on the muggers, Eileen could be distracting the investigative team from their purpose: to find Grant's killer. Since no one else seemed to share Geraldine's view, she kept it to herself. And now that they had possibly claimed a second victim, the hunt for the gang of muggers was set to continue with increasing urgency.

12

'SO WHAT? SO BLOODY what?'

Daryl stared at Carver through lowered lids, wondering whether he was as relaxed as he appeared. Casually, Carver flicked open his knife and yawned, displaying yellow teeth. Putting the knife down on his leg with the blade exposed, he rolled a spliff and lit up. Leaning back in his comfortable armchair, he puffed at the ceiling. After several botched attempts he managed to blow a nearly perfect smoke ring. Watching it float lazily above his head, he clicked his fingers in triumph.

'See that?' he crowed.

Nelson nodded, his narrow head bobbing up and down with exaggerated enthusiasm. 'Sure, I seen it. Nice one, bro.'

'Am I the man, or what?' Carver twisted round suddenly to face Daryl. 'Well? Some dude brodied your tongue, boy?'

'No, no,' Daryl mumbled, dropping his eyes. 'That is, yes, yes, sure I seen it, and it was –' He hesitated, groping for words. 'It was cool, really cool, man.' He heaved a sigh of genuine regret. 'Wish I could blow smoke rings like that.'

'Takes practice,' Carver said. 'And skill. You practise enough, you'll get to blow smoke rings. Not as good as mine, but good enough. You just got to keep trying.' He smiled complacently. 'You try hard enough, you can do anything you want.'

Daryl watched a fragile column of ash lengthen on the end of the reefer, until Carver shifted in his seat and the ash dropped. Oblivious to its fall, Carver inhaled noisily and blew out a series of untidy puffs of smoke, none of which formed a circle. Frustrated, Carver flicked his reefer butt across the room. Daryl watched its glowing flight, tensed to jump up and grind it under his heel if it landed on the carpet. The butt fell on the concrete floor where it lay sending delicate threads of smoke eddying upwards through the dusty air. He wished Carver would stop lobbing burning cigarette ends, but he held back from complaining. It wasn't smart to challenge Carver.

Several months ago, on the first occasion Daryl had been invited into the garage, he had rashly sat down on the one armchair.

'That's my seat,' Carver had told him, speaking so quietly Daryl hadn't sensed danger.

'Well, I don't see your name on it,' he had replied, with an insolent grin.

Carver's movement was so swift Daryl scarcely had time to raise his arm in front of his face. The scar was hardly visible now, a thin white line running along the back of Daryl's left forearm from his wrist to an inch above his elbow. Neither of them ever mentioned the incident, but the memory hovered between them, a stain on the carpet and an unspoken threat.

'This is my place,' Carver liked to say, as though the derelict garage was a castle.

And, in a way, it was.

Watching the others closely, Daryl realised he wasn't the only one feeling edgy. Nelson was fidgeting with the ring he always wore on his right hand, a sure sign that he was jumpy. When a car horn beeped somewhere close by, his eyes widened almost imperceptibly. Daryl caught his eye and Nelson looked away, casting a furtive glance at Carver. But Carver was sprawling in his chair, apparently oblivious to his companions' nerves.

'So...' cautiously Daryl returned to what he had been saying before Carver was distracted by his smoke rings, 'I still think we need to lay low and keep out of sight for a while. That's all I'm saying. And maybe we shouldn't hang out together until this blows over.'

Nelson looked at Daryl and licked his lips, as though he was about to take a bite out of him.

'You saying you're gonna stay away from us, man?'

As he asked the question, Nelson jumped to his feet and paced up and down the garage, with a sneaky sideways glance at Carver to check he was listening.

'You gotta be joking, man,' Nelson went on. 'Where you gonna go? Who you gonna hang with? We're family, bro. You can't walk away from us. You can't never walk away from us.'

Nelson turned to Carver, waiting for him to join in. Sensing a crafty motive behind Nelson's outrage, Daryl tried to back down.

'I'm not saying we stay away from each other,' he stammered. 'That's not what I meant.'

But he could see from Nelson's flicker of a grin that it was too late to retract his words.

'Not for long,' he pressed on desperately. 'Just for a few weeks, maybe.'

All the time Daryl and Nelson had been talking, Carver had remained silent, his eyes closed, as though he was asleep. Now he spoke, still without opening his eyes.

'What kind of shit are you talking here, Daryl? What kind of wuss are you anyway?'

Daryl took a deep breath. 'I just think we should stay out of sight until all this goes away. That's all I'm saying.'

'It ain't never gonna go away if you don't conquer your fear, blad,' Carver said, opening his eyes slowly to stare coldly at Daryl. 'This shit is all in your head, man. You gotta cut it out.' He leaned forward, and spat on the carpet. 'I don't want bad blood between us, man.'

'No, no, no bad blood. Of course not,' Daryl replied, lowering his eyes, and struggling to keep his voice steady.

'Shut the fuck up then. And you,' Carver turned to Nelson, 'stop prancing around like a dog on heat.'

Carver leaned back in his chair again as though to indicate

the discussion was over. Nelson sat down on a wooden crate and stared at the floor. Daryl pressed his lips together and wondered what he should do now.

'There's no need for us to do anything different,' Carver said softly. 'The pigs don't know us, and we don't know them, and that's how it's gonna stay. Suits us fine, because they got no idea who we even are.' He threw his head back and laughed, and his yellow teeth shone in the light from the bulb overhead. 'We move in the shadows,' he whispered, straightening up.

'We move in the shadows,' Nelson repeated.

The words had a certain ring to them. Even though it wasn't cold in the garage, Daryl shivered. If the other two thought there was nothing to worry about, perhaps they were right and he was behaving like a girl. But it was equally possible his companions were cretins. There had always been a risk they would be caught by the police, only now they might be accused of murder as well as mugging. He wished he knew how to persuade Carver to take the threat seriously. But Carver was frowning with concentration as though blowing smoke rings was the only thing that mattered. Not for the first time, Daryl wished he had never met Carver and Nelson. The trouble was, his companions were never going to allow him to walk away from them. He knew too much. His grandfather used to tell him that knowledge was power, but this knowledge enslaved him.

13

'WE NEED TO FIND out who she was,' Eileen said.

'We're searching for her dental records with all the local surgeries,' Geraldine replied. 'Her teeth are in good condition and she seems to have taken care of herself, so it's likely she went to the dentist regularly. Let's hope so anyway. It's a good reason for making regular visits to the dentist.'

'What? So that you can be identified if you're killed and your wallet is stolen?' Ariadne asked, laughing. 'I can think of better reasons for going to the dentist.'

Geraldine's optimism proved justified when the dental records of the second victim were traced. A primary school teacher living on her own, Felicity Dunmore had been twenty-seven when she died. The man who had stumbled on her body at the river's edge came to the police station to make a formal statement. Geraldine had the impression he was quietly excited by all the unexpected attention he was receiving. To be fair, he hadn't seen the dead woman's face, only the back of her head as she was lying in the water. He had been kept well back while the body was recovered, even before the rescue team were aware of any necessity to protect the site as a crime scene. Shielded from the disturbing sight of a dead body seen at close quarters, he appeared to be treating the incident as a kind of day out at the police station, where he was offered tea and biscuits and an attentive audience. She wondered if he lived alone. Seeing a gold band on his wedding finger, she guessed he was a widower, and his first words confirmed her impression.

'I often walk along by the river,' he told her. 'My wife used to like it there, and the river helps me remember her. She's been gone fifteen years and it's sometimes hard to keep hold of the memories.' He gave an apologetic shrug, as though he had confessed too much. 'It's something to do, anyway,' he added in a brisker tone. 'We're all just filling in time to distract ourselves from the human condition, aren't we? That's the best we can do, on our journey from birth to death.'

Touched by his bleak outlook, Geraldine asked whether he had any family.

'I've got a daughter, but we don't see one another anymore. She fell out with my wife.' He paused. 'Some people just can't seem to accept when their children aren't cast in their mould.'

'There's nothing to stop you getting in touch with her again. She might be pleased?'

He shook his head. 'It's too late for that. I made my choice.'

'It's never too late,' Geraldine said.

They both knew that wasn't true.

She felt a wave of sympathy for this man who looked so small and frail. He was right. Thinking about the transience of existence *was* depressing. The irony of using the deaths of strangers to distract her from thinking about her own mortality was not lost on her. Shaking off her despondent musings, she snapped back to the job in hand. Another distraction.

'Can you tell me exactly what you saw when you found the body?'

'Well, it's like I told your constable, the woman was just there, in the water. It was only by chance that I happened to see her because she wasn't that easy to spot from the footpath. I think I noticed her legs first, or maybe it was her arms. Anyway, I went a bit closer because at first I thought I was imagining it, and then I saw it was a dead body all right, so I called 999 straightaway, and I have to say they responded very quickly.'

Geraldine did her best to find out whether he had noticed anything unusual, but he had nothing of any interest to tell her.

Thanking him for his help, she left him quietly sipping tea in the company of a constable. It was time to take a closer look at the victim.

Ian decided to accompany her to hear what Jonah had to tell them, but he was so silent in the car, she wished she had gone alone.

'Are you sure you want to come along?' she asked and was rewarded with an incoherent grunt.

'It's nothing to do with you,' Ian said, after a few minutes.

She didn't respond that she hadn't thought it was, but waited to hear what he was going to say next. For a while neither of them spoke.

'Bev's been in touch,' he said at last, as though in answer to her unspoken question.

Geraldine took her eyes off the road long enough to observe the firm set of his jaw, and the tension in his hunched shoulders.

'Do you want to talk about it?' she asked when she couldn't bear the silence any longer.

He didn't answer and they drove the rest of the way in silence.

The anatomical pathology technician, Avril, looked slightly flushed when she let them in.

She flashed a broad smile at Ian. 'Haven't seen anything of you for a while,' she said, addressing him as though Geraldine wasn't there. 'I was beginning to think they'd thrown you out.'

Geraldine was tempted to point out that *she* had been there four days ago, but she held her tongue. There was no need to remind Ian about her recent trip to the mortuary. Besides, Avril's flirting might cheer him up. He had always been quick to respond to such banter before, but on this occasion he barely seemed to notice Avril and strode past her, his expression sombre. The pathology technician drew in a sharp breath and opened her mouth, then thought better of it and closed it again. Geraldine followed Ian, pretending not to notice Avril's disappointment.

'Aha, the wanderer returns,' Jonah greeted Ian jovially.

'Been taking a holiday from the grim reaper's carryings-on this time around, and leaving your sergeant to shoulder the burden?'

'Something like that,' Ian replied. 'Although sometimes life can be harder,' he added almost under his breath.

'True enough.' Jonah winked at Geraldine. 'Sounds like our inspector's in trouble. A case of cherchez la femme, is it? Oh well, nothing like an interesting cadaver to take your mind off your problems.' He turned his attention to the body. 'She wasn't in the water very long, I'd say less than twelve hours. Overnight anyway.' He indicated a gash on the left-hand side of the dead woman's chest, just below her breasts. 'Whoever stabbed her was aiming for her heart. Either that, or it was a lucky strike.'

'Lucky?' Ian queried.

Geraldine didn't comment. She had heard Jonah make a similar comment about the other recent corpse.

'There was no trace of frothing in the mouth, no water in the lungs; our girl here was dead before she reached the water.'

'The scene of crime officers seemed to think she was dragged to the water's edge and fell from the bank after a brief scuffle.'

Jonah nodded. 'Makes sense. So we have evidence of a scuffle?' He raised his head, his eyes alert with interest.

Geraldine nodded. 'Yes. But so far all we know is that the killer was wearing new Wellington boots which might not have been the right size as he seemed to slip around a bit in the mud. So they don't necessarily reveal very much. There's not a lot of point trying to follow up everyone who's recently bought Wellington boots. We don't even know it was a recent purchase, or that he bought them locally.'

'Or she,' Jonah added. 'A woman could have been wearing boots that were too large for her to throw us off the scent.'

'We're pretty sure the killer was a man,' Geraldine said. 'Forensics have found a trace of DNA at the scene –'

'And it matches the DNA found on Grant's sleeve?' Jonah

interrupted her, his eyes brightening with excitement although he kept his voice steady.

'Yes,' she told him. 'So we now suspect the killer is a blond blue-eyed man and, if we're right, he has killed twice in a week.'

'Well that narrows it down a bit,' Jonah said, raising a quizzical eyebrow at Ian. 'Rules out me and Geraldine at any rate.'

Jonah grinned. He could afford to be cheerful, Geraldine thought. He could go home confident that he had been thorough and his work was finished, while the detectives' job had scarcely begun, and they were still casting around for leads.

14

FRUSTRATINGLY, THE SECOND DNA sample they had obtained gave them no more information than they had already gathered. Although it matched the trace that had been found on Grant's body, they were still no closer to finding the culprit. A team of officers had been patrolling the areas where youngsters were known to hang out, asking around. Although the police suspected their targets might no longer be in full-time education, they also visited schools and colleges in and around York, trying to pick up information about the muggers. The intelligence officers gathered little about the local gangs that they didn't already know, and no one shared any information that gave any positive leads to the identities of the three youths who had been responsible for the recent muggings.

Armed with a vague description of the gang, Geraldine and Ian questioned the head teachers at several local schools, but they too drew a blank. Whoever the muggers were, they had succeeded in keeping a low profile. Since none of the boys known locally as troublemakers matched the details the police had been given, they wondered whether the members of the gang might have come to York recently. Students in higher education wouldn't be known at any of the local schools, so Geraldine and Ian visited the vice chancellor of the university.

'This is going to be a waste of time,' Geraldine muttered as they waited in the hushed corridor outside the office.

'I feel as though I'm back at school and have been summoned to see the headmaster,' Ian whispered, with a smile. 'I bet you were never in trouble at school.'

Geraldine returned his smile. He was right. She had been an exemplary pupil, but she hesitated to admit it for fear of sounding boring. Instead, she turned the implied question around.

'I bet you were always in trouble,' she replied.

'Oh no, you don't get out of answering that easily. I'm intrigued now.' He leaned forward, his blue eyes alight with amusement. 'Tell me honestly, what was the naughtiest thing you ever did at school?'

'Naughty?' she repeated.

Before she could say any more, they were summoned to see the vice chancellor. Breathing a sigh of relief, Geraldine wondered whether Ian would remember their unfinished conversation and challenge her again.

The vice chancellor of the university was a charming man who seemed genuinely dismayed at being unable to help them.

'My role is largely nominal,' he explained, with an apologetic smile, as though he was somehow letting them down. 'Sadly I don't enjoy much contact with the main body of students here. It's not like being a head teacher in a school. But I had a long discussion with the dean, who has spoken to all the tutors, and we just can't come up with any suggestions for you.'

'He almost seemed disappointed that he's not aware of any students who are running around mugging people,' Geraldine said as they drove away.

Ian nodded, seemingly lost in thought. Only as they reached the entrance to the police station car park did he say, 'I haven't forgotten, you know.'

'Forgotten what?'

'You still haven't told me what you got up to at school.'

She laughed. 'I'm afraid that would be another disappointment for you.'

Later that morning, the team scanning through hours of CCTV footage picked up a blurry image of the female victim making her way down towards the river, shortly before she was killed. She was instantly recognisable from the billowy skirt she was wearing.

'It's definitely her,' a constable said when Geraldine went to see the images for herself.

Registering her colleague's excitement, Geraldine felt a pang of regret, recalling her own enthusiasm when she herself had been a young officer. Increasingly these days she was feeling dull and slow, as though she had lost her edge. She had never really been driven by ambition so she didn't think her fading enthusiasm for her job was due to her demotion. Perhaps she was just getting too old for her chosen career.

'Do you ever feel you've been in this job too long?' she had asked Ian one day.

He was the only colleague she knew well enough to share her feelings with, but his blank stare made it clear that he hadn't really understood what she was talking about.

'It's not just the skirt, but the way she walks is quite distinctive,' the VIIDO officer said.

Geraldine leaned forward to study a grainy image on the screen, noting the woman's gait as she disappeared down steps leading from Lendal Bridge to the river path below. It was probably the last time anyone had seen her alive – apart from her killer. As she watched, a second figure walked across the bridge, right at her heels.

'Did you see that? There was someone behind her,' Geraldine said. 'Go back. Play that again.'

She hadn't been mistaken. A figure shrouded in a long hooded coat turned off on to the bridge just after the woman in the full skirt started down the steps.

'We need to enhance that image,' Geraldine said.

'We did our best,' the constable replied. 'The hood gets in the way. There isn't a clear shot of his face.'

Geraldine studied the moving image. Stilled, it was too blurred to make out any details. It wasn't even clear whether they were looking at a man or a woman. She swore softly.

'Work backwards,' she suggested. 'We need to find an image of this figure before he or she reached the bridge, an image where you can actually see the face.'

'We've tried,' the constable assured her. 'We've scoured all the footage we can find of the streets leading to the bridge, searching for an earlier shot.'

'Try harder,' Geraldine snapped.

She knew she was being unreasonable. The visual images team were doing their best. Everyone was doing what they could, but it was frustrating to be so close to the face of a witness who might be able to describe the killer, yet not be able to see it. It was even possible they were watching the killer as he followed his victim down to the river.

'Just keep looking,' Geraldine said as she turned to leave the room.

The constable scowled. 'I told you, we've looked everywhere.'

Nevertheless she must have persisted because barely an hour later she called Geraldine.

'It's a woman,' she said.

'What?'

'The person who followed the victim down off the bridge was a woman. We traced her back through town and a CCTV camera picked her up as she was passing a lighted shop window. We've got a shot of her face, although it's not very clear even after we enhanced it. But someone might recognise her,' she added uncertainly.

It was disappointing, since they were looking for a man, but beneath the anonymous figure's hood it was just about possible to make out long dark hair and dark lipstick. The woman also appeared to be wearing fairly heavy eye make-up, although that could have been shadow. Looking at the image Geraldine could see why the constable had sounded unsure. It was unlikely anyone would be able to identify the woman from that fuzzy image. Still, it was possible the unknown woman had seen the killer and would be able to help them with a description. Instantly, Geraldine thought of the dark-haired woman who had been spotted near the scene of the first murder. They had to try and find her.

'And there's no sign of a gang of youths,' Geraldine added, when she told Eileen about the sighting.

The detective chief inspector chose to ignore the last comment. Geraldine wasn't even sure if Eileen had heard her.

That afternoon, Eileen prepared an urgent television appearance in which she appealed to the unidentified witness to come forward.

'We'll be inundated with false information,' she grumbled.

They were doing everything possible to find the woman who had followed the victim. Even so, Geraldine wasn't optimistic. If the missing woman had witnessed the murder and not reported it at the time, she was hardly likely to come forward now.

'Perhaps she was scared,' Ariadne suggested.

'Why would she be less scared now?' Geraldine asked.

'Or maybe she saw the killer approaching, but had no idea what he was intending to do. I mean, it's hardly what you'd expect to see, is it? Anyway, once she's seen the TV appeal, or heard about it, she'll know this is a murder investigation, and she might decide to show up. There's a chance, anyway.'

And without any other leads, they needed to follow up any chance they had.

15

THE NEXT MORNING THERE was a predictable flurry of spurious phone calls and people arriving in person at the police station to describe their experiences of walking by the river. Most of them claimed to have been followed and even accosted by strangers who were clearly harbouring murderous intent. All were able to give quite detailed accounts of the person they had encountered. The only common feature in the diverse descriptions was the manic expression in the killer's eyes which were variously blue, brown or green, 'like a snake', one witness said.

'Do snakes have green eyes?' Ariadne asked Geraldine, who just shrugged.

This was the downside of appeals to the public. Extra officers were drafted in to cope with the calls, but Eileen's appearance on television resulted in a mass of conflicting reports. Everyone was aware that most, if not all, of the calls were going to be a waste of time, but they persisted, knowing that in among the false allegations and trumped-up descriptions, there could be one nugget of truth that would lead them to identify the killer. He had already struck twice. They couldn't let him claim another victim.

At lunchtime, Geraldine went to look for the long-haired woman who had been filmed walking near Pope's Head Alley. The house where she appeared to live belonged to a landlord who let his house on six-month contracts. The woman Geraldine was looking for had been in residence for three months, and her six months' rent had been paid in advance, directly into the landlord's account. The tenant's name was Lindsey Curtis, a name that wasn't known to the police. Geraldine rang the bell but again there was no response from inside the house.

The following morning Ian listened more attentively than Eileen had done to Geraldine's suggestion that the long-haired woman might be a witness in Grant's murder case, and could possibly have been there when Felicity was attacked.

'Do you think she's working with the killer?'

Geraldine shrugged. 'I don't know, but we need to speak to her.'

Ian shared Geraldine's disappointment that she had not yet managed to speak to the potential witness.

'No matter,' he said. 'We'll question her sooner or later. Hopefully sooner. Well done on tracking her down.'

At a briefing that afternoon, Eileen reiterated her belief that a group of young muggers were responsible for the two recent fatalities. It was certainly possible, but it still remained only a theory.

'It could be coincidence,' Ian said.

'Stabbing isn't that uncommon,' Geraldine agreed.

'Two people stabbed to death in less than a week within less than half a mile of each other? I hardly think that's common. This isn't London,' Eileen said, looking pointedly at Geraldine. 'Of course you could argue it might be coincidence, two fatal stabbings so close together, if it wasn't for DNA evidence telling us one person was present at both attacks. It must have been the same killer. And the only lead we have so far is this gang of muggers. So come on, let's find them.'

Geraldine didn't point out that there was actually nothing to link the muggers to the two stabbings other than that witnesses had reported seeing the youths carrying knives. There was nothing wrong with looking for the muggers. Apprehending them would certainly be a good thing, but it wasn't the job of the murder investigation team, and Geraldine was concerned that they were spending their limited resources hunting for the wrong criminals. She decided to sound Ian out about it but before she could raise the subject he brought it up himself.

They had gone to the pub for a quick drink after work. Geraldine had the impression Ian wanted to talk to her and she wondered if he wanted to vent his feelings about his estranged wife. But it turned out Ian only wanted to discuss work.

'Do *you* think we should be spending so much time questioning all the youngsters in York?' he asked her as soon as they sat down.

She hesitated. Her relationship with Ian was slightly complex. On the one hand they were old friends, but at the same time he was her superior officer and neither of them was yet used to that relationship. When they had first met, she had been an inspector and he had worked as her sergeant. Although their positions were now reversed, Geraldine didn't regret her demotion. By taking the place of her identical twin in an encounter with a dangerous drug dealer, Geraldine had put her own life on the line. She had survived the incident, but had ended up being arrested in place of her twin. In exchange for Geraldine risking her career, Helena had agreed to go into rehab and so far seemed to be managing to control her cravings. They had both had to give up the lives they had known, but Geraldine knew it had been harder for Helena than for her. At least she still had a job.

In addition to their long friendship, Ian had been working in York for years and knew Eileen better than Geraldine did. So for that reason as well, she felt she had to be circumspect in her comments.

'What do *you* think?' she replied.

Ian gave her a sympathetic smile, as if to say he understood the reason for her caution.

'It's all right, you know,' he said quietly. 'We're not on duty now. You can say what you like. No one else is going to know.'

Geraldine wondered if he was referring specifically to Eileen.

'For what it's worth,' she replied, 'I think we're possibly barking up the wrong tree, wasting resources on a wild goose chase.'

'Why don't we cut out the intermediate step and just bark at the geese?'

Ignoring the flippant interruption, Geraldine pressed on, determined to make her point now that she had begun. 'Even if we manage to find those muggers, or when we do I should say, how is that going to help us solve the murder case? There could be something that connects the two victims apart from the DNA of their killer, and that's what we ought to be investigating. Perhaps the woman was killed because she knew something?'

'About the first murder, you mean?'

'Yes. What if she was a witness to the first murder, or somehow found out about it, and so the killer decided it was necessary to silence her. We know the two stabbings are related, so that would make sense, wouldn't it?'

He nodded. 'If these muggers are involved, perhaps she knew the members of the gang who've been attacking people on the street, only once someone was killed she decided to go to the police, but it was too late because the muggers got wind of her intentions and got to her first to stop her talking to us.'

'So you're saying you still think the muggers are our killers?'

He shook his head. 'I don't know. I just don't know. What exactly are you saying?'

'This is just between us?'

He nodded.

'I actually think these murders were carried out by someone far more skilful than some young kid with a blade would be,' Geraldine said. 'I could be wrong, but it's just a feeling I have. And if you ask me, I don't think we'll find our murderer by tracking down the kids who've been carrying out all these low-level muggings. Those are crimes specifically of property. Kids snatching stuff they can sell. The murders have a different feel about them than any of the muggings.'

Ian nodded. 'Eileen thinks the two may be related.'

'Well, they're certainly connected. We know that from the DNA found on the bodies.'

'No, I mean she seems convinced the muggings and the murders are related.'

'I know. But just because they've been going on at around the same time, that doesn't mean these victims were attacked by the gang of muggers. It could be someone else entirely who's killed them. We ought to be searching for a connection between the two victims, as well as looking for the muggers, which could turn out to be a waste of time.'

Before Ian could respond, another voice interrupted them.

'What's a waste of time?'

Geraldine spun round. Standing behind her, Naomi was smiling across at Ian. Geraldine wondered whether it was coincidence that the young constable always seemed to turn up at the pub whenever Ian was there.

'Come and join us,' he said.

Naomi pulled a chair over and sat down between him and Geraldine.

'So what's a waste of time?' she repeated, leaning towards Ian ever so slightly.

He gave a dismissive shake of his head. 'It's nothing.'

Naomi's laughter sounded fake. 'You're discussing *nothing*?'

For a few seconds none of them spoke.

'Am I interrupting something?' Naomi asked.

Geraldine felt sorry for her colleague who had been chasing Ian for months without much obvious success. She always seemed to turn up wherever he was, and she hung on his words, while he appeared oblivious to her attention. But Geraldine was also irritated with the constable for interrupting her own conversations with Ian.

'No, no,' Geraldine assured her quickly, concealing her

disappointment. 'I was just going.'

'You haven't finished,' Ian said, glancing at her glass.

'I meant I need to push off soon, once I've drunk this. I'm knackered.'

Naomi smiled. 'The night is young,' she said.

'Yes, and so are you, but sadly I'm not and I need to get home to my bed soon,' Geraldine smiled.

'OK, granny,' Naomi grinned. She turned to Ian. 'Are you hungry? We could grab a bite –'

'No, I need to get going as well,' he replied without even turning to look at Naomi.

Seeing how crestfallen the constable was, Geraldine swallowed a sigh. In many ways life was tough for a single woman in her early forties, but she didn't remember it seeming any easier when she had been in her twenties, as Naomi was. She finished her drink and gathered up her coat and bag.

'I'll see you tomorrow,' she said as she stood up.

In the door she turned and saw Naomi still sitting beside Ian. She was leaning forward, her pose suggesting she was listening intently. But Ian was staring gloomily at the table, and he wasn't saying anything.

16

THE LOCAL PAPERS THE following day were full of sensational reports of a 'crime wave' hitting the city. It was nothing new, but the mood at the police station was tetchy and the usual banter and chat were noticeably absent despite the fact that it was Friday and the sun was shining outside.

'It's like working in a morgue, sitting here,' Ariadne grumbled.

Geraldine smiled at that, because Jonah was far more cheerful than any of her colleagues at the police station that day. Her own mood darkened when she learned that Felicity's parents were coming over from Leeds that afternoon to formally identify the body, and she was tasked with meeting them at the mortuary.

She set off in good time and arrived about twenty minutes before the Dunmores were due to arrive, but they had caught an earlier train and were already there, waiting to be shown in to view the body. The visitors' waiting room at the mortuary was decorated in light grey and pink, and sensitively furnished. There were a few plants and several boxes of tissues placed on the tables within easy reach of all the armchairs, which were upholstered in soft grey. Mr and Mrs Dunmore were sitting together on a sofa, holding hands, their anxiety almost palpable. They both looked young to have a daughter in her late twenties.

'You don't have to do this,' Mr Dunmore said to his wife when Geraldine offered to take them to see their daughter's body. 'I can go. You can stay here if you want to.'

With positive confirmation from her dental records, it was almost impossible the body had been wrongly identified.

'No, no, I want to see her,' his wife replied in a voice that was barely louder than a whisper.

Both her parents had dark hair so Geraldine guessed the dead woman's blond hair had been dyed. It had still been streaked with mud and dirt when she had seen the body previously. Observing the corpse after it had been cleaned up, Geraldine could distinguish a few traces of dark roots under the hair. She was relieved the girl had been stabbed in the chest, because her face was virtually undamaged. Only a few skilfully concealed minor scratches and abrasions remained from her contact with the river bank. Her make-up had been restored, the redness of her lips contrasting starkly with the pallor of her cheeks.

Mrs Dunmore let out a faint yelp, like a cry of pain. Tears slid unchecked down her own pale cheeks. There was no need for words. Mr Dunmore put his arm around his wife as though to support her, and turned to nod at Geraldine.

'Yes, that's her. That's our Felicity.'

His voice cracked as he spoke the name, and as though that was her cue, his wife began to wail. Geraldine led them back to the visitors' room and waited for their initial shock to subside.

'I'm so sorry. We're doing everything we can to find out who did this, and rest assured we will find the person responsible. Now, we can do this another time if you prefer, but I would like to ask you a few questions.'

'What can we do to help you find whoever did that to our daughter?' Mr Dunmore asked, his eyes bright with emotion.

Mrs Dunmore had already collapsed on a sofa where she was sitting weeping silently, but her husband seemed to have his grief in check for the moment. Geraldine spoke to him.

'Please, sit down. I just want to ask whether you know of anyone who might have had cause to feel angry with your daughter? A jealous ex-boyfriend perhaps?'

She hesitated to add that Felicity had clearly been a very

attractive woman. Mr Dunmore was more likely to keep control of his emotions if they avoided talking about his daughter directly. From the sofa, Mrs Dunmore mumbled incoherently and her husband nodded.

'She had an argument with someone recently,' he said and hesitated.

Geraldine waited, deeming it wise not to hurry him.

'They met at a club or a bar somewhere.'

His wife muttered inaudibly.

'They were in a relationship for a while,' he continued awkwardly. 'But he was no good. We knew that the moment we laid eyes on him. He was a smart looking boy, but I can't say we were impressed when he told us he was between jobs.' He drew in a deep breath. 'Between jobs, that's what he said. Anyway, you can probably tell where this is heading. He spun her some sob story and she ended up lending him money.' He paused. 'Quite a lot of money, in fact. More than she could afford. He was supposed to be paying her back monthly, but that didn't last long. And nor did their relationship once he'd got what he wanted.'

'So he owes her money?'

'Not any more. She took me to see him, and I threatened him.'

'Threatened him?'

He frowned. 'It was very vague. I just said if he didn't pay her back, I'd deal with him myself. That was all.'

'And did he pay her back?'

He shook his head. 'He said he would but now of course he can't.'

He dropped his head in his hands and his shoulders shook with sobs. His wife pulled herself together.

'This wasn't your fault. I don't think he did it, Barry. He wasn't like that. He wasn't violent. You said he was scared when you threatened him. He would have run off, he would never have done something like this.' She turned and appealed to Geraldine for corroboration that her husband wasn't responsible for what had happened to their daughter.

'It's extremely unlikely,' she agreed. 'But I would like you to give me details of where I can find this ex-boyfriend as we'd like to speak to him.'

Mr Dunmore's voice was muffled behind his hands. 'Of course. I can't tell you his address right now, but I've got it at home.'

'Can he email the details to you?' his wife asked, stepping in to take control as her husband broke down sobbing at her side.

'Yes, of course. Please email me when you get home. And I'm so sorry, once again. We'll do everything we can to find out who did this. I know it can't bring her back, but we might stop it from happening to someone else.'

Feeling helpless in the presence of such raw grief, Geraldine left the couple weeping silently, side by side. Beyond comfort, they were no longer holding hands.

17

Mr Dunmore was as good as his word. At nine o'clock the next morning Geraldine received an email with details of a man called Tom Parker who lived in Leeds. She drove straight there, hoping to catch him before he went out. As it was Saturday, she thought he might not be up and out early. She left the young constable who had accompanied her in the car with instructions to follow her after five minutes, and wait at the gate. With that backup in place, she went and rang the bell. The girl who answered the door looked about sixteen.

'Is Tom here?'

'Why? What's he to you?'

Geraldine looked younger than her forty years, but she could still have been the girl's mother. Even so, the girl scowled and looked at her through narrowed eyes, as though she thought Geraldine might have a personal interest in Tom.

'Why do you want to see him?'

Geraldine hesitated. The girl looked shrewd, and Tom was likely to be slippery.

'We have a mutual friend,' she said.

It was half true.

'What friend?' the girl asked sharply. 'Who is she? What's this "friend" called?'

Geraldine sighed. There was nothing more annoying than a potential witness who refused to co-operate. With a sigh she pulled out her identity card. But before the girl had a chance to look at it, a young man appeared in the hallway behind her. He was tall, with dark hair and pointed features.

'Yes?' he said. 'What's this about, Lily?'

Geraldine took a step forward to put one foot across the threshold. The young man's expression darkened and he pulled the girl backwards, so that she was standing directly in front of him, like a shield.

'What do you want?' he asked.

'I'd like to talk to you about Felicity Dunmore.'

'Oh fuck off, will you?' He took a step back. 'Shut the door, Lily.'

'You can talk to me right now, or I can call for a car to come and pick you up and bring you along to the police station. Your choice.'

The young man looked startled, and he stared more closely at the card Geraldine was holding up. Understanding who Geraldine was, he cleared his throat.

'I thought you were a debt collector. Look, I owe the girl some money. So what? I said I'd pay her back and I will. I was never not going to pay her back. I told her father I'll give her the whole lot as soon as I get a job and in the meantime I'll pay what I can. But I don't see what on earth any of this has got to do with the police.'

'Who's Felicity?' Lily demanded.

'Oh bloody hell,' Tom burst out, exasperated. 'Now look what you've done. I'll get hell from her now. Oh shit. Can't you people mind your own business?' He turned to his new girlfriend. 'Felicity's history. She's just someone I was seeing for a while, that's all, but if you think you're going to be in any way threatened by her, you couldn't be more wrong. Honestly, Lily, I wouldn't cross the road to speak to her. In fact, I'd make a point of crossing the road to avoid her because she'd only be on at me for money. She won't come between us, I promise.'

'That's true, at least,' Geraldine said.

Tom and Lily both turned to look at her.

'She might say that now –' Lily began.

'Oh, I can guarantee she won't be bothering you again.'

Geraldine looked directly at Tom above Lily's head. 'Felicity's dead.'

His eyes widened. 'Felicity's dead? But –'

'Where were you on Tuesday night?'

His shocked expression altered as he registered the implications of the question.

'I was –I was –' he stammered.

'He was here with me,' Lily said quickly.

As Geraldine had suspected, the girl was sharp. Lowering her gaze to look at Lily, she was met by a cold stare.

'Lily,' she said gently, reminding herself that the girl was very young. 'It's never a good idea to lie to the police. We have all sorts of ways of finding out the truth – witnesses you're not aware of, DNA, and CCTV. So there's really no point in lying about where you were. You don't even remember what you were doing on Monday night, do you?'

The girl bristled. 'Don't tell me what I can and can't remember. Are you calling me a liar? I told you Tom was with me on Tuesday night, and that's where he was.'

Geraldine sighed. 'Tom,' she said, 'I'm afraid you're going to have to answer a few more questions. Would you like to accompany me now?'

Tom was about to speak when his attention was caught by something over Geraldine's shoulder. The constable had arrived at the gate. Tom's jaw tensed.

'I can't go out like this,' he muttered.

He pushed Lily aside and Geraldine saw that beneath a long sleeved sweatshirt he was wearing only underpants. Without taking her eyes off Tom, she gestured for the constable to join her.

'Mr Parker needs to put some clothes on,' she said. 'Would you accompany him please?'

Her colleague went into the house and disappeared upstairs behind Tom, leaving Geraldine alone with Lily.

'You won't get away with this, you know,' the girl said.

Geraldine looked at her in silence.

'I know you're trying to pin something on Tom, but just because he knew that girl doesn't mean he had anything to do with her death.'

Geraldine inclined her head. 'Of course it doesn't, and that's why he hasn't been arrested. But he knew the dead girl and we need to find out if there's anything he can tell us that we don't already know about her, like who she associated with, and where she liked to go. And of course we want to eliminate him from our enquiries.'

The girl glared at her. While they waited for the two men to come back downstairs, Geraldine found out Lily's full name and her work place. She grinned as she admitted that her parents had been extremely unhappy when she had moved in with a man nearly twenty years older than her. A moment later, Tom came trotting downstairs with the constable at his heels, ready to lunge if he tried to barge past Geraldine who was standing in the doorway. They drove Tom to the police station without any further conversation, and by eleven o'clock, Geraldine and Ian were facing him across an interview table.

'My client has not been charged,' the duty lawyer said in an unpleasant nasal voice, shaking her blond head as though she disapproved of the situation.

Ian took no notice of her. 'Where were you on Tuesday evening?'

Tom shrugged, in a transparent attempt to appear nonchalant. 'I was at home, and Lily can corroborate that.'

The steely-eyed blond lawyer gave an almost imperceptible nod. Her client had clearly remembered the instructions he had been given.

'Where were you a week last Friday?' Geraldine asked.

Tom looked surprised. 'What? How should I know?'

He turned to the lawyer with a panicked expression, and she held up one hand to silence him. Geraldine suspected the lawyer knew perfectly well what had happened on that Friday night.

'My client is not prepared to answer that question.'

'If your client refuses to answer our questions, we'll have him arrested for obstruction,' Ian replied.

'I'm not refusing to answer, but, really? Two Fridays ago?' Tom repeated, sounding baffled. 'I can't remember. I mean, Lily and I usually go out for a few drinks on a Friday night, and sometimes we meet up with friends, but –' He shrugged. 'It's not like we have a regular arrangement or anything.'

'Please, think carefully, two Fridays ago, where were you that night?'

'What did Lily say?'

'I'm asking you.'

He shrugged. 'We would have gone out drinking, or stayed at home. I can't remember.'

'Are you sure you were together?'

He nodded uneasily, unaware that he was talking himself into being regarded as a suspect. It hadn't taken a constable long to establish that Lily had been visiting her parents in Hertfordshire on the weekend of Grant's murder. She had left York straight after work on Friday, returning on the Sunday evening. So Tom's alibi for the Friday evening when Grant had been murdered was discredited. Either Tom had a very bad memory, or else he was lying. And if he was prepared to lie about one evening, he might also be lying when he claimed to have been with Lily on the night Felicity had been killed. Eileen decided to keep Tom locked up overnight, despite his lawyer's objections.

That evening the atmosphere at the police station was cautiously optimistic. Lacking only incontrovertible proof, they seemed to have caught the killer. All it needed was for Tom's DNA to match that found on the two dead bodies.

'Why did you do it, Tom?' Ian asked when Tom's DNA had been sent off for processing.

The suspect just shook his head and shrugged his shoulders, insisting he had never killed anyone.

'Felicity and I broke up,' he repeated, in a trembling voice. 'But I never hurt her. I never hurt anyone. I couldn't. Ask Lily. She'll tell you. Ask anyone. This is all a mistake.'

Geraldine found it hard to believe Tom could be guilty.

'What on earth's your problem?' Ariadne asked her.

'I don't know, he just doesn't seem the type to go around killing people. He seems so —' She paused, struggling to find the right word for what she meant. 'So gentle,' she concluded.

Ariadne raised her eyebrows. 'You can't tell whether someone's a murderer or not just by questioning them. You know that. And this man you're defending is living with a teenager half his age.'

Geraldine nodded unhappily.

'That's true,' she replied. 'It was just the impression I had, but I'm probably wrong.'

Ian was walking past as she spoke. He raised his eyebrows at her when he heard what she said.

'It's not like you to be wrong,' he said.

'Are you saying I won't admit when I'm wrong?' she began indignantly.

'I think he meant you're not often wrong,' Ariadne interrupted her. 'Surely it was meant as a compliment?'

Geraldine began to stammer an apology, but Ian had already moved out of earshot. Usually so shrewd in her understanding of other people, somehow she was flustered by Ian. Her confusion over her feelings towards him seemed to be spilling over into her professional life too, so that where formerly she would have trusted her instincts, she now seemed to be floundering.

'I suppose Tom could be the killer,' she conceded. 'I just had this impression... I probably had him all wrong.'

Her bewilderment must have been apparent, because Ariadne gave her a curious look.

'For goodness sake, Geraldine,' she said, 'why are you so down about it? This is it! He's stabbed two people to death and in a few hours we'll have the proof we've been waiting for!'

18

As soon as she arrived at the police station the following morning, Geraldine went along to the custody suite to have a word with the suspect, hoping to satisfy herself of his guilt.

'Looking for a room for tonight?' the custody sergeant called out when he saw her approaching. 'We have guest accommodation available. It may not be the most comfortable hotel you'll ever stay in, but you won't be disturbed by loud music late at night, and privacy is guaranteed. And it's absolutely free, all in, breakfast, lunch and dinner.'

She laughed. 'What's on the menu today?'

'You've missed breakfast, but there's some sort of meat pie and mash for lunch.'

'You certainly make it sound attractive. Can I see the wine list?'

'Champagne for you, Madame? Oh, drat, we seem to have run out.'

Even though there was still a lot to do, the atmosphere at the police station felt more relaxed now that Tom was securely locked in a cell. Seated on his hard bunk, staring at the floor, he started up when the door opened to admit Geraldine.

'Well?' he asked. 'Can I go now?'

His face looked paler than when she had last seen him, and his eyes were bloodshot.

'Tom,' she said, 'you know we're going to keep talking to you until you tell us the truth.'

He sat down, and stared dully at her. 'I've told you the truth,' he said. 'I can't remember what I was doing that night. You

100

can ask me and ask me, but if I can't remember then I can't tell you, can I?'

There was no point in continuing the conversation so she left, resolving to keep her reservations to herself. If it turned out that Tom was guilty, as seemed likely, she would only damage her reputation with her colleagues by insisting she believed he was innocent. And if he really was innocent, the truth would emerge soon enough. Frustrated by the way her gut feelings had let her down, she decided to take advantage of her day off and visit her twin sister in London.

Geraldine had cancelled their last meeting, which always annoyed her twin, so it was with some trepidation that she set off. She decided to take the train to London as it was faster than driving and she could reread the witness statements on the way. The results of Tom's DNA test would be back soon to hopefully put an end to all her speculation. In the meantime the gang of muggers remained at large and she wanted to read through all the witness reports again. It was possible there might be a detail that had so far been overlooked. She devoted the entire journey to reading the different accounts, and reached London without having given much thought to her sister. It was probably better that way. She would only have become stressed if she had spent the time worrying about how she was going to be received. Geraldine understood it was difficult for Helena to control her cravings, but her erratic behaviour was challenging.

'You're doing your best for her,' Ariadne had said when Geraldine had complained about Helena in very general terms. 'If she's going to get angry with you for not giving her everything she wants from you, then you need to set firm boundaries for yourself. Decide how much is reasonable for you to do for her, and do just that. But you shouldn't feel guilty for not doing more than is reasonable, or even possible. Don't let her manipulate you with her disappointment and anger. It's not your fault she's had such a hard time of it.'

Geraldine knew Ariadne was right, but that didn't make it any easier. Her underlying fear was that Helena might revert to her drug abuse if she didn't feel she was receiving enough support. Trying to feel strong and confident, she strode along the street where Helena was living in a flat Geraldine rented for her. Helena opened the door straightaway. Stepping over a pair of boots lying in the doorway, Geraldine followed her sister into a dingy living room. Helena had not yet cleaned the carpet or upholstery, nor had she washed the grimy windows or replaced the once smart curtains that were now mottled with mildew. The room could easily have been smartened up with a coat of paint, clean curtains and a new rug on the stained carpet. Living in careless squalor didn't seem to bother Helena, but Geraldine found the place depressing. She was relieved when they left to go out for lunch.

Geraldine took her sister to a restaurant around the back of Kings Cross station that she knew from her years spent living not far from there in Islington. It was a fairly smart place, but Geraldine was fed up of the tacky cafés Helena frequented and wanted to take her somewhere more comfortable. Helena didn't comment as they went in the restaurant and were shown to their seats. She seemed as at home in a slightly upmarket restaurant as she was in a cheap café, and Geraldine realised that her twin didn't actually pay much attention to her surroundings. Someone as unobservant as her would make a poor detective. It was strange how similar they were in appearance, yet how different in inclinations and temperament. She wondered if they would ever reach enough of an understanding to become really close.

Helena seemed relatively cheerful, and for once they didn't argue. Although Helena was skinny, Geraldine was pleased to see that she still had her appetite, eating twice as much as Geraldine.

'I don't know where you put it all,' she laughed, as the pile of food on Helena's plate rapidly vanished.

For a second Geraldine was afraid she had said the wrong thing when Helena didn't respond, but she was only finishing a mouthful. Swallowing, she grinned, displaying chipped teeth, before she carried on eating.

'That was good,' she said at last, wiping the last crumbs from her plate with the side of her knife. 'You didn't eat much.' It sounded like a criticism.

Geraldine hesitated. 'I had enough,' she said at last. 'I ate breakfast on the train.'

Still, the lunch passed without incident and Helena thanked her with genuine appreciation in her voice.

'I know I'm not what you might call the best of sisters,' she added. 'I know I'm not perfect.'

'Who is?'

'You are.'

Helena's retort sounded like an accusation.

Geraldine laughed it off. 'I wish,' she said. 'Honestly, Helena, I'm just like everyone else, struggling to make sense of my life and keep on top of things.'

'But you *do* stay on top. That's just the point, innit? Me, I hit rock bottom. If it weren't for you, what the hell would've happened to me?'

Helena paused, perhaps remembering the vicious drug pusher who had been threatening to shoot her until Geraldine had stepped in to save her, at the cost of her own career prospects.

'Oh, I know it's not just me,' she went on. 'Everyone's got their shit to deal with. And don't think I'm not grateful to you for bailing me out like you done. But it's hard sometimes, trying to move on. Because the past is always there, innit? "So we beat on, boats against the current, borne back ceaselessly into the past." I been doing some reading. One of my new friends put me onto that. It's a good book. *The Great Gatsby*. You heard of it?'

Geraldine nodded, hiding her surprise. 'I've read it, but I wouldn't be able to quote from it.'

Helena shrugged. 'I don't suppose many people could, but I seem to remember useless shit like that.' She shrugged. 'Not that it's going to do me any good.'

Encouraged by their conversation, after lunch Geraldine invited Helena to accompany her to the British Museum. When she had lived in London she used to enjoy wandering around the exhibits on her days off.

Helena laughed at the suggestion. 'A museum? Me? What the fuck for? I've never been inside a museum in my life and I'm not about to start now. Bloody hell. What do you think I am?'

Geraldine smiled her regret. 'Another time then.'

'Not bloody likely.'

'You will be careful, won't you?' Helena asked as they said goodbye. 'I mean, with all those killers you're chasing after. Don't let them get you, will you?'

Geraldine was more touched by Helena's unexpected concern than she admitted. After reassuring Helena that as a police officer she was well protected, she left. Glancing round, she saw Helena still standing outside the restaurant, watching her walk away. All in all, it had been a satisfactory meeting. They had actually got on quite well, and there had been none of Helena's usual recriminations. Geraldine hoped this might mark an improvement in their relationship which, so far, had been strained. She felt a burst of optimism and even allowed herself to hope the case would be resolved soon.

But by the time she arrived back in York early that evening, the report had come back on Tom's DNA. There was no evidence he had been present at either of the murder scenes, and the identity of the man who had left his DNA at both remained a mystery. Geraldine called in at the police station to see what was happening in the aftermath of the report. Eileen was prowling around with a long face, snapping at anyone who spoke to her. Tom had been released, and even the most cheery of officers were subdued because they were back to casting around for leads in a case that seemed to be going nowhere.

'We have to be patient,' Ian said when she saw him.

'If it wasn't for the DNA evidence, we might have convicted him,' Geraldine replied. 'I wonder how many false convictions there were in the days before DNA evidence.'

It was a sobering thought to which neither of them had an answer.

19

WHENEVER WENDY WAITED UNTIL one o'clock to go out, she had to waste half of her lunch hour queueing for a sandwich, so she decided to take an early break. The sun was shining and she didn't want to be stuck in a shop for the little time she had away from the office. As it turned out, she was doubly pleased with her decision because not only was there no queue in the sandwich shop, but they had just taken a fresh tray of sausage rolls from the oven. The smell was irresistible so she bought three and scoffed one before setting off to find a bench in the sun, clutching the paper bag with the rest of her lunch in one hand, and her handbag in the other. As she turned off the main road, she was faintly aware of the sound of footsteps behind her. Someone was in a hurry. She was about to move over to the side of the pavement to allow them to pass when she felt a violent tug on her handbag.

'What the hell –' she burst out, tightening her hold on her bag and trying to yank it away.

Looking round, she saw a stocky boy staring at her. Caught by a ray of sun, the blade of a knife glinted brightly in his hand. Two other boys were standing on either side of him, glaring at her, and she now saw it was one of them who had caught hold of the strap on her bag. The third boy looked younger than the other two, and she thought he looked scared. At any rate he seemed to be trembling, and his dark eyes stared wildly at her as though he was afraid she was going to hit him. The boy who had attempted to snatch her bag was taller than the other two and very skinny, with untidy dark hair. He shuffled nervously from one foot to the other, as though he was incapable of keeping still. Only the boy who was brandishing a knife didn't move a muscle but just stood there, gazing coolly at her.

'Come on, hand it over,' the tall boy said.

He pulled the bag but again failed to dislodge it from her arm. For a second no one spoke. No one moved.

Wendy gave the strap a sudden tug. 'Get your hands off!' she shouted, too outraged to care that she might be in danger. 'Help!' she cried out, more loudly. 'I'm being robbed!'

The street was deserted. The boy with the knife took a step closer, and another. When he spoke his voice was so quiet, she had to strain to hear. 'Shut your trap or I'll shut it for you.'

His eyes gleamed with suppressed excitement and she realised he was high, and unlikely to respond rationally to anything she said or did. Her thoughts racing, she clutched the bag of sausage rolls more tightly and, in that instant, the boy lunged forward. A point of cold metal tickled her skin as the tip of his blade touched her neck. She was conscious of the warmth of the sun on the back of her head, and a few flecks of white fluff floating high overhead in a bright blue sky. Slow resentment unfurled inside her like a cat flexing its muscles. It was never wise to react in anger, but all her life she had been pushed around – by her parents, by her teachers, by her boss. Now even these imbeciles thought they could bend her to their will.

She had to resist their assault, if only to protect her painstakingly constructed self-esteem. But there were three of them, and at least one of them had a knife. All she had was two sausage rolls and her handbag. Even if she had been carrying a weapon, she wouldn't have been able to reach for it because her hands were full.

She stared at the boy who was threatening her, gauging his weight and height. If it wasn't for the knife, she might have stood a chance, even against three of them. None of them looked particularly fit. But the sharp metal point was pressing against her neck, and she didn't know whether the other boys were armed. Holding her breath, she edged backwards until the tip of the knife was no longer in contact with her skin.

'OK,' she said, lowering her head submissively, but keeping her eyes fixed on the boy. 'I don't want any trouble. I'm not stupid. I can see there's no point in trying to resist. But put the knife down, for heaven's sake. If I slip, there could be a nasty accident, and I don't think you want to end up drenched in my blood, do you? I'm a haemophiliac,' she added, with sudden inspiration, 'and that means even the tiniest cut makes me bleed a lot. And I do mean a lot. I have to go straight to hospital or I can bleed to death in minutes.'

She was talking nonsense, but it seemed to work because the youngest boy muttered something about not wanting to have a murder on their hands. The boy holding a knife grunted and lowered his arm. Seconds later he was lying flat on his back, winded, and staring up at the sky with his mouth hanging open. He wouldn't have known what hit him. As he flipped over he had let go of his knife, which had gone skidding into the road. She was afraid he might have cracked his head on the pavement when he landed, but there was no time to worry about that. Before the other boys could take in what had happened, she turned and sprinted back to the main road, still clutching her handbag. She had dropped the sausage rolls, but the boys who had tried to rob her were welcome to them.

After glancing up to check there was a camera facing the doorway, she darted into the first shop she came to and whipped out her phone. On the point of reporting that she had been mugged, she hesitated. She might have injured the boy who had been waving a knife in her face. It was possible she had killed him. She was confident she had been justified in using her martial arts skills to defend herself, but if she had actually hurt her assailant, perhaps seriously, she could end up in trouble. The law was tricky, and she had heard of people being prosecuted after innocently fighting to defend themselves from attack. On balance, she decided it might be best to keep quiet and not report the incident at all. If by some horrible accident she had actually killed her attacker, she might lose a lot more than a couple of sausage rolls if she was apprehended and prosecuted. As it was, there was no way the assault could be traced back to her.

Thoughtfully she put her phone back in her bag and made her way to the office. She hadn't even been away for an hour.

'Had a good morning?' one of her colleagues asked as she went back inside.

She nodded, and gave a tight smile. 'Oh, you know. Same old, same old.'

20

TOM WAS SENT HOME, threatening to complain about wrongful arrest and police brutality. No one took any notice of him, least of all the impervious custody sergeant who had heard such accusations many times before.

'Well, he wasn't a happy man,' the sergeant told Geraldine cheerfully, 'and he certainly wasn't at all pleased with us, I can tell you that much.'

She shrugged. It couldn't have been easy for Tom, finding himself imprisoned like that, completely out of the blue. Admittedly he had only spent a single night in a cell, but he had originally been locked up for an unspecified period. That must have been a terrifying experience, especially for someone who had little reason to feel confident in the police. After all, they had taken him in for questioning and then accused him of a double murder he hadn't committed. It was understandable he might have been afraid he was being stitched up as, without an alibi, he had little defence against the power and credibility of the police. He was probably still feeling stunned by the whole experience.

After lunch the team assembled to discuss the latest development. Eileen was doing her best to sound encouraging, but she couldn't conceal her disappointment.

'We have to put this behind us and move forward,' she said. 'With Tom in the clear, we must redouble our efforts to find the muggers. They are now back to being our main suspects.'

Geraldine glanced around the room. Her colleagues were all gazing at Eileen, and most were nodding earnestly. No one seemed prepared to challenge what she was telling them. But just because Tom had been exonerated didn't automatically mean that the muggers were guilty of murder. Worried that she was alone in her silent criticism of the detective chief inspector's focus, she went to look for Ian to find out whether he shared her opinion. There was no one else with whom she felt comfortable sharing her private views about the way their senior investigating officer was conducting the case.

Ian dismissed her reservations straightaway. 'What would you do in her position?'

Geraldine took a deep breath. They both knew she would never rise to the position of detective chief inspector after her demotion to sergeant. The fact that she had once been a likely candidate for promotion made her position harder to bear.

'I just think we should keep an open mind,' she replied, trying not to sound bitter. 'When we thought Tom was guilty, we abandoned the idea that the muggers were responsible without a moment's thought. So how plausible does that make them as suspects in a murder investigation? Why are we suddenly so convinced they are our killers, just because it wasn't Tom? Isn't it possible there's someone else out there who killed those two victims? Why are we being so limited in our search?'

'It's not true we abandoned our attempts to find the muggers. And I don't see why the killers wouldn't also be muggers.'

'That's hardly a reason to think they *would* be.'

'The victims were stabbed to death, and we know the muggers carry knives.'

'Again, why is that a reason to suppose they are the same people? Are knives so difficult to come by?'

'Well, the plain fact is, we don't have any other leads.'

'That's exactly my point. Instead of devoting all our resources to looking for people who may or may not be implicated in the murders, we ought to be searching for the actual culprits. It might be the muggers, it might not. We just don't know.'

'But what else can we do?'

'For a start, we could be searching for anything that connects the two victims. And how about taking DNA samples from anyone matching the profile we have got, Caucasian, male with blond hair and blue eyes.'

'You really think we should be taking DNA samples from every blond adult male in York? That would be an impossible task. And we don't even know if the killer lives in York.'

'But why are we only pursuing these muggers?' Geraldine insisted.

'I would have thought the reason was obvious. If Tom *was* guilty, then it wasn't the gang who've been out mugging people. But now we know he's not the killer we're after, they *could* be guilty. That's all. It seems perfectly simple to me.' He stared at her with an intensity that made her feel uneasy. Doing her best to conceal her disquiet, she lowered her gaze. 'It's understandable you're feeling disappointed about your position in the team, Geraldine,' he went on, 'but you must guard against letting that feeling turn into resentment against the DCI. You could have been in her shoes, but you're not. You need to get past that and concentrate on the job.'

Geraldine's face felt hot. 'Is that what you think of me? That I'm so unprofessional I'd let myself be influenced by my feelings about my own career?'

He frowned, but before he could respond she spun round and left his office. She wasn't sure she could trust herself not to snap at him. She had never felt so despondent at work before.

'What's wrong?' Ariadne asked, catching sight of Geraldine's scowl when she returned to her desk.

'Oh, nothing, it's just this case.'

'I know. It's driving us all nuts. Fancy a coffee?'

Geraldine nodded. 'Might as well.'

They went down to the canteen together. Sitting over steaming mugs of coffee, they discussed the likelihood that the muggers and the killer were one and the same. In its own way, Geraldine found Ariadne's reaction to her reservations even more depressing than Ian's. While he had accused her of being distracted by her own personal disappointment, Ariadne didn't even seem that bothered by what Geraldine was saying.

'It's what the DCI wants us to do,' she replied, when Geraldine questioned their focus on the muggers.

'But what if these muggers have got nothing to do with the murders at all? We could be wasting valuable resources and time in searching for them. We've spent hours studying CCTV footage of the areas around the scene of their attacks, questioning the victims of the muggings, trying to trace the goods that were stolen, and asking around in all the locations where youngsters hang out. What if we've been looking in the wrong place all along?'

Ariadne shrugged. 'Then it's the DCI's head on the block, not ours.'

'But surely the most important thing is to find these killers?'

'Yes, of course it is, but we're part of a team and we can only do what we're told.' She gave Geraldine a curious look. 'I know you were an inspector, and you're used to having more say in what goes on, but well, you're just a sergeant like me now, and we can't question what a DCI tells us to do, can we?'

Geraldine had no answer to that. It seemed that any time she questioned the detective chief inspector's views, she was accused of insubordination. She genuinely believed she was right to challenge Eileen's judgement, but perhaps Ian and Ariadne were right and she was actually voicing a resentment she couldn't acknowledge, even to herself. If that was true, then she could no longer trust her own objectivity.

'You're right,' she told Ariadne. 'We can't question our superiors. We just have to follow orders.'

She hoped she hadn't sounded bitter, but the words sickened her. She stood up abruptly and hurried back to her desk, leaving her half-drunk coffee on the table.

21

IT WASN'T THAT THEY had failed to profit from their intended victim. That would have been depressing enough, but it wouldn't have been the first time they had messed up an attempt to mug someone. Once, they had approached a man who had turned out to be homeless and destitute. Not only that, but they hadn't noticed he had a dog. The hobo had chased them down the road, waving a bottle, while his dog barked and worried at their legs. Another time, they hadn't realised that a young man had been lagging behind a crowd of his friends. As soon as he called out, more than half a dozen youths had come bounding towards them and they had barely managed to escape a thrashing.

So it wasn't the defeat itself, but the uncomfortable nature of it that had thrown them into disarray. Carver had always boasted that he was invincible. As long as he had his flick knife in his hand, no one could touch him. Now, not only had he had been beaten in a fight, he had been overpowered by an unarmed woman who had tossed him over her shoulder as easily as she would a child. Daryl could still picture Carver flying through the air, his fair hair splayed out around his head, his arms and legs flailing helplessly, his eyes glaring wildly, and his mouth stretched wide in silent outrage. The incident had lasted no more than a second, but the image was indelibly stamped on Daryl's mind. If the butt of the joke hadn't been Carver, it would have been funny.

After the woman had fled, Daryl stood gazing helplessly from Nelson to Carver, and back again, wondering what to do. Refusing to meet Daryl's eye, Nelson scurried to retrieve Carver's knife from the middle of the road. Daryl trotted past Carver without looking down at him and picked up the white paper bag the woman had dropped. Smelling food, he glanced inside and saw two sausage rolls. Between Carver and Nelson, he didn't suppose he would get so much as a bite, but Nelson had come back and was eyeing him suspiciously.

'What you got there?'

Resigned, Daryl held up the bag. 'Must be her lunch,' he said.

Nelson reached forward and snatched the bag from him.

'Hey! Give that back. I found it.'

Ignoring Daryl's protest, Nelson picked a sausage roll from the bag and took a bite.

'Not bad.' He crammed the rest of it in his mouth.

Neither of them dared go over to Carver to check he was all right. Daryl was afraid he was dead. He had certainly landed on the pavement with a loud thud.

'We should split,' Daryl said. 'She's bound to call the pigs.'

Nelson frowned. 'Fuck her. We'll say we never seen her before.'

'But what about him?'

As though he knew they were talking about him, Carver groaned. They both turned to look at him. He was lying on the ground where he had fallen, but now his eyelids were flickering. Nelson walked over to him, still holding the knife, and the bag with the remaining sausage roll.

'Here you go,' he said, dangling the knife above Carver's face.

Carver stirred. Slowly he heaved himself into a sitting position and glowered up at his two companions, before clambering to his feet. He stood upright for a moment, swaying almost imperceptibly, then grabbed his knife from Nelson and slipped it in his pocket.

'What's that you got there?' he growled.

Nelson barely hesitated. Able to move and speak, Carver was the leader once more.

'It's a sausage roll. It's for you.'

He held out the bag.

Carver looked perplexed. 'What the fuck you doing with a sausage roll?'

Nelson didn't answer.

'She dropped them,' Daryl said.

'Who?'

'The woman.'

'What woman?'

'The woman –' Daryl broke off, realising his mistake.

Nelson turned to him, head on one side, as though he was genuinely interested in hearing what Daryl had to say.

'What woman?' Carver asked again.

'Yeah, what woman?' Nelson repeated.

'Just some woman who walked by. She saw us and she was scared so she dropped the bag as she ran away and it had –' Daryl glanced at Nelson. 'It had a sausage roll in it,' he finished lamely.

'Here.' Nelson held out the bag with the sausage roll in it.

Carver took the bag and sniffed it. 'Smells like shit,' he said.

'It must have been her lunch,' Daryl said pointlessly.

He watched Carver take a bite out of the sausage roll.

'Not bad,' Carver admitted.

He took another bite and then chucked the rest of it on the pavement.

'I think I'm going to puke,' he said.

Daryl watched as a stray ant discovered the bonanza and began scurrying around in a frenzy. It was a waste of a perfectly good sausage roll, but he didn't dare retrieve it.

'Let's go and do it then,' Carver said.

He seemed to have no recollection of the humiliation he had just suffered.

'You feeling OK then?' Daryl hazarded.

'Sure thing. Why not?' Carver answered.

'You just knocked yourself out,' Daryl said.

Carver halted and turned to stare at Daryl through half-closed lids. 'What did you say?' he hissed.

Nelson folded his arms and leaned back on his heels, watching, with a faint grin on his lips.

'I just wanted to make sure you're all right.'

'I'm all right. Why wouldn't I be, halfwit?'

It wasn't clear whether Carver was refusing to acknowledge his defeat, or genuinely had no recollection of what had happened. Whatever the truth, Daryl realised it wasn't a good idea to mention it again.

'No reason,' he muttered. 'Nothing.'

'Imbecile,' Carver said, cuffing Daryl on the side of his head. 'Stop talking shit.'

After that, they had better luck. Back in the safety of the garage, they set to work dividing up their spoils: two handbags stuffed with goodies, and a brief case. Having tipped all the contents out on the floor, Carver put the three bags down.

'One each,' he said.

There was a beautiful crimson handbag, which Daryl really wanted, but Carver put that one aside. Nelson had next pick. He chose the brief case, leaving a brown leather handbag for Daryl.

He smiled. 'Wicked.'

Watching him, Nelson burst out laughing, rocking backwards and forwards. 'What you doing with a handbag, you fucking gay!'

He hadn't made fun of Carver, but Daryl didn't retort. The handbag looked expensive, and had a gold name on the front.

'It's for my girl,' he said.

Nelson laughed harder. 'You telling us you got a girl? In your wet dreams, boy.'

Daryl just shrugged. He knew who he was going to give the bag to, and he didn't care what Nelson thought.

'My girl's gonna love this. She got style,' he said quietly.

Nelson sniffed and turned his attention to the money and phones, keys and cosmetics, credit cards and iPads and purses spread out on the floor between them. Carver watched closely as Nelson rifled through all the items, sorting them into piles and then counting the money, starting with the notes.

'Nearly two hundred quid,' he announced at last. 'Fuck all this plastic. Why can't people carry their money in cash? Fucking perverts. What use is all this plastic shit?'

Carver nodded complacently.

'Not a bad day's work,' he said.

Daryl wanted to know what his share of the cash would be, but he hesitated to ask. Impatiently he watched Carver pull out a cigarette and light up. Leaning back in his chair he began blowing uneven smoke rings at the ceiling.

22

ONLY SOMEONE WHO WAS a dedicated killer would devote so much thought and care into taking lives. Given the preparation he had taken, it was hardly surprising he hadn't been caught. From all the accounts he had read in the papers, they had no idea who he was. That was really down to him, leaving no clues behind. All the same, he lived in constant fear of hearing the police banging at his door. Now, more than ever, he needed to be careful.

It was barely a week since his last kill, and the second one had been rash. Sometimes he had been forced to wait for years between kills, until he felt it was safe to continue. Those periods of inactivity were tough, with only his memories to sustain him. But this time, he had killed two people in the space of a week. That was unprecedented for good reason.

He hadn't planned to make the second of his two recent kills so soon after the first one, but an opportunity had arisen and he had given in to the temptation. Down by the river, in near darkness, with no one else around, the impulse had been too strong to control. He would have to watch that, and exercise greater restraint in future. An impetuous kill, when he wasn't out hunting for a victim, was far too risky. He had been stupid, allowing himself to be carried away in the excitement of the moment. It had taken seconds to slip into his protective clothing and strike. With hindsight, he resolved never to carry his rucksack with him again unless he was planning to use it, carefully and deliberately.

If the police weren't preoccupied with looking for a gang of muggers, he might not have got away with it. So while he had no intention of stopping, he knew he had to be more careful. It would be wise to wait a while before his next venture. For at least a year he would keep his head down and stay out of sight. He would be cautious and resist his urges, however powerful they became.

Not that he was seriously worried, because there was no way the police were going to find him. They were looking in all the wrong places.

23

GERALDINE WAS STILL HOPING the woman she was looking for would remember seeing a blond man near Pope's Head Alley on the evening of Grant's murder. If so, she might be able to give the police a description of the killer. That could be just the lucky break they were looking for. There was even a chance the woman might be working with the killer and so could lead them directly to him. Geraldine called at her house again on her way to work early the following morning, but there was no answer.

It was unlikely, yet the figure who had followed Felicity down to the river *could* have been the same woman. Geraldine wondered whether it had really been a coincidence that the same woman might have been in the vicinity on both occasions. The fact that no one had responded to a television appeal for the woman in question to come forward, combined with the fact that she wasn't answering her door, suggested that she might indeed be hiding something. Another possibility had also occurred to Geraldine. Because if this woman *had* seen the killer, there was also a chance *he* had seen *her*. And if he had, that might explain why she was impossible to find.

Determined to investigate further, Geraldine went to speak to Ian.

'What is it?' he asked, with more than a hint of impatience in his voice.

She hovered in the doorway. 'Is this a bad time? I can come back –'

'No, no. You've disturbed me now. So, what do you want?'

She went in and shut the door. 'I want to talk to you about the case.'

'Go on. I'm listening.'

When she explained her concern that the dark-haired woman sighted on CCTV might also have been murdered, Ian shook his head.

'You've brought this up before, Geraldine. She's probably just gone away. Maybe she walked out on her partner. Women do that all the time,' he added with a touch of bitterness in his voice. 'It's not our job to go chasing after them.'

'If she was nearby when Felicity was killed, she might have witnessed what happened and become a victim herself.'

'If that was the case, there'd be a body –'

'They were right by the river. Felicity was found in the water. What if the other woman's body was also thrown in the river? She could have become caught up in river weeds and got trapped beneath the surface.'

Ian shook his head again, understanding her drift. 'SOCOs found no signs of anyone else being involved in any sort of scuffle, and we can't justify the expense of dredging the river without any evidence. Geraldine, what you're suggesting may perhaps be plausible, but it's nothing more than vague supposition. I can't go to Eileen with a half-baked idea like that and expect her to sanction the resources we'd need to dredge the river. Let's work from what evidence we have, and not go running off after some theory concocted out of thin air.'

'This is not just a haphazard theory. The woman's been missing since the second murder and it's possible she saw the killer both times. He might have felt it was necessary to get rid of her.'

'Oh please,' Ian interrupted her. 'What are you basing this on? A woman goes away. So what? It's hardly a case for a serious crime investigation, is it? She could be on holiday. And people walk out on their partners all the time. There's nothing to suggest a crime's been committed, is there? Look,' he went on a little more gently, 'there's nothing to stop you going to speak to her, to see if she can tell us anything. It does no harm to speak to her, if you can find her. That's up to you.'

'Ian –' She hesitated again, hating the way he made her feel so unsure of herself. 'Ian, if there's anything else you'd like to talk about, anything at all, you know you can speak to me as a friend. We've known each other for a long time.'

He gave a brisk nod. 'Thank you. I'll bear that in mind.'

'I mean, about Bev.'

At the mention of his ex-wife's name, his frown deepened. 'Is that all? This is all very well, and I appreciate your good intentions, but I have work to do, and so do you.'

She nodded and left the room quickly, uncertain whether to feel annoyed, or anxious. Ian had been understandably devastated when his wife had left him. He hadn't even known she was having an affair when she had fallen pregnant by another man. At the time his marriage had broken down, Geraldine had been working in London. They had met up as friends and equals, and Ian had confided freely in her. Now that Geraldine was working with him, he rarely spoke to her about his personal situation. Although she missed the intimacy of their former friendship, she was reluctant to pry, and already regretted having brought up the subject. Feeling despondent about the whole situation with Ian, she left the room and went to speak to Eileen.

The detective chief inspector listened solemnly to Geraldine's fears.

'You're suggesting this woman saw the killer at the scene of both murders just around the time they were committed?'

Geraldine nodded. 'So I wonder if she's been killed as well, to protect the killer's identity.'

Eileen frowned. 'There's no body.'

When Geraldine pointed out that Felicity had been killed by the river, Eileen shook her head.

'I see where you're going with this, but is there any evidence to suggest there might be yet another body in the river?' she asked, as though they had already discovered multiple bodies floating in the water. 'No, Geraldine, this may be an interesting theory, but it certainly can't justify the expense of dredging the river. If any evidence turns up to support your idea, of course we'll get on to it straightaway.'

Geraldine returned to her desk, disappointed that both Ian and Eileen had dismissed her theory, even though she knew they were right. Without evidence, there was no case to investigate.

'Cheer up,' Ariadne said, seeing Geraldine's expression. 'It's not that bad. We'll crack this case sooner or later. We'll get him through his DNA.'

Geraldine nodded, but it wasn't the investigation that was making her feel low. The truth was, she hated seeing Ian looking so miserable, knowing there was nothing she could do to cheer him up. An awkwardness had arisen between them and they didn't seem able to talk to each other like they used to. At one point she had hoped their relationship might develop into more than friendship. She was afraid Ian might have picked up on that, although she had been careful to conceal her feelings. Whatever the reason, he was keeping her at a distance, and she was sad to have lost their former closeness. She would have liked to tackle him about it, but she wasn't sure how to approach the subject. So she kept her disappointment to herself. It didn't help that she was unable to discuss her feelings with anyone else. Even Ariadne knew nothing about the situation.

'I know,' Geraldine replied, returning Ariadne's anxious smile. 'It just feels as though we're going nowhere.'

'It does feel like that. I don't know about you, but I really thought we'd got our man when we arrested Felicity's ex. He was such an obvious suspect. It's a pity he was a false trail. The obvious suspect usually turns out to be the one we're after. Shame it didn't turn out that way this time. It would have been nice to get this wrapped up, after two deaths.' She looked apprehensive and she lowered her voice. 'You don't think there'll be any more, do you?'

'Who knows? But I don't see why there should be.'

'No, you're right, but it's a worry, isn't it? And the media don't help, with all their scaremongering.'

Geraldine shrugged. 'We just have to keep on keeping on, and hope for the best.'

24

INSTEAD OF GOING STRAIGHT home after work that evening, Geraldine drove to Gillygate once again to find out whether the missing woman had returned home yet, but once again no one answered the door. Geraldine felt that Eileen had dismissed her concerns fairly peremptorily. Even Ian hadn't taken her seriously. Meanwhile, they were no closer to questioning the woman who might hold the key to the investigation. A few cranks had walked into the police station to insist they had been present on the night of one or both of the murders, but they had promptly been dismissed. There had been no response from anyone credible. Meanwhile, Geraldine felt increasingly uneasy about the woman who had seemingly vanished.

The following morning a woman came into the police station claiming to have been mugged. She seemed fairly coherent. The constable who initially spoke to her was aware that the team were keen to find out as much as they could about the muggers, so he passed her on to Geraldine. She greeted the woman, Wendy, who was about twenty-five and wiry.

'I wasn't going to come forward. I don't want my mum to know about this or I'll never hear the end of it. But there's been so much in the local news about muggings that I thought I really ought to report what happened. They tried to snatch my bag right off my shoulder. If it wasn't for my training in martial arts, anything could have happened.'

She lowered her eyes, waiting for a response.

'Are you saying you resisted them taking your bag?'

'Oh yes. I –' Wendy hesitated. 'I threw one of them,' she admitted.

'Threw? As in –?'

'As in judo. I threw him to the ground. I don't think he was hurt, but I didn't hang around to find out. It all happened so quickly. There was no time to think. I was so scared, I just wanted to defend myself and get away as quickly as possible.'

'You were clearly acting in self-defence,' Geraldine reassured her. It was surprising that so petite a woman could have taken anyone on in a fight, let alone a violent assailant. 'Can you describe your attackers?'

'Describe them?' Wendy repeated.

'Yes, we're trying to track them down and the more information we have, the sooner we'll find them.'

'Yes, yes, of course. Let me think. There were three of them…'

Wendy paused for a moment, her eyes screwed up with the effort of remembering.

'It's difficult, you know. In the moment I was so shocked… and then I was focused on getting away.'

'Yes, I understand. But anything you can tell us might be helpful. How old were they? Can you give me an idea of how tall they were?'

Geraldine was concerned when Wendy told her one of the youths had threatened her with a knife.

'Are you telling me you attacked a man who was armed?'

'I said I'd give them what they wanted, but he had to lower his knife first, and he did. He didn't see what was coming,' she added with a sly smile.

Wendy had been stopped by three boys. The oldest carried a knife and seemed very calm. The other two were both skinny and not yet out of their teens, and jumpy. Wendy's description tallied with what other witnesses had told the police. It was obviously the same gang that had been reported before. This time the victim was able to add one detail that hadn't been mentioned yet. One of the boys had a bad case of acne.

'Are you sure of that?'

'Absolutely. I can picture him in my mind. The brawny one who was armed, he seemed to be the ringleader. I can't really remember his face, because I was so shocked, but he had a growly kind of voice, as though he had a throat infection, and he had fair hair. I think the second one was tall and skinny, although he was hovering at the edge of the group and I didn't see him so clearly, and the third one, the one with acne, looked terrified.' She paused. 'I think he was scared of the other boys. I looked at him when the one who had threatened me was on the ground. He must have been about sixteen, and younger than the other two. He was really frightened.'

'How old were the others?'

'I'd guess they were about eighteen or twenty, but I don't really know. I only saw them for a few seconds, and I was distracted, wondering how I was going to escape unharmed. And then I ran.'

'Thank you. That's been very helpful.'

Geraldine summoned a constable to take a formal statement from the witness while she wrote up her own notes on the meeting. After that she went to find Ian. She wasn't sure what kind of greeting she would receive, but he gave her a cautious smile when she opened his door.

'Geraldine,' he called out to her, 'I've been meaning to come and speak to you.'

She waited.

'Please, come in and shut the door. I wanted to apologise,' he went on, awkwardly. 'I'm sorry if I came across as abrupt with you yesterday, and – well, it was uncalled for.'

She smiled with relief. 'That's OK. These are tricky times.'

She wasn't quite sure what she meant by that, but he returned her smile, obviously also relieved to be on good terms again.

'I have been meaning to talk to you about Bev at some time,' he went on, 'but really there's nothing to tell. She's still living with this other man, and our divorce is in the hands of the lawyers. And that's all there is to it, really.' He looked at her with a tentative half smile. 'Time for a new beginning, and a new life.'

Hearing him talk of new life reminded Geraldine that his estranged wife was pregnant, but she didn't like to ask whether she had given birth yet. She tried to tell herself that she was glad about the divorce solely for Ian's sake, and not in any way for herself. Bev had never made him happy and he was better off without her. He might even have a chance of finding happiness with someone else now. In the meantime, she was careful to remain appropriate in her response.

'I'm sorry to hear about the divorce,' she lied.

'Well, it's for the best,' he replied, curt again. 'Did you want something?'

He seemed vexed, although she couldn't imagine how her words could have caused him any offence. Impassively she told him about the latest victim of the three muggers.

'Which confirms there are three kids,' she concluded. 'Admittedly one of them is fair-haired, but I still have my doubts about whether they could really be the murderer we're looking for.'

'Is that all?'

Geraldine hesitated. There was so much more she could have said, but none of it had anything to do with the case.

'Yes, that's all.'

Spurred on by Ian's dismissal of her views, she read through the reports received so far. Thinking about her own adoption, she wondered whether they had been hasty in concluding the apparent match to the DNA found at the crime scenes had been an error, and went to see Eileen.

'So, one of our gang is blond,' Eileen greeted her, with a smile, 'and we know he carries a knife. The net is closing in.'

Geraldine nodded. 'I had another thought.'

'What's that?' Eileen asked, expansive in her good mood.

'What if Peter Drury had another brother no one knows about?'

The detective chief inspector's smile vanished. 'Yes, I suppose it's possible.'

'His father might be able to tell us.'

'Edward Drury's already been questioned.'

'But a local constable might not have realised the importance of getting to the truth.'

Eileen gave Geraldine a hard stare. 'I take it you're suggesting you go and speak to Mr Drury yourself?'

'This could be important,' Geraldine said. 'Too important to be left to a local officer who's not even working on the case. He could easily have missed something. What do we even know about the officer who went to speak to Edward Drury? He could have been incompetent.'

'I'm sure he was thorough,' Eileen retorted frostily.

'I just mean it might be as well for an experienced officer to question him. The constable who went might not have appreciated the significance of his errand.'

But it was too late for Geraldine to retract her implied criticism of Eileen for delegating the task to an unknown officer, just as it was too late to recall the constable who had already spoken to Mr Drury. The detective chief inspector looked at her screen for a moment as though signalling it was time for Geraldine to leave. But as Geraldine turned to go, Eileen spoke.

'Yes,' she said, 'I think you had better go and talk to Peter's father, just on the off chance that you might be able to get more out of him than a young constable managed to do.'

It was tantamount to an admission from Eileen that she had made an error.

'I'll get onto it right away,' Geraldine replied.

'Geraldine –'

'Yes?'

Eileen hesitated. 'Nothing.'

They both knew that Geraldine could easily have been in Eileen's position if circumstances hadn't dictated otherwise. Had their roles been reversed, Geraldine liked to think that she would have been willing to acknowledge her mistakes. As it was, she could only nod and leave the room without comment.

It took Geraldine all afternoon to reach Edward Drury's house on the outskirts of Oxford. He sighed when Geraldine introduced herself, but he invited her in and offered to put the kettle on.

'I hardly ever have any visitors, and now this makes two in less than two weeks. But I don't know how I can help you. I've already told your constable what little I know. I'm sorry I have nothing more to say.'

Edward confirmed that he had only had two sons, and that neither was still alive.

'Jamie left home soon after my other son, Peter, was taken away.'

'Do you mean when he died or –'

'I mean when he left home,' Edward replied sharply.

'That was nearly ten years ago. And what happened to Jamie after that?'

Edward shook his head. 'Peter's prison sentence wrecked all our lives. We were a family before that. My poor wife didn't survive the shock. She took her own life.'

'I didn't know. I'm so sorry.'

'She said she'd raised a monster and couldn't live with herself. She did, she kept on for another ten years, but she was never the same. None of us were. The family was finished. Peter was never violent before he started taking drugs, and that only started when our daughter died. After that, he changed completely. He behaved monstrously.'

He let out an involuntary sound, like a whimper.

'What happened to your daughter?' Geraldine asked gently.

'She fell into the weir and drowned. Poor thing, she didn't stand a chance. She was only eight and could hardly swim.

They fished her out, but she was past help by then. My wife never got over it. None of us did. It was an accident, but the boys never recovered from seeing her fall off the bridge. They were both there when it happened. Peter couldn't cope with the guilt so he blamed his brother. Peter was the oldest, you see, so I think he felt responsible for what happened, and that's why he lashed out at Jamie. Then he turned to drugs, and ended up dying behind bars.' He sighed and shook his head. 'My Norma kept going as long as she could but in the end she took an overdose. And after that Jamie left, without a word, and I never heard from him again. To be honest, if you told me you were bringing his body home it would leave me cold. Too much has happened. I can't feel anything anymore.'

'So your wife died ten years ago? I'm so sorry.'

He nodded. 'Jamie and me, we were the only ones left. I don't think he could take it. And soon after that, he upped and left, and that's the last I saw of him.'

'Didn't you try to find him?'

The old man shrugged. 'What was the point? I suppose I could have made an effort to look for him, but he knew where I was. He could have got in touch if he'd wanted to. But he never did. The last I heard from him was a phone call telling me he was in Australia and intended to stay there. I thought he was probably better off, making a clean break, you know, putting it all behind him. We –' he hesitated. 'My wife and I, we were never close to him. He always kept himself to himself, you know. Even as a teenager he was out to all hours, and we never knew where he was or what he was doing. He never told us anything. And then I had a phone call from Thailand informing me Jamie had died of a respiratory infection and I could fly out and get his body if I wanted it. I told them they could dispose of him however they wanted. I hadn't seen or heard from him for years by then.' He shook his head. 'That was two years ago. And that was the last I heard of him.'

Geraldine pumped the old man gently, but he was adamant that was all he knew.

'He could be buried anywhere on the other side of the world,' he said sadly. 'I like to think he found some happiness before he died, was making a life for himself away from all this. I would have liked to see him again. Until I heard he was dead, I used to hope he would come back and see me, one day. But he never will now.'

Geraldine wondered what it was like to live without any hope for the future, and whether he had finally been able to find a kind of peace.

As though he could read her thoughts, he said, 'At least now I don't have anyone to worry about or fret over. I live very quietly, with no disturbance.'

Once again they had been pursuing a lead that went nowhere.

25

ALEXA THREW A RAPID glance around, taking in all the aisles within sight. Signs flashed by her: FROZEN FOOD, STATIONERY, FRESH PRODUCE. She slowed down beside two middle-aged women who were deep in conversation. They didn't even glance at her.

'He never did,' she overheard one of them say as they passed her.

Hovering by a stand of glossy magazines, she gazed at a row of models taunting her with their unblemished skin, sleek hair, and flawless bodies barely concealed in gorgeous clothes, a million miles from her own scrawny figure dressed in faded jeans, baggy sweatshirt and dirty plimsoles.

'It was way past time,' Alexa heard one of the women say.

'Yes, I've told her and told her,' the other replied. 'It had been going on for long enough.'

'Too long.'

The women moved out of earshot. Neither of them paid any attention to a skinny fifteen-year-old loitering in front of the magazines. As soon as the two women disappeared around the end of the aisle, Alexa approached the shelf. In contrast to her shuffling feet, her hand moved swiftly, before anyone else came along. Clutching her bag under her arm, she walked to the next aisle where several young women were sifting through hangers of brightly coloured clothes. Alexa strolled along the aisle, her eyes darting from side to side, assessing what was in stock. Having picked out what she wanted, she took up her position and waited while another woman rummaged through the rail. At last the woman moved away. In a flash, the embroidered shirt in Alexa's hand was stowed away out of sight, along with the magazine, several bars of chocolate, and a bottle of rum. She struggled to close the zip of her bag after cramming so much inside it.

No one paid her any attention as she bypassed the row of cashiers and headed for the exit with her bag over her shoulder. Too late she spotted a fat security guard near the doorway. She swore under her breath, but she couldn't turn back. His eyes moved lazily towards her, and on without a pause. She let out a silent sigh of relief. If he tried to interfere with her, she would have no trouble outrunning him, even with her heavy bag over her shoulder. It was gorgeous, real leather, with a leather tassel and 'Burberry' written in gold letters on the front. One strap went over her shoulder, and there was a second shorter strap so she could carry it over her arm.

'I didn't know if you'd like it, because it's so plain,' Daryl had said when he showed it to her.

'Are you having a laugh?' She had been unable to take her eyes off the bag. 'It's bloody beautiful. It's the most beautiful bag I've ever seen.'

'Really? I mean, yes, it's a nice bag, it's real leather and everything. I only meant you might not like it because it's brown, so I thought you might think it's boring. I wanted to get you a nicer one. I thought you might've liked a red one better because it would be, well, brighter.'

She shook her head, laughing at his stupidity.

'What the fuck would I do with a red bag? It would be like, hey, everyone, look what I got. And then someone would want to know where I got such an expensive bag, and then what would I say? No, this is just perfect. No one's going to take any notice of a bag like this. Really, it's perfect and I love it. And it's got a strong zip. Bags like this, they make them properly, not like them shitty ones in the market.'

She was so pleased with her new bag, she let him kiss her

and touch her where she'd never let his hands go before. She touched him too, until he wet his pants with excitement. It had been worth it, for her at least. His thrill was over in a minute but she walked away with a new bag that was going to last for ages, it was so strong and well made.

What with the bottle of booze and the magazine and everything, the bag was heavier now than when she had first set out with it over her shoulder. Without watching the fat security guard, she was conscious of his presence. Some sixth sense warned her that he was on to her, but she ignored it. As long as he didn't move, she only needed to keep walking steadily towards the door. Logically, there was no way he could suspect what she was up to. He hadn't even been watching her while she was lifting things from the shelves. It wasn't as if she had taken a lot, anyway. Only the bottle cost more than a tenner. Altogether she had probably helped herself to less than forty quid's worth of gear, but she knew she could be in trouble for nicking even a fiver's worth of goods. It was so unfair. What the fuck difference did it make to a supermarket if it lost out on a few quid now and again? As for the store detectives, they were a bloody menace, poking their noses into other people's business. Nobody wanted them around.

The fat security guard fixed his eyes on her as she approached. When she drew near him he shifted position, so he was standing between her and the door. Without looking at him, she concentrated on keeping her pace steady and her expression blank as she changed course slightly to walk past him. Without looking round, she made for the door that was further away from her. Having bypassed the guard, she didn't dare look round to check whether he was following her. Her heart was racing and she felt breathless although she was still walking quite slowly. As soon as she was through the door, she would run, knowing he wouldn't be able to catch her.

The automatic door slid open. She stepped through it and glanced over her shoulder, tensed to run, but there was no sign of the guard pursuing her. With a grin, she relaxed and walked right out of the store. The fat guard was standing in front of her, blocking her path. His face was damp with sweat and she realised he must have run along the outside of the store to reach the far door before her. If she had moved faster, he might not have got there in time to grab her.

He took a step towards her and seized her by the arm. She caught a whiff of his sweat.

'Please come with me,' he growled.

His eyes were nearly hidden in creases of skin, as though he was half asleep, but his grin was triumphant. The grip on her arm tightened.

'Let go!' she shrieked. 'Get off me! Help! Help! I'm being attacked!'

A few passersby looked round in surprise. One or two people smiled at her performance, but no one was taken in by her protestations. Unable to wriggle free of the vicelike hold on her arm, she was nicked.

'I'm only fifteen,' she told the guard.

They stared at one another for a second, sizing each other up. The weight of her bag on her shoulder reminded her of Daryl and his desperate gratitude. The guard was fat and sweaty and unattractive. He wouldn't be getting any, that was for sure.

'I'll give you anything you want,' she said, smiling at him. 'I know what men like. You got a fantasy? Something that could be our secret?' She licked her lips. 'You know I could really go for a strong man like you.'

He listened to her with an expression of growing disgust. 'You just told me you're fifteen. So, what would my wife and kids say if I was caught playing around with an underage tart? First thing anyone would want to know is what the hell I was thinking of, messing with a scraggy little whore. Come on, let's get this over with so I don't need to touch you for any longer than I have to.' He gave a cold, cruel smile, and tugged at her arm. 'Now come on, I'd like you to accompany me to the office. You can tell your story there, to the police.'

There was nothing more she could say, so she spat at him. A round globule of spit clung to his uniform, a tiny bubble of hatred. She watched it as he marched her back into the supermarket, down the first aisle, and through a door at the back of the store. Facing Alexa across a desk that was too large for his tiny office, the store manager scowled. He was a small balding man, with a face that looked squashed, as though sitting in the cramped office day after day had made him shrink. In front of Alexa the contents of her bag were spread out on the desk. Behind her, the security guard had taken up his position at the door, blocking her escape. There was no other way out of the room.

'It's a bloody lie,' she blustered. 'I never took them things. He put them in there.' She pointed at the fat guard standing imperviously in the doorway. 'And anyway, that bag's mine. He had no right to take it off me. He's a bloody thieving bastard. Give it back. You can keep your fucking crap, I don't want any of it. It's all shit anyway. But you've got no right to nick my bag. Give it back!'

She was devastated at the prospect of losing her bag. She had only owned it for a day, and it was one of the few presents she had ever received.

'Sit down and stop screeching,' the manager snapped. 'Now, let's get this sorted.' He pulled out a form. 'First of all, what's your name and where do you live?'

'That's none of your business.'

'Listen, kid, we need an adult to come here and take responsibility for you.'

'I don't need anyone to be responsible for me. And don't call me a kid.'

'Who do you live with?'

'That's none of your business either.'

'Where do you live?'

Alexa crossed her arms and shut her mouth.

'All right then,' the manager said wearily. 'Have it your way. The police can deal with you.'

'Good,' she replied, hiding her fear. 'They can deal with you as well, because from where I'm sitting, you just nicked my bag.'

Muttering about wasting his time, the manager picked up his phone.

Alexa wasn't bothered. If the manager was narked, it was his own stupid fault. If she had her way, she would be out of there already, and no one's time would need to be wasted at all. The manager was welcome to his things: the magazine, the shirt and the bottle. That was all it came down to. He was the one making a stupid fuss about it, so it served him right if *his* time was wasted. But what about *her* time? She had been through crap like this before when she was younger. For a while she had been scared off, but the temptation had proved too strong, and it was easy to help herself. It was a long time since she had been caught, and lately she had grown careless. Still, there was nothing the police could do to her. They might lock her in a cell for a few hours, and give her a warning, but then they would let her go again. Her mother would be cool about it. If anything, she hated the police even more than Alexa did. As for her father, it was so long since Alexa had seen him he wouldn't even recognise her if he passed her in the street.

'Go on then,' she said, 'do your worst. You don't scare me.'

But she did want her bag back.

26

IN HER LUNCH BREAK, Geraldine took a quick look at the list of recent arrests. There were only a couple for relatively minor infringements. A drunk had been brought in the previous evening and left in a cell overnight. It wasn't the first time he had been brought in for brawling in a pub. On this particular occasion he had been too sozzled to end up in any real trouble, but one day he was likely to have his head bashed in. A patrol had brought him in as much for his own protection as to stop him causing a nuisance. Other than that, a young girl had been caught shoplifting and had been brought in to give her a scare. This wasn't her first offence. There was nothing new or interesting in any of it. But just as she was closing the report, her attention was caught by one detail.

'Look at this,' she called out, to no one in particular.

Ariadne was sitting opposite her. 'What have you found?'

Geraldine directed her to the report.

'Oh, a girl was caught shoplifting.' Ariadne didn't actually say 'So what?'

'Never mind the shoplifting,' Geraldine said. 'Look at the details. Look at what she had on her.'

'A bottle of Captain Morgan, a shirt, a magazine and some chocolate,' Ariadne read aloud. 'OK, I've looked at the list. What now?'

'That's not all. Look again.'

'Geraldine, there isn't anything else.'

'The bag,' Geraldine replied, unable to conceal her impatience. 'She had a bag with her. Look!'

'Oh yes, I see, she had a Burberry bag. Very nice. So you're saying she was stealing from other places as well as the supermarket? Well, that figures.'

'Yes, but she said the bag was given to her.'

'OK, she lied about it. That's hardly any surprise, is it?'

'What if she wasn't lying?'

'Geraldine, I've no idea what you're talking about. Who would give a fifteen-year-old girl a Burberry bag? I don't even know if *I* could afford one of them. Do you know how much they cost?'

'How much?'

'Oh, I don't know, but enough to know that she stole it. And the question remains: so what? I daresay the shop takes out insurance against –'

'The significance of the bag is that one of the victims of the recent muggings was carrying a brown leather Burberry bag which was stolen. So when a young shoplifter turns up with a brown leather Burberry bag and claims it was a gift, perhaps we should try and find out who gave it to her.' She stood up. 'I'm going to speak to Eileen while the girl's still here. Whatever else happens, we've got to find out who gave her that bag.'

'One of the muggers!' Ariadne said, finally catching Geraldine's drift.

As soon as Eileen understood the significance of the Burberry bag, she sent Geraldine to question the girl.

'She'll be a hard one to crack,' Ian told Geraldine when they met outside the interview room. 'These youngsters think they're untouchable. The borough intelligence team recognised her name straightaway. She's tough for all that she's only fifteen.'

'They know her?'

'Yes, but don't get your hopes up. They don't know who her associates are.'

'That's a pity.'

'Yes, all they have is a record of her shoplifting and some

alleged minor drug offences. At one time she was suspected of soliciting but they never discovered the identity of her pimp. She was under surveillance for a short time but these kids are slippery and they concluded there was nothing serious going on so she dropped off the radar. Until now.'

'It's a pity they don't have the names of her associates,' Geraldine repeated.

'I know, but once she understands what's at stake, we should be able to crack her all right. She thinks we're only interested in her pilfering. We need to make it clear that if she persists in obstructing us, she'll be treated as an accessory to murder. That should put the fear of God into her, if nothing else does.'

'She's only fifteen,' Geraldine reminded him.

'We're looking for a murderer, and this kid might be able to help us find him.'

Geraldine rather hoped the girl would lead them to the muggers so that they could finally establish the gang wasn't responsible for murdering Grant or Felicity, leaving the team free to focus their attention on searching for the actual killer.

The girl was seated beside a sharp-faced woman, not her mother but a local lawyer who specialised in defending underage youngsters.

'Good,' Ian said, smiling grimly at the lawyer, 'I'm very glad to see you. With such a serious accusation pending, we need to do this by the book.'

'Alexa has been accused of petty shoplifting,' the lawyer replied in a tinny voice. 'That's hardly a serious accusation. It's her first offence –'

'She was cautioned for the same offence two years ago,' Geraldine interjected.

'When she was thirteen. As I've already pointed out, this is hardly a "serious accusation",' the lawyer repeated evenly, still looking at Ian.

'You can't touch me,' the girl piped up.

The lawyer gave her a warning frown, reminding her to

keep quiet. With a sullen glare, the girl lowered her head and sat motionless, staring at the table. Geraldine gazed at streaks of pale scalp showing through the girl's thin hair. She looked a lot younger than fifteen, possibly because she was scrawny and flat chested. Her skin was very pale, making her look sick. Perhaps she was. For all her swagger, Geraldine thought she was frightened.

'Where did you get your bag?' Ian asked suddenly.

The girl glared across the table but she didn't answer.

Ian repeated the question. 'You'd not be wise to obstruct us in *this* investigation,' he added.

It was almost a throw away remark but the lawyer's expression altered and she glanced thoughtfully from Ian to Geraldine and back again. A detective inspector and a detective sergeant working in serious crime were hardly likely to be interested in a teenager who had been caught shoplifting. Finally the penny seemed to be dropping, at least with the lawyer.

'Answer the question, Alexa,' she instructed her young client.

'I told you, my boyfriend gave it to me. Which means it's mine, doesn't it? And I want it back. They can't keep it, can they?'

Ian leaned forward slightly, his low tone menacing. 'And where did your boyfriend get hold of such an expensive bag?'

The girl shrugged. 'He must've found it in a charity shop,' she replied coolly.

Ian sniffed. 'Very well. We need the name and address of your boyfriend and then you're free to go.'

Alexa shook her head. 'He's called…' Her hesitation was pathetically transparent. 'He's called Harry.'

'And where does Harry live?'

'I don't know, do I?'

'Where do you meet him?'

'I just see him around.'

That might even be true, Geraldine thought. But Ian was

growing impatient.

'We have evidence that your bag was stolen in the course of a serious crime,' he said firmly, glaring at the lawyer. 'If your client persists in obstructing us in our enquiries by withholding information, she is likely to end up accused of being an accessory to a serious crime.'

'Shoplifting isn't a –' the lawyer began to trot out a predictable response.

'We're investigating a murder,' Ian interrupted her roughly. 'I suggest you recommend your client starts talking to us or she's going to find herself facing a very serious charge.' He turned to Alexa who was looking baffled. 'Even your clever lawyer here won't be able to save you if you decide to join your boyfriend on a murder charge. We'll give you a moment to reconsider.'

He nodded at Geraldine to pause the tape.

'Let's hope she does actually know where we can find this so-called boyfriend,' Geraldine said after they had left the girl to discuss her position with her counsel.

Ian nodded. 'This could be it,' he said softly, speaking more to himself than to Geraldine.

He didn't need to explain.

27

CARVER WAS SPRAWLING IN his armchair when Daryl arrived. Nelson had bagged their new acquisition, a rickety yellow kitchen chair, leaving a wooden crate. Daryl would have preferred the chair, but he didn't complain. The crate was better than the floor. At least he was more or less on a level with the others. In new jeans and sweatshirt, and expensive new trainers, Carver was listening to an iPod Daryl hadn't seen before. Nelson was also kitted out in new gear. Only Daryl was still in worn jeans and old trainers, because his mother had nicked all his dosh. She called it rent, and promptly spent it all on booze.

'How did your mother like her new bag?' Nelson sniggered when they were all seated.

Daryl felt his face go red. 'I didn't give it to my mother.'

'Wanted to keep it for yourself?'

'I gave it to my girl,' Daryl blurted out, stung by the mockery.

'I gave it to my girl,' Nelson mimicked him, flapping his hands stupidly in the air. 'Ooh, I gave it to my girl.'

'Fuck off,' Daryl muttered. 'Just fuck off, will you? What the hell?' He scowled and heard his own voice grow shrill with anger. 'What? You think I can't have sex with my girl any time I want? We're not all like you.'

He hadn't really had sex with Alexa yet, but he had gone as near as possible, short of actual penetration. He figured it counted. He got excited just thinking about it.

'What's that supposed to mean?' Nelson asked, jumping to his feet, his fists clenched.

'Fuck you,' Daryl snarled.

He stood up and turned to face Nelson.

'Enough,' Carver interrupted them quietly.

Daryl and Nelson both turned to look at him. He didn't need to speak again. Nelson slumped back down on his chair, sulking. As Daryl took his seat on the crate he experienced an unexpected rush of pride because it was true. He did have a girlfriend. Never having stood up to Nelson's taunts before, he had just batted the other boy's gibes away without even thinking about it. He felt suddenly free, able to do anything.

Carver's keen eyes missed nothing. 'What are you grinning about?' he asked.

Daryl shrugged.

'Thinking about his imaginary girlfriend,' Nelson suggested with a sly grin.

On the point of responding, Daryl thought better of it. Sometimes silence made a powerful statement. He had never felt so much energy coursing through his veins without getting high. Nelson would never intimidate him again. There was nothing so special about Nelson, anyway. If anyone was special it was him, Daryl. He had just never recognised it in himself, until now. With a rush of elation, he threw his head back and laughed.

'What the fuck?' Nelson said.

'Ignore him. He's just a dick,' Carver drawled.

And just like that, Daryl's excitement fizzled out. But he knew he would never tolerate Nelson's goading again. From now on they were going to be equals. Only Carver would continue as their leader because, well, he was Carver and he had killed a man. They spent the rest of the evening discussing their plans for the future. It was frustrating. They had been doing so well and now they were having to be careful on the streets, just because some other idiot had killed a few people. It was so unfair. The recent murders had nothing to do with them. Nelson suggested they shift their operations to Leeds where the police weren't out looking for them.

'I bet the Leeds police are all here in York, helping to look for us. So we'd be safer there.'

Carver dismissed the idea. The beauty of what they had been doing until now was that they had their garage, he said. As soon as they lifted the goods from someone on the street, they withdrew to their bolt hole. Mugging on the streets of Leeds would mean returning to York, and all the time they were travelling they would risk being picked up. They all agreed it wasn't a sensible idea to mug people elsewhere, but none of them could come up with a solution to the problem of York which seemed to be teeming with police officers, all hunting for them. Carver's pride at being newsworthy had given way to a sullen rage.

'They've screwed us up royally, and we've done nothing to deserve it,' he raged. 'Nothing!'

Failing to reach any conclusion about what to do next, they split up for the night. By the time Daryl arrived home, his mother was snoring in the living room, an empty bottle of Scotch at her feet. In a food-encrusted bowl on the arm of her chair, a cigarette butt sent tiny spirals of white smoke into the air. Daryl's father had left them years ago. Now his older brother had gone, leaving only Daryl and his mother in the house. As soon as he could, he would be off too. If the old cow was left on her own, she had only herself to blame. He was going to find a place with Alexa and sleep with her every night. She had told him exactly how it was going to be. He wasn't keen on the idea of a baby, but she had explained that was the only way they were going to get their own place, and had promised him it wouldn't stop them having sex every night. Proper sex. So that was all right. In the meantime he had to put up with living with his mother. At least he no longer had to sleep in the living room, now his brother had gone. He went upstairs to bed and fell asleep almost at once.

He was woken by a loud noise. At first he thought he was having one of his nightmares, but then he heard the banging again. He sat up. He certainly felt as though he was awake. If this was a dream, it was horribly real. Again he heard banging, this time accompanied by voices.

'Open up! Police!'

A few seconds later, he heard his mother shrieking. 'What the fuck are you doing? It's the middle of the night! Fuck off out of here!'

A deep voice answered her, 'Where's your son? Where's your son?'

His mother had the presence of mind to shout that her son had left home. Meanwhile, Daryl was scrambling out of bed. He was naked. His mind raced as he pulled on jogging pants. There was only one small high window in his room. He ran out on to the landing intending to run to his mother's room, but he was too late. Heavy footsteps were pounding up the stairs. He fled, but before he reached his mother's room his arm was grasped and twisted up behind his back so sharply he thought his shoulder would be dislocated. Screaming he fell to his knees and felt a hand pressing down on the back of his head, forcing him to the floor. The carpet stank of vomit.

28

THE BOY WAS SKINNY, with a severe case of acne and cavernous dark eyes that made him look older than his sixteen years. Geraldine watched him, noting how his eyes flitted away every time he glanced at her. He fidgeted constantly with the frayed cuff on his sweatshirt, and appeared unable to sit still. At his side, his mother gazed vacantly across the table. She could have been stoned. All at once she jolted, seeming to realise where she was. At Daryl's other side was a legal representative who specialised in defending underage offenders.

'What's this all about then?' Mrs Bowen asked, brushing her straggly fringe out of eyes as cavernous and dark as her son's. She turned to Daryl. 'What have you got yourself into this time, you fucking pillock? You're nothing but trouble.'

Without warning her hand snaked out to clout her son on the side of his head. He barely flinched. Only his glittering eyes revealed his anger, or perhaps they were shining with unshed tears. He was barely more than a child.

When her son didn't respond, Mrs Bowen turned to Ian. 'I asked you what this is about. My boy here is only fifteen. This should be illegal, what you're doing to him. He wants to go home. This is harassment. You can't keep him here.'

'Please, be quiet and let them say what they have to say,' the lawyer remonstrated quietly.

Ignoring the advice, Mrs Bowen carried on. 'This is no place for a child. You've got no business putting the wind up him like this. Can't you see he's scared out of his wits?'

'I'm not scared,' the boy muttered. 'Nothing scares me. And I'm sixteen.'

He cast a quick glance at his mother, as though to check she wasn't going to hit him again. She stood up and he scrambled to his feet beside her.

'You can leave when we've finished with him,' Ian said. 'Sit down, both of you.'

'Please, just listen, and leave the talking to me,' the lawyer insisted.

The constable beside the door shifted his weight from one foot to the other, ready to move. Mrs Bowen hesitated and then sat down, and the boy followed suit.

'What's he supposed to have done this time? Go on, what stupid nonsense has he got himself involved in?' Mrs Bowen demanded.

There was a faint pause before Ian spoke, very quietly. 'Would you describe murder as stupid nonsense?'

The lawyer opened her mouth to speak but closed it again abruptly. For a moment no one spoke.

'I asked you a question.'

'What the fuck are you talking about? My son's got nothing to do with any murder. He's a kid. He's a good kid.' Her eyes narrowed. 'He just gets a bit high spirited, that's all. Nicking my fags and stuff like that. It's harmless nonsense. He's never broken the law, have you, Daryl? He shouldn't be here.'

'We have reason to suspect that your son is involved in a gang who have been mugging people on the streets at knife point. Two victims have been fatally stabbed,' Ian said.

'That's got nothing to do with Daryl! What are saying? You can't pin this on him!' The woman's voice rose in a shriek. 'You can't take him away from me. What am I supposed to do on my own?'

'We're not accusing Daryl of being directly involved in the murders,' Geraldine interrupted her gently. 'But we do have reason to suspect he knows the gang who are doing this.' She turned to speak to Daryl directly. 'If you can tell us who these muggers are, then you can go home and that will be the end of it.'

The lawyer nodded at the terrified boy. 'Go on, Daryl. If you know the boys they're talking about, you need to speak up.'

'My son wasn't brought up to be a thief,' Mrs Bowen burst out furiously, glaring at the lawyer. 'You're supposed to be on our side!'

'Daryl, you know a girl called Alexa, don't you?' Geraldine asked.

Underneath his acne, Daryl's face reddened. He shook his head.

'Who is this girl?' the lawyer asked. 'What does she have to do with Daryl?'

Ignoring the interruption, Ian spoke to Daryl. 'We know Alexa received a bag stolen during the course of a mugging.'

Geraldine was watching Daryl's reactions very closely as Ian mentioned Alexa, and she now suspected the girl could be a way of putting pressure on him.

'It's a very expensive brown leather bag,' Geraldine added. 'A Burberry. Alexa could be in very serious trouble, if you don't help her, and we'd have to tell her you refused to help her just to save yourself from being questioned.'

'No!' Daryl cried out. 'You can't say that. She hasn't done anything. She wouldn't. You leave her out of this.'

Ian threw Geraldine an appreciative glance.

'You gave her that bag, didn't you?' Ian asked.

'No. No.'

'Oh dear,' Ian said. 'Now Alexa is in worse trouble than before, because she told us you gave it to her. So she's not only been receiving stolen goods, but she's lied to the police about it.'

'Withholding information, and obstructing the police in a murder investigation.' Geraldine shook her head. 'Those are very serious charges.'

She turned to Daryl. 'Well, that will be all.'

'What?'

'You can go now.'

Ian nodded. 'We'll just have to get to work on Alexa and get the truth out of her, whatever it takes.'

'Yes, we'll have to get back to her and tell her we know she's lying about where she got that bag. She's in a lot of trouble now for lying to us. Serious trouble.'

Mrs Bowen stood up. 'Come on, Daryl, you heard them. We can go.'

All the colour had drained from the boy's face making his acne show up more brightly. He stared at Ian, making no move to follow his mother.

'Daryl, come on, we're going home.'

'No!' It sounded like a cry of pain.

Mrs Bowen turned in surprise, her eyebrows raised. Once more she appeared about to remonstrate, but she hesitated and sat down again.

'Don't speak, Daryl,' the lawyer warned him. 'Don't say a word.'

Like his mother, the boy took no notice of the lawyer's advice. 'It was me,' he said.

It was his mother's turn to cry out. 'No! It can't be true. It's not true.' She appealed to the lawyer. 'He wouldn't – he couldn't… you have to do something.'

'You gave that bag to Alexa, didn't you?' Geraldine responded.

Daryl's mother let out a long shuddering breath as she realised what Daryl had admitted to.

The boy nodded, and answered in a whisper. 'Yes, yes, I gave her the bag. I did. She wasn't lying. It was me.'

Recovering her senses, Mrs Bowen snapped at him to be quiet.

'Don't say any more, Daryl. You heard what the lawyer said. Shut the fuck up. They'll tie you up in knots.'

Geraldine leaned forward and spoke as gently as she could.

Unattractive as they were, Daryl and his mother were both clearly frightened.

'We just want to know where that bag came from, Daryl. Don't be frightened, you're not in any trouble.'

'I'm not frightened of you. Nothing scares me…' he began but his protest petered out.

'You could end up in very serious trouble if you withhold information from the police,' the lawyer said. 'I suggest you tell them where the bag came from.'

Daryl shrugged and looked helplessly at his mother who advised him to keep his trap shut.

'You just told us you gave a very expensive leather bag to your girlfriend,' Geraldine said.

'She's not my girlfriend.'

At her side, Geraldine heard Ian sigh impatiently.

'You told us you gave an expensive leather bag to your friend, Alexa,' she amended her statement. 'Where did you get that bag from?'

'I found it,' he replied.

'Found it?'

'Yes. In – on a rubbish dump. Someone had thrown it away. So it wasn't even stealing.' He smiled in an attempt to look friendly, as if to emphasise how accommodating he was.

'Someone had thrown it on a rubbish dump?' Ian repeated, his tone scathing. 'Where is this rubbish dump?'

'No, I mean it was dumped in the rubbish. In one of the bins outside Sainsbury's.'

It was pathetically obvious he was making his story up as he went along, and making a very unconvincing job of it.

'I wonder who would throw out a perfectly good brand-new very expensive bag,' Geraldine said slowly.

'People throw out all sorts,' Daryl's mother said. 'Can we go now?'

'Not until Daryl tells us the truth.'

'Oh bloody hell, he told you, didn't he?'

Geraldine and Ian exchanged a glance.

'Let me help jog your memory, Daryl. That bag was stolen when its owner was mugged in the street,' Geraldine said.

'Do you have any evidence that links Daryl to the mugging?' the lawyer asked. 'You don't have to say anything, Daryl –'

'It wasn't stolen by him,' Mrs Bowen interrupted. 'That must be why they threw it away,' she went on with a crafty expression. 'Whoever stole it didn't want to be caught red-handed. They must have taken all the cash from inside it and dumped the bag. That's what they do, isn't it?'

'You tell me,' Ian replied drily. 'You seem to know all about it.'

The woman scowled and muttered something about having read about it in the local paper.

'If you keep on lying like this,' Geraldine said, 'we'll have to believe you were lying about giving the bag to Alexa. Which means she lied to us as well.'

Ian nodded, catching her drift at once. 'That girl's going to be in a lot of trouble.'

'You leave her out of it!' Daryl shouted.

Ian's expression didn't alter, but Geraldine knew he must be as pleased as she was to have succeeded in finding a way to persuade Daryl to talk.

'Tell us the truth then, Daryl. Where did you get hold of that bag? We know you didn't find it in a rubbish bin.'

'You need to answer the question,' the lawyer said. 'Tell the police what you know.'

'He said –' his mother began but Geraldine pressed on loudly, ignoring the interruption.

'Did you mug someone for it? It was because you wanted to get a nice present for Alexa, wasn't it? You wouldn't be the first boy to do something like that.' She smiled at him. 'What you did is understandable, but wrong.'

'No, no. I never mugged anyone. I was just the...' He broke off. His mother was hissing at him to shut up, but it was too late.

Once he started talking, Daryl became surprisingly garrulous. His mother sat at his side, alternately swearing at him and growling at Geraldine and Ian, but even she was powerless to stop him talking. The one message that came across clearly was that he would refuse to share any names with the police unless they could offer him protection from the other gang members.

'You don't know what they'll do to me,' he kept repeating, his voice trembling with fear. 'I can't tell you, I just can't.'

In the end he agreed to divulge the location of their hideout on the condition that he was present when the police arrived, and was treated in exactly the same way as the other members of the gang. It was a reasonable request, and Ian agreed. Geraldine was surprised to learn there were only three boys in the gang.

'Is there anyone else? A leader who doesn't meet you very often?' Ian asked, evidently sharing Geraldine's reaction.

Daryl shook his head, puzzled by the question. 'No, I told you, it's just the three of us. The other two and me.'

'If there is anyone else, now's the time to tell the police,' the lawyer said.

'Oh, shut up,' Daryl's mother said. 'And I bet I know who one of the other toerags is. I bet it's that boy who used to walk to school with you, when –'

'That's history,' Daryl interrupted her. 'No one cares about junior school anymore.'

'What's his name?' Ian asked, but Mrs Bowen shook her head and claimed she couldn't remember.

It didn't matter. If Daryl's information was correct, the whole gang – all three of them – would be interviewed at the police station before the day was over, and samples of their DNA would be taken and analysed. Geraldine doubted that a match with the murderer would be found, but at least they would have apprehended the muggers.

29

CARVER LEANED BACK IN his seat and surveyed his domain. Walls once white were coated with a film of grey filth. Streaks of dirt merged with shadows cast by the solitary light bulb until the two were indistinguishable. He turned his attention to his stubby fingers, the pads engrained with grime, the knuckles on his right hand swollen and split from a recent brawl. As long as his opponent came off worse, Carver was never bothered by trivial injuries sustained in a fight. And there was no question that his opponent had come off worse this time. Carver had left him writhing in a gutter, eyes already swelling above his smashed nose, body bent double over injuries concealed beneath his clothes. Carver chuckled at the memory.

Flexing his fingers, he winced slightly when his right hand smarted at the movement. It had been a tough fight. Although he wouldn't have admitted this to anyone, for a moment he had been afraid he was going to be thrashed. The fleeting doubt had made his eventual victory all the sweeter, and he was still elated by his triumph. His humiliation at the hands of a girl earlier in the week had ceased to rankle once Nelson had explained how she had taken advantage of him.

'How was anyone supposed to know she was some kind of martial arts expert?' Nelson had demanded.

Nelson was right. It hadn't been a fair fight. From now on, Carver would trust no one.

Nelson came in, shaking his head and grumbling about the rain.

'Man, you're always whining. You were born complaining,' Carver said.

'Where did you get that?' Nelson asked, catching sight of Carver's injured hand. 'You look like you been in a fight.'

'It was epic. You should've seen him.' Carver threw his head back and laughed.

'We're supposed to be keeping out of trouble,' Nelson said, scowling. 'What if he'd called the cops?'

Carver grinned. 'He's not gonna be talking to anyone for a while. Bring me that chair.'

Carver put his feet up on the old yellow chair, leaving Nelson to sit on the wooden crate. Between Nelson and Daryl, the yellow chair was taken on a first come first served basis. This evening, Nelson had missed out on the chair even though he had arrived before Daryl. Still, the crate was better than nothing. Daryl would have to sit on the floor.

'Where's the boy?' Carver asked.

Nelson shrugged one shoulder, one eyebrow raised in disdain.

'How should I know?'

'Where the hell's he at? Don't tell me he's decided to stay home after I told him to be here. Shit, where is he?'

Nelson scowled. 'That boy's trouble. I been saying it all along. He's got trouble written all over him. We ought never to have brought him here. We were doing just fine before he came along. Now everything's fucked up.'

'Fuck me, if he don't show up, I'm gonna –'

As he was speaking, there was a knock on the door. The two boys froze, listening, their eyes fixed on the door. Since the recent stabbings reported in the news, they had all become jumpy. They heard another tap. And another. As the boys recognised the pattern, the tension in the air slipped away. Carver's grip on the arm of his chair loosened.

'I knew it was him,' Nelson said, smiling with relief.

'Like fuck you did. Well? You gonna let him in or what?'

Carver tossed him the key, and Nelson jumped up to open the door. Carver waited until the door was locked and the key returned to him, before addressing Daryl.

'You're late, boy.'

Daryl glanced at his phone to check the time. 'It's not even eight yet,' he protested, his fear of Carver momentarily swept away by indignation.

'I said you're late,' Carver repeated, raising his voice slightly.

The time was immaterial. If Carver said it was late, then it was late. Daryl ducked his head and muttered an apology. From his perch on the crate, Nelson watched, grinning. Daryl looked all around, and then sat on the floor close to the wall, hugging his knees to his chest.

'So what we gonna do?' Nelson asked.

'We'd better stay here,' Daryl replied, glancing anxiously towards the door. 'We're safe in here. No one knows about this place.'

Nelson sniggered. 'You planning on spending the rest of your life hiding in here?'

'What you laughing at, boy?' Daryl demanded.

Fuming, he stood up and glared at Nelson who jumped to his feet. A tiny cloud of dust rose from the floor, scuffed up by his movement.

'For fuck's sake sit down and shut up,' Carver said. 'I got no time for your yapping. I got to think. Just as well someone around here does.'

When they were both sitting down, Carver stared from Daryl to Nelson and back again. Then he lit a cigarette and sprawled in his seat, his feet resting comfortably on the yellow chair. For a few moments no one spoke. The dust settled on the floor once more.

'We gonna stay here all night?' Nelson asked.

Daryl scowled at him but didn't answer. Then he turned to watch Carver, who was blowing smoke rings at the ceiling. Some of them were quite neat.

'That's a good one,' Daryl said with fake admiration.

'We going out or what?' Nelson said.

'You can't ever just sit still, can you?' Daryl said.

'What you complaining about? Anyway, we can't just sit here all night doing nothing.'

'What's wrong with staying here?' Daryl asked.

'What we gonna do hanging in here all night, big mouth?' Nelson persisted.

Carver was watching the other boys through lowered lids. Without a word he pulled out his knife and began flicking the blade in and out, in and out.

'Nobody's gonna bother us,' he crooned, his eyes on his knife. 'I'd like to see some fucker try.'

The blade slid in and out, in and out, with a faint clicking sound. The tension grew fierce as Nelson and Daryl glared at one another. And all the while the blade flicked in and out, in and out.

'We can stay here and make plans,' Daryl said at last. 'Talk about what we're gonna do when it's safe to go out there again.'

'And when is it gonna be safe enough for you?' Nelson clucked and flapped his elbows.

'How about when the killer's been caught, and the streets aren't crawling with pigs, looking for us?'

'Ooh, I'm scared,' Nelson said, slapping his hands to his cheeks and stretching his eyes open wide.

Absorbed in blowing smoke rings, Carver took no notice of them. He leaned back and closed his eyes. Nelson shook his fist at Daryl who scowled, but neither of them broke the silence.

At last Carver spoke. 'So here's what we're gonna do.'

He spoke very slowly as though working out what he was going to say while he was speaking. But he got no further because, without any warning, there was a resounding thump and the garage walls trembled. Carver sat bolt upright. The trail of smoke rising from his cigarette drew a jagged line in the air.

'Open up! Police! Come out with your hands in the air! The garage is surrounded!'

Carver leaped from his chair as though he had been stung. Nelson was already on his feet, and Daryl scrambled up from the floor.

'What the fuck –' Carver cried out.

Daryl had never seen him looking scared before. Carver's eyes glared wildly around the room and Daryl trembled as they darted past him.

30

THE THREE BOYS HAD attempted to escape but with several burly officers in uniform blocking the doorway, and no other way out, their efforts had been futile. Geraldine frowned as she read the report logged by the arresting officer. After the door had been kicked in, Daryl had fought as hard as the other boys, and had been dragged to the police van in handcuffs, still kicking and struggling. He was terrified of the boy he called Carver, so concealing his collusion had been a condition of Daryl's co-operation with the police. Even the officers at the scene had been unaware that he was an informer. He must have done a good job of convincing his friends that his resistance was genuine.

'If Carver finds out, I'm dead,' he said several times when Geraldine and Ian questioned him.

The words might have been an exaggeration, but his fear was genuine.

Arriving at the police station, the boys were charged separately. All three of them strenuously denied being involved in any wrongdoing, and a search of the garage and each of their homes found no stolen goods. Obdurate even after lengthy questioning, Nelson admitted only that the boys had hung out together, talking, smoking cigarettes, and drinking beer. If he was to be believed, they spent most of their time sitting in the garage trying to blow smoke rings.

'You can treat me like a big shot villain if you want, but kids hanging out in a garage isn't a crime, is it?' he had asked, opening his eyes wide in fake surprise that the police would be interested in him.

Ian gave an impatient laugh. 'You're a big shot villain like I'm Father Christmas.'

'So why am I here?'

Ian leaned forward suddenly, a menacing scowl on his face. 'Just because you've been nicking phones doesn't mean you don't have information that could be of use to us. And if you don't co-operate with us, you'll find yourself facing a charge of obstructing the police in a murder enquiry, and then the justice system *will* treat you like a serious villain, and you'll find yourself in prison for a very long time. And I can promise you, if you don't start talking, you're going to be sorry, because that's what's going to happen to you. We'll make sure you're locked up for a long time.'

Nelson turned to his lawyer. 'What does he mean? Why is he talking to me like that?'

The stout lawyer sitting beside the boy roused himself, blinking. He could almost have been fast asleep with his eyes open.

'My client is becoming distressed,' he said, throwing out a generic objection. 'He's not been charged with any crime and he's young –'

'Eighteen. He's old enough to understand exactly what's going on,' Ian interrupted, 'and he's refusing to co-operate.' He nodded at the constable at the door. 'Take him to the cells and bring him back when he's prepared to tell us the whole truth, and not before.'

'You can't keep me locked up. I haven't done anything.'

'Charge my client or let him go home,' the lawyer said, yawning behind a plump white hand.

'Take him away,' Ian repeated. 'You'll be charged as an accessory to murder if you don't start talking.'

It was pointless posturing. Nelson couldn't be forced to talk to the police, and there was nothing they could do about it. They all knew he would be released within twenty-four hours unless they could come up with evidence placing him at one of the murder scenes.

The oldest boy gave his name as Carver. He insisted that was the only name he had, but the local borough intelligence officers knew him as Billy Whitelow. Their records showed that his mother was dead and his father had abandoned him when he was in his early teens, since when he had been in and out of care until he had disappeared off the radar when he reached sixteen. When he was brought in to the police station he was carrying a switchblade and there was a collection of other knives stashed in a rusty filing cabinet in a corner of the garage, all of which bore his fingerprints. The boys' appearance matched several descriptions that had been given independently by victims of recent muggings. There was no doubt these were the three boys who had been active on the streets, stealing bags and wallets at knife point. Finding the hoard of knives raised everyone's hopes that the killer had been found, and the following day the team at the police station went about their work in a mood of suppressed optimism. No one dared mention that Carver was blond and Caucasian, for fear of jinxing the enquiry.

When the forensic report came back, the cheery bubble burst. None of the blades discovered in the garage matched the murder victims' stab wounds and, worse, none of the boys' DNA matched that found on the victims. Even Carver's DNA wasn't a match. The identity of the owner of the DNA found at the crime scenes remained unknown.

'We've found the muggers, but we're no closer to the murderer,' Eileen said grimly, when she called the team together that afternoon. She glared around the room as though each of her team was personally responsible for her strategy of focusing on finding the muggers. 'All we've managed to do is finish the job for the team supposed to be cleaning up the muggings,' she added crossly. 'And although we all know they're guilty we can't even charge them with theft, because we haven't found any proof of their guilt. Meanwhile, we're still nowhere further ahead with our own investigation. Two weeks' work, and that's all we've come up with: three teenage thugs who've been out on the streets helping themselves to other people's wallets.'

'Maybe the team who are supposed to be finding the muggers will discover the murderer for us?' a young constable piped up.

'Don't talk nonsense. If we can't find him, no one can,' a sergeant replied.

'Of course we can find him. It just takes time,' Ariadne said.

'Be quiet, all of you,' Eileen snapped, and the chatter ceased. 'I've arranged to have those thugs identified this afternoon. Let's hope someone recognises them and then at least we'll have a conviction for thieving, if nothing else.'

The line-up turned out to be as disappointing as the lack of DNA evidence linking the boys to the murder scenes. No one was able to identify any of the boys with any certainty. 'It all happened so fast,' the victims of the muggings kept saying. 'It could have been him, but I can't say for sure.' Even Wendy, who had given a relatively coherent description, was reluctant to confirm these were the boys who had attacked her. Several young police officers were picked out, along with other boys who vaguely resembled the suspects. It was inconclusive, so the three boys were released.

'That's harassment, that is,' Carver protested, when the custody sergeant warned them the police would be keeping an eye on them.

'Come on, officer, they're good boys,' the lawyer interrupted, with an oily smile. 'Don't worry, boys, it's just talk. You're free to go.'

Along with the rest of the team, Geraldine was disappointed. But at least they had hopefully put an end to the recent spate of muggings. When Ariadne suggested that at least one of the gang was potentially young enough to be successfully rehabilitated, Eileen grunted.

'Let's hope they all learn a lesson from this, and stop before they really do hurt someone,' she concurred.

Miserably they all agreed that their time hadn't been completely wasted in tracking the gang down. Geraldine didn't mention that she had been convinced all along that they had been misguided in focusing their resources on searching for the muggers. Their job was to find a killer and, so far, they had failed. Discovering the identity of the muggers had no bearing on their investigation. Somehow the temporary excitement, and subsequent disappointment, made it even harder to continue an investigation with which they were making no headway.

31

No one else seemed interested in finding out what had happened to the missing long-haired witness, Lindsey Curtis, but Geraldine still clung to the possibility that her fate might be somehow tied in with the murders.

'It seems too much of a coincidence, her disappearing like that, just after she might have seen two murders being committed.'

'Are you saying you still think she was somehow involved?' Ariadne asked. 'There's no evidence for that.'

'No, I'm saying I don't think it's necessarily a coincidence that she's disappeared just now.'

'Women leave home for all sorts of reasons,' Ariadne replied.

Despite her colleagues' lack of interest in the missing woman's fate, on her way home from work that evening, Geraldine called at the house once again. Sooner or later she hoped to find out what, if anything, the woman had witnessed on the nights of the two murders. In addition to that, even though no body had been discovered, Geraldine remained uneasy about her fate. If no one answered the bell again, she would question the missing woman's neighbours to see if they could tell her anything about her. It was possible one of them knew her and might be able to suggest where she could have gone. Perhaps she had confided in a member of her family, or a friend. It was unlikely, but worth following up, because it was possible.

Geraldine drove to the address in a side turning off Gillygate. Claremont Terrace was narrow, and several cars were parked along the kerb. Parking a few doors away from the house, she walked up and rang the bell. No one answered so she walked past paved front yards as far as the adjoining property. The man who came to the door there was at least seventy, with a balding head and a round face. He smiled kindly at Geraldine.

'Yes? Can I help you?' he greeted her with old-fashioned courtesy.

She was pleased his smile didn't falter when she held up her identity card. Increasingly, members of the public clammed up or became hostile when she introduced herself as a police officer. When she asked him whether he knew his neighbours, he nodded thoughtfully.

'You mean next door?' He jerked his head in the direction of the house where the elusive woman lived. 'Oh yes. That is, I don't know her, exactly, but I've seen her once or twice, coming and going. She isn't often around. I don't think I've seen her more than a few times and never to speak to. Why? Has something happened that I ought to know about?'

The neighbour told her that the woman rarely seemed to go out.

'At least I don't see her go out much during the day,' he added, pulling a face.

'Do you mean she goes out at night?'

The old man sniffed. 'It's not for me to pass any comment on how other people live their lives, but yes, I've seen her going out after dark far more often than I've seen her go out during the day.'

'Do you mean she works shifts?'

'I don't think she'd be going to work, not in a respectable job, not dressed like that. I've seen her traipsing down the road at all hours, off for a night out, dressed up to the nines in tight skirts, with her hair all done up in curls.' He sniffed again. 'I can't say I hold with such carryings-on.'

'What time did she usually go out at night?'

'Oh, don't get me wrong, I only saw her going out late once or twice. I go to bed early as a rule.'

'And on those few occasions when you did see her going out at night, what time was that?'

'I'm afraid I couldn't say what time it was, exactly. But it was after dark anyway. I wish I could be more helpful.'

'And was she on her own?'

'Always.'

Geraldine had the distinct impression he disapproved of his neighbour and what he referred to as her 'carryings-on', but it was important to keep to the facts. People's opinions could be misleading. Having found out what she could, she thanked the neighbour and moved on to the property on the other side. The woman there was about sixty and slim, and voluble. She seemed eager to help.

'Well, I probably shouldn't say it, but she's a bit of a dressed-up tart. Sorry, I shouldn't say that, should I? I hardly know the woman. But the way she dresses! Talk about over the top. I'm guessing she's a lot older than she looks.'

'How old does she look?'

'I don't know that I can say, really. I've never seen her close up.'

'What's she like? Can you describe her?'

The woman shook her head. 'I don't know. She's got long hair, I can tell you that much, but I've never spoken to her, and I can't say I want to either. I see her once in a while when I'm putting the rubbish out at night, stalking past with her nose in the air. I'm not saying she's any better than me, only she looks as though she thinks she is. Why else would she ignore me? The first time I saw her going out, I called out, just to say hello, as you do, and she completely blanked me.'

'Perhaps she's deaf.'

The woman frowned. 'I hadn't thought of that. But I don't think so. I think she's just hoity toity. So, how is it the police are interested in her all of a sudden? What's she done?' Her eyes glittered with curiosity.

As Geraldine questioned other residents of the street, a picture emerged of a vulgarly dressed woman who was rarely seen during the hours of daylight. It was interesting, but none of it helped further the investigation into her disappearance, or into the recent murders. No one seemed to care that the woman might have gone missing. It was depressing that a human being mattered so little to the people living around her. Geraldine hadn't met any of her own neighbours. She wondered who would notice if she herself ever disappeared.

32

CARVER TAPPED RHYTHMICALLY ON the arm of his chair making a barely audible thud with each impact of a stubby fingertip on the upholstery.

'The whole lot,' he fumed. 'The whole bloody lot.' His head whipped round and he glared at his companions. 'Do you know how long it took me to collect them all?'

'No,' Nelson muttered, without meeting Carver's eye. 'I don't know. How long did it take?'

Daryl merely shook his head, wary.

'I don't fucking know, do I?' Carver replied. 'I've been collecting them for years. Years! They couldn't even open it properly like any normal person. They're worse than animals. Ignorant fuckers! Don't they know how to use a key?'

The three boys all turned to stare at the metal cabinet, its bent door hanging uselessly on one rusty hinge where the police had busted the lock.

Nelson hazarded a question. 'Did they take them all?'

'You know they did. The bastards. Cowards!'

Carver was working himself up into a rage, and when he was angry he was dangerous – but not as dangerous as he had been when he was wielding a knife. Daryl was frightened, but also slightly excited when Carver leapt to his feet and began prowling around the garage. Nelson was vicious, but Daryl could be handy with his fists if he needed to be. Without weapons, if it came to a fight, it would be a question of numbers. Between them, Nelson and Daryl could easily take Carver down. That was a thrilling thought. But Daryl knew that Nelson was never going to turn against Carver. It wasn't safe to antagonise the two of them.

'What do you want us to do?' he asked Carver. 'Whatever's going on, I'm your man.'

'You're my man?' Carver repeated, the words sounding like a sneer.

Daryl nodded, licking his lips which suddenly felt dry. 'That's right,' he said. 'That's what I said. I'm your man.'

There was a slight hiatus during which none of them spoke.

'What did you need to say that for?' Nelson challenged Daryl at last. 'What makes you think we might suspect you're not one of us?'

Daryl shook his head, suddenly fearful. He felt a rush of anger against Nelson for stirring things up against him. It wasn't the first time he had tried to make trouble for Daryl.

'I never said that,' he protested. 'I never suggested anyone was thinking I wasn't in. Why would I say that?'

He turned to Carver who was watching him without blinking, one hand resting proprietorially on the broken cabinet.

'What the fuck are you talking about then?' Carver asked him.

Daryl shrugged. 'I don't know. I just thought…'

'And?' Nelson prompted him. 'What were you thinking?'

Carver answered for him. 'You know your problem? You try and think. It doesn't suit you. And you know why? Because you're a cretin. That's why.' He laughed. 'You are a cretin.'

Carver stared at Daryl, as though weighing him up. He glanced over at Nelson who was already poised to pitch in if it came to a fight. There was little doubt that Nelson would support Carver in any kind of conflict. Carver tapped his toe on the dirty floor, his eyes fixed on Daryl.

'Well?' Nelson pressed him, taking a step closer to Daryl.

'No point in us falling out,' Daryl muttered. 'It's the pigs who done it, not any of us.'

As it happened, he wouldn't have minded falling out with

the other two. In fact, he would have been very happy to know he was never going to see either of them ever again. But he had to tread warily. The last thing he wanted was to find himself caught up in a fight with them. It would be two against one and he would suffer a bad beating, if he even survived. They were dirty fighters, both of them, and strong with it. Carver let go of the cabinet and took a step forward. Spellbound, Daryl watched him move closer.

Carver's voice was low, and his words hung suspended in the air. 'But who was it brought them here is what I want to know.'

His eyes gleamed as he glared from Daryl to Nelson and back again.

Sensing danger, Nelson grunted. 'What the fuck?'

Carver's voice was a hoarse whisper. 'What's that you said?'

'No one would be that stupid,' Nelson spluttered in alarm. 'For fuck's sake, Carver, you can't think one of us would do a thing like that. Bloody hell, it makes no sense. Why would we want to get in trouble with the filth? What would be the point? And you know we got in trouble the same as you. If you think it was one of us told them where we hang out, you're fucking mental, man. Fucking hell.'

'You're doing a lot of talking,' Carver said.

'To you, man, to you. I don't talk to anyone else.'

Nelson sat down on the yellow chair, muttering.

'And you?' Carver turned to Daryl. 'You're keeping very quiet. You think I've forgotten you?'

'No, no,' Daryl stammered. 'I don't think you forget anything.'

Until Carver armed himself with a new blade he was a toothless tiger, so Daryl took courage and spoke up.

'I never talked to anyone. Why would I? What do you think I am?'

Nelson muttered something about a cretin.

Daryl ignored him. 'Someone must've followed us here. Someone must've seen us.'

Carver scowled. 'If I ever find out who led the pigs here, he's dead.' He rolled both his hands into fists and pummelled the air. 'Worse than dead. I find out who squealed on me, I'll rip his tongue out with my bare hands. I'll smash his balls.'

'They never got us though, did they?' Nelson said, grinning.

'They said they'd be watching us,' Daryl reminded him.

'Even that fat bastard lawyer said the pigs were full of shit,' Carver replied.

'He was full of shit,' Nelson said.

Daryl nodded in agreement, licking his lips and doing his best to remain calm. With a final snarl of fury, Carver sat down again. The soft drumming on the arm of his chair resumed.

'Here, boss.'

As he spoke, Nelson drew a large bottle out of each of his jacket pockets and held them up above his head: vodka in his left hand, whisky in his right.

'Fuck me,' Carver burst out. 'You had those on you all this time and you never mentioned it!'

'I know how to keep my trap shut,' Nelson said pointedly.

Opening the whisky, he tipped his head right back, and his Adam's apple bobbed up and down with each gulp. At last he straightened up, his eyes watering slightly, and handed the bottle to Carver who was waiting impatiently for it. Daryl watched anxiously as Carver took his turn, seeming to pour the liquid down his throat without even swallowing. When he lowered the bottle, he waved it at Daryl who sprang over to take it from him.

'Hey,' Nelson blurted out. 'Tha's my whisky. 'Smine.'

He slid off his chair, and opened the vodka.

Carver held out his hand to Daryl who returned the whisky to him, wiping his mouth on his sleeve.

'Hey,' Nelson called out, 'didn't I just say 'smine?'

Ignoring him, Carver resumed drinking. After a while he

dropped the empty whisky bottle, and reached out to Nelson for the vodka. He drank noisily, then leaned back in his chair, and stared blankly up at the ceiling. Meanwhile Nelson was lying curled up on the floor in a foetal position and seemed to have fallen asleep. Daryl began to giggle, and once he started he couldn't stop. The other boys took no notice of him as he crawled across the floor and reached for the empty whisky bottle. His head was pounding and the light bulb hanging from the ceiling had become painfully bright. The crate where Daryl had been sitting was a long way off, and the room was spinning. He tried to drag himself over to the yellow chair, but it was too much effort, so he lay down where he was and closed his eyes. He was still giggling.

33

GERALDINE HAD INTENDED TO go and see her sister in Kent on Sunday, but during the week she called to cancel her visit. It was a long way to travel, and Celia had long ago given up grumbling that, whenever Geraldine was involved in a murder investigation, her work took priority over everything else.

'It's OK, really,' Celia had replied, her tone growing plaintive as she added, 'I understand you have to put your work before us.'

'As soon as the case is over I'll come and see you all,' Geraldine had promised. 'You know I can't wait to see the baby again. He must be growing so fast.'

Celia had chattered for a few minutes about how much weight the baby had gained, and how long he slept at night, before airing her ongoing anxiety over Chloe.

'Honestly, Geraldine, I don't know what to say to her. I mean, it can't be easy for her, you know, sibling rivalry and all that, but I thought she was fine. And now this. It has to be a reaction to the baby's arrival.'

Geraldine had laughed at her concern. 'You're looking for problems where there really aren't any. It's perfectly normal and natural, and it's got nothing to do with the baby. She was going to become interested in boys at some point.'

'But she's so young,' Celia had wailed. 'I don't remember being interested in boys at her age, do you?'

'She's probably more interested in copying what her friends are doing, and some of them are probably copying older sisters.'

'Oh well, I suppose you're right. Anyway, how are you getting on?'

Geraldine hadn't admitted that although the case was going nowhere, a lead could turn up at any moment, and she was keen to be there if it did. Visiting Celia took up a whole day, and she didn't want to be away from York for that long. A few of her younger colleagues had begun muttering about the possibility that this might be one of those cases that was never solved, but she remained optimistic.

A team had been deployed conducting door-to-door questioning throughout the city, starting in the areas around Pope's Head Alley and Lendal Bridge, and approaching anyone walking or cycling along the river bank. So far no one had reported seeing anything suspicious or even unusual, but the investigation continued as vigorously as ever. Meanwhile, long drawn-out forensic analysis of any potential evidence found at the scenes of both murders continued, but nothing had yet been discovered that furthered the investigation. Random cigarette butts had been collected and sent off to be tested for DNA, footprints analysed, and hour after hour of CCTV footage scrutinised, but there was no evidence placing the same person at both scenes, other than the unidentified DNA they had found, and a barely distinguishable image of a long-haired woman that Eileen had dismissed as irrelevant.

Along with her colleagues, Geraldine was feeling frustrated at the lack of progress. She had spent hours poring over reports, studying everything that had so far been thrown up. The only loose end she had come across was the case of the woman who had been spotted on CCTV and then gone missing, part way through the investigation. Were it not for the timing of Lindsey's disappearance it would have been unremarkable but, as it was, Geraldine couldn't help wondering whether it might be significant. In the absence of any other leads, on Sunday morning she decided to call on the woman again. Her house wasn't far out of Geraldine's route from her flat near Skeldergate Bridge to the police station. There was no answer when she rang the bell so, after waiting for a few minutes, she left.

'We're just not getting anywhere,' Ariadne grumbled, when Geraldine arrived and sat down opposite her.

'Something will turn up,' Geraldine replied. 'Something always does. And there's still the long-haired woman we haven't managed to find yet. Who knows what she might have to tell us?'

But Ariadne didn't hold out much hope that a witness would ever be found.

'It can't have been the same woman,' she said. 'The one who followed Felicity down to the river could be anywhere, and we don't know the one we traced on CCTV even lives in York. She could be miles away by now. Granted it would be perfect if she did contact us and told us she had seen the killer, and gave us a detailed description of him, but what are the chances? We might as well wait for hell to freeze over.'

Geraldine's other colleagues seemed equally sceptical, and it was true that so far they had very little to go on. All they knew was that a long-haired woman was renting a house in York, and she had possibly walked near at least one of the victims shortly before a murder. Not only was it a very tenuous lead, but they hadn't been able to find her.

'Perhaps she's on holiday,' Ariadne suggested. 'But she's probably got nothing helpful to tell us anyway.'

Geraldine shrugged. Once they managed to find the missing woman, she would hopefully admit to having seen the attack in Pope's Head Alley. But it was stretching plausibility to believe that the same witness could really have been present at the scene of the second murder as well. Seeing a second long-haired figure descending from the bridge just after Felicity must have been a coincidence. Still, one or other of the women might have seen something and been too scared to come forward, or perhaps hadn't yet realised the significance of what she had seen that night.

Geraldine was beginning to regret having cancelled her visit to Celia that Sunday when Eileen summoned the team for a briefing. Everyone gathered in an atmosphere of expectation, but it turned out that Eileen had nothing new to report. She just wanted to review what they knew so far.

'We must be missing something,' she said. 'We've been searching for something that links Grant and Felicity but other than the fact that they were both school teachers, there doesn't seem to be any connection between them. They trained in different institutions and have never worked in the same school. Now, what about the Drury family?'

'We haven't managed to trace Jamie's death certificate yet,' a constable said. 'We know he went to Australia, according to his father, and our enquiries there haven't come up with anything, but Edward Drury seemed to think his son died in Thailand. We've been in contact with the authorities there, but they aren't the easiest to deal with, to put it mildly. To be fair, we haven't given them much to go on, because we don't know exactly when or even where he died. We're chasing them, but don't hold your breath for a response.'

'Anything else?' Eileen asked.

Geraldine brought up her concern about the long-haired woman spotted near the scenes of both murders, and how she seemed to have vanished.

'She could have just gone away,' Eileen replied, 'and, in any case, we don't know she's connected to the case at all, or even if it was the same woman recorded on film on both occasions. But yes, do keep looking for her, Geraldine.'

Ignoring Eileen's patronising response, Geraldine determined to continue looking for the long-haired woman. Once again, she felt a frisson of anxiety about Lindsey's fate. There was no evidence to connect her to Grant's murder, but something about her hurried gait as she had walked away from Pope's Head Alley worried Geraldine, and she couldn't shake off her unease.

34

'YOU FUCKING FINISHED IT!' Nelson roared. 'Tha's mine! What you doing with it anyway?'

He staggered to his feet, red-faced with fury, and ready to lash out. Normally Daryl would have cringed and kept his eyes lowered, in a craven attempt to avoid attention, but the drink had loosened his tongue. At the same time, it was making him incoherent.

'No, no, no, it was empty,' he replied. 'It was empty.'

'It's empty now,' Nelson snarled.

'Listen, I'm telling you, the bottle was empty when I found it –' Daryl insisted, struggling to form the words.

'Found it?' Nelson interrupted him. 'What you on about, you found it? You mean you fucking stole it off me.'

Nelson leaned over and grabbed the bottle. Clutching it, he staggered to his feet and brandished it in the air, glaring wildly at Daryl as he yelled. 'What the fuck are you doing running after us all the time, boy? You need to grow some balls if you want to hang out with us. Why don't you find some kids your own age to pester? We're sick of a whining kid like you trailing after us all the time.'

'I'm not the one whining,' Daryl pointed out. 'You haven't stopped whining since you woke up. You're a brat,' he added under his breath.

Nelson muttered about being a man not a snivelling boy.

'Oh fuck you,' Daryl replied.

Carver sat up. 'Shut the fuck up, both of you,' he snarled. 'It does my head in the way you two carry on, always snapping at each other. There's no peace with you two around.'

'Get rid of him then,' Nelson replied promptly. 'We don't need him. We were fine before he came along. He's nothing but trouble. You said it yourself. He'll get us busted.'

Daryl started, afraid Nelson had discovered his betrayal.

'Well?' Nelson persisted. 'Why is he always hanging around here?' He turned to Daryl. 'Why are you still here?'

'I got as much right to be here as you,' Daryl replied, deciding to tough it out.

He turned his back on Nelson to show he wasn't scared of him.

'Why are you still here?' Nelson repeated, his voice suddenly quiet.

'For fuck's sake,' Carver burst out. 'You're as bad as he is, yapping at him like a fucking girl. Why don't you have it out like men?'

Behind Daryl there was a loud crash. As he spun round to find out what had happened, he saw Nelson's eyes blazing beneath a glittering rainbow. Dazzled, he realised a shattered bottle was forming an arc of light in the air. Without warning, he felt dizzy and his legs gave way. Through half-closed lids he saw the floor, covered in a carpet of blood-spattered shards of glass. A veil of darkness gathered as Nelson and Carver leapt back, glaring wildly at him. Carver was yelling something about a busted door.

'Anyone could get in and see him!' he was shouting.

His voice reached Daryl through a dense fog. Daryl wanted to tell him not to worry, no one could see him in the darkness, but Carver changed tack suddenly. He turned to Nelson and grabbed him by the arm, shaking him. 'We got to split, man, get away from here and never come back.'

He kicked the broken bottle into a corner of the garage.

'Oh shit. I never meant to kill him,' Nelson stammered. 'I just wanted him to piss off.'

Daryl had stopped wheezing, and a pool of blood beside him glowed in the light.

'Well, you done for him. He's not getting up again. Come on, let's get out of here.'

'No,' Nelson cut him off firmly. 'We're not gonna run. That's the last thing we want to do.'

'What are you talking about, man? We can't let them find us here. They'll bang us up for sure.'

'No, they won't *find* us here because we're gonna call them.'

'Call? Call who? What the fuck, man?'

Carver was staring open-mouthed at Nelson who was staring down at Daryl with a curious smile on his lips.

'Listen,' Nelson's voice came at Daryl through the mist, dry and clipped. 'This was an accident. He was coming at me with a bottle and he tripped and fell on it.'

'What are you saying, man?'

'We call the pigs, exactly like we would do if we were innocent, and we act like we're shocked at this terrible accident. There's two of us and no one else to say anything different to what we tell them. As long as we get our story straight, we're in the clear.' He leaned forward and lowered his voice so Daryl struggled to distinguish his words. 'There's gonna be no other witness, is there?' He seemed unable to tear his eyes away from Daryl. 'Most people would've slashed at him but I stuck that glass right into his neck, like it was a knife stabbing him. Like as if he was so pissed he lost his footing and fell right on to it.' A slow smiled spread across Nelson's face. 'We can do this, as long as we stick together.'

'We could say it was self-defence?'

'No, listen to me, man, and concentrate, will you? It was an *accident*. You need to get that into your head. I dropped the bottle by mistake and it smashed. I was busy picking up the pieces, just tidying the place. He was so pissed, he tripped and fell on top of me, and I had that broken glass in my hand.' Nelson's voice rose. 'Before I realised what the fuck was going on, he fell right on to the broken glass and it went right through him.'

Carver nodded.

'Repeat it.'

'He tripped and fell,' Carver said. 'It was an accident.'

'That's it. That's the story and we never change it, not one detail, or they'll nail us for murdering him for sure.'

Carver staggered over to his chair and sat down. 'So what happens now?'

'We wait until he bleeds out and then we call the pigs and the ambulance and whoever else we can think of. Remember, we're panicking, right? Our bro here just had an accident, a fatal accident. We're in shock. Think how shocking it is. So look shocked. Cry if you can.'

Carver gave a bark of laughter. 'Cry? What are you talking about? You cry if you want to.'

'You think I'd cry over this little shit. He was always trouble, right from the start.'

'You never liked him.' Carver narrowed his eyes. 'It was you done this, remember, not me.'

Nelson turned and gazed coolly at Carver. 'If you tell them it was me, I'll say you're lying. I'll say it was you done it. And if we both go accusing each other, chances are we'll both go down. They're going to find both our prints all over that bottle. They won't know which one of us did it, and those bastards aren't going to let it go, are they? But listen, if we stick together there's a way to save both our skins. Only we've got to do this together. They're gonna split us up and question us until we're ready to drop, until we're ready to say anything just to make it stop. And they'll catch us out if they can. So we got to keep it simple. Tell the truth about everything else. It was my bottle. We were all sharing. Here's what happened and we got to tell it right, so listen. I got this figured out now, so pay attention, man. Daryl was out of control. A kid like that, he couldn't hold his booze. He smashed the bottle and went for me. We struggled but he was unsteady on his feet and I managed to wrest the bottle from him. We were both laughing at him. That made him crazy and he lashed out with his fists, stumbled, and that's when he tripped and fell on to me. Only I was still holding the broken bottle. And that's how it happened. That's what we say. Nothing more.'

The room seemed to spin as Carver nodded his head. Daryl wanted to protest at their lies, but he couldn't move. All around his head lights glittered and flashed. A loud rushing noise filled his head, drowning out the voices of the other boys, and then all sensation faded and he slid into a pool of blackness.

35

By the time Geraldine and Ian arrived at the derelict lock-up where Daryl had been killed, a cordon had been set up to prevent members of the public contaminating the scene. A young man was standing outside the police tape taking pictures on his phone. It was a pointless exercise, since the garage was out of sight around a bend that led past a row of disused garages due to be demolished.

'Is this a murder scene?' the young photographer asked, darting forward to intercept them, his eyes alight with excitement.

Geraldine returned his gaze coldly. 'I suggest you leave immediately. There's nothing to see, so there's no point in loitering here.'

'You can't tell me there's nothing going on because I can see they've put up a forensic tent. It's all going on over there, isn't it? Can't I just have a quick look? One photo is all I'm asking, and then I'll be out of your hair –'

Ian interrupted the speaker firmly. 'If you put one foot over this line, you'll be leaving here in police custody. Consider yourself cautioned for wasting police time.' He nodded at a constable who was standing nearby. 'Take down this man's details and send him packing.'

'Oh, forget it,' the youngster snapped. 'I can find out what's happened without your help. It'll be all over the internet by tonight. There's no way you can hush it up if there's been another murder.'

'Nothing's being hushed up, we're just doing our job –'

Geraldine began, but the disgruntled young man was already hurrying away.

'Shall I go after him, sir?' the constable asked.

'No, stay here. And make sure no one gets past you.'

'Sir.'

Turning a corner in the driveway, Geraldine saw the furthest door stood open. After pulling on protective clothing she approached the garage where scene of crime officers were already occupied, photographing and collecting evidence. Although Daryl's death had been reported as an accident, the place was being treated as a crime scene.

She put a hand on Ian's arm to stop him at the threshold.

'You don't think we're in any way responsible for this, do you?'

'What are you talking about?'

'Daryl told us where to find him, and now he's dead,' Geraldine said.

Ian didn't answer.

'What if they found out Daryl had informed on them?'

'How?' Ian replied with a worried frown. 'He was hardly going to tell them, was he? And no one else would've known what he did.'

'But what if he told someone? There was a girl, wasn't there? He might've told her.'

'Then he would've been even more of a fool than we thought,' Ian snapped.

'He wasn't exactly Brain of Britain. But the point is, if Carver and Nelson learned how we discovered their hideout, and their knives –' She paused.

Ian stared back at her uneasily. 'I don't suppose they found out what he did.'

'But they killed him,' she protested. 'Why else would they have done it?'

Ian shook his head. 'We're talking about vicious thugs, high on drugs and booze, obsessed with knives and violence. This was bound to happen sooner or later. Come on, let's get this over with.'

The dead boy was lying on his back, arms and legs outstretched. One side of his spotty face was scored with tiny jagged scratches where he had been lying on broken glass, and his throat was hidden beneath a choker of dried blood. A larger pool of blood formed a dark halo around his head, and specks of dust and dirt flecked his clothes. Geraldine drew near and stared down at him. Despite his lacerated face he looked younger than when she had last seen him, jittery and nervous at his mother's side. He couldn't have experienced much of life. It was deeply disturbing to see him lying dead at her feet when he had been facing her across a table only three days before. For an instant she felt a rush of rage against his two friends, but they too were barely adults. And besides, it was possible they had been telling the truth and Daryl's death really had been an accident.

'What terrible lives they all led,' she said out loud, to no one in particular.

A scene of crime officer standing nearby turned to look at her. 'Sorry, were you talking to me?' he asked, pausing in what he was doing.

Geraldine shook her head and he returned to his work, scrutinising, judging, and bagging evidence.

'Have you found anything interesting?' Geraldine asked him.

He raised his eyebrows and jerked his head in the direction of the body. 'Isn't that interesting enough for you?'

She gave an uneasy smile. 'You know what I mean. Have you found anything that could help us to establish exactly what happened here?'

'You already know the boy died from a wound inflicted by a broken bottle?'

Geraldine drew closer to him and lowered her voice, even though her question was hardly confidential.

'What we're trying to ascertain is whether this was an accident. Is it possible he was attacked? We know one of his friends went around with a knife.'

The scene of crime officer shook his head. 'This was no knife wound.'

'I know that. But I'm asking if this wound could have been inflicted deliberately.'

'Well,' her colleague paused and gave the question some thought before answering. 'Either someone smashed a bottle and went for him intending to kill him, in which case you're looking at the victim of a vicious assault, or else he had an extremely nasty accident.'

'Is it possible to tell which it was?' Geraldine asked patiently.

The scene of crime officer shook his head. 'Not from where I'm standing.'

Geraldine sighed. She could see he was trying to be helpful, but she wasn't learning anything from talking to him. So far the other two boys who had associated with the victim had independently stated that Daryl had been drunk and had tripped and fallen on to Nelson, who had been holding a broken bottle in his hand at the time. It was plausible, if unlikely, but although Geraldine didn't believe their account, it was difficult to disprove. If their claims were true, the death of their friend had been a terrible accident. They were both clear about what had happened and, in the absence of any other witnesses, it might be impossible to disprove their statements.

Geraldine gazed around the dingy garage. Even under bright forensic lights the place looked grey, with heavy cobwebs obscuring every corner of the grimy walls. According to Nelson's statement, on discovering the garage was empty Carver had established himself there, securing the door with a strong lock. Although the garage had temporarily been his illegal hideout, Carver had refused to add to this account. Nelson claimed the three boys had used their den for drinking and smoking cigarettes and storing their collection of knives.

He had insisted that none of them had ever taken a knife out of the garage.

Discoloured with rust and dirt, the cabinet where the knives had been stored stood empty, its door hanging loosely on one hinge. Stepping carefully along the established approach path, Geraldine went as close to it as she could. Even though it was empty there was something horribly depressing about it. She turned and gazed around. The broken bottle had been sent away for forensic examination, but fragments of glass still littered the floor. Among the splinters an occasional blood spot glowed, a ruby among diamonds that twinkled like scattered stars under the brilliant lights.

36

JONAH LOOKED UP AND heaved a sigh that seemed to shake the whole of his body. Geraldine had met the tubby pathologist several times, but never had she seen him looking so solemn, his face under the bright lights almost as pale as Daryl's. Without his usual cheeky grin, he was an unattractive little man.

'He hadn't even outgrown his adolescent acne,' Jonah said, shaking his head mournfully. 'Look, his face is covered in it. You might not believe this, but I had acne just like that when I was a teenager. Terrible, it was, terrible. To be disfigured like that at such a self-conscious age, hiding at home, when all you want to do is go out and impress girls.' He heaved another sigh. 'It's very hard. And now this poor lad will never have a chance to get past it. He dies with his pimples emblazoned on his face.' He paused and took a step back, frowning with concentration as he studied the dead boy's features. 'I could probably cover it up, make it less obvious. At least he could lie here with some dignity. Oh well,' he went on, more cheerfully. 'Only the good die young, eh? I should be around for a while then.' He gave a low laugh. 'Can't help feeling sorry for him though. Still, I guess it looks worse than it is, highlighted under these lights.'

'He won't care about his acne now,' Geraldine said. 'And if he *could* think about anything, I dare say that would be the least of his worries. This is all very well, your reminiscing like this about your tortured adolescence, and it's beautiful the way you're empathising with the victim, really beautiful. I had no idea you were such a sensitive soul. But I wonder, could we possibly postpone this touching nostalgia and get back to the business in hand?'

Jonah held up his hands in mock surrender. 'Far be it from me to waste your valuable time.'

'Can you add anything at all to what we already know about how he died?' Geraldine persisted, ignoring the good-natured jibe.

Jonah nodded and heaved another sigh. 'It's not a nice thing to suffer, that's all I'm saying. But now, OK, let's get down to the business. You know you're a hard task master, Sergeant. Steel by name, steely by nature.'

Geraldine was relieved to see Jonah had returned to his usual positivity. She wondered whether he was so relentlessly cheerful at home, or if he was more at ease dealing with the dead than the living. With a shiver, she realised that such a characterisation might apply to her. Dismissing the gloomy thought, she forced herself to focus on what Jonah was saying.

'Well, you know the tox report's not back yet, but even a stuffed-up nose can detect there was a quantity of alcohol in his bloodstream, and there wasn't much food in him either. I'd say our boy hadn't eaten since lunchtime – a kebab that must have looked rather nasty even before it was ingested – and he knocked back a fair amount of liquor about six hours later. So, basically, our boy was drinking heavily on an empty stomach.'

'And he was quite possibly not yet a hardened drinker. He was only sixteen,' Geraldine added.

'So I gather, and physically immature. I'd have hazarded a guess at thirteen.'

'You say he'd drunk a fair amount of liquor? Is it possible to be more precise about what he was drinking just before he died?'

Whatever it was, she hoped it had numbed the pain when he had received his fatal wound.

Jonah wrinkled his nose in disgust. 'From the smell, I'd say he was drinking whisky.'

'The murder weapon was a broken vodka bottle.'

'Drinking one spirit doesn't preclude drinking another,' Jonah replied.

'So he was drinking whisky and vodka, and he hadn't eaten much that day. And the cause of death was that blow to his throat?'

'More of a cut than a blow,' Jonah replied.

'Was there more than one injury?'

'No, just the one.'

'Does that mean the defence that he fell on a broken bottle is feasible?'

Jonah nodded, frowning.

'Is it likely he would have fallen in such an angle that the bottle would have slashed his neck like that?'

Jonah shrugged. 'A drunk toppling over can land awkwardly. It's not impossible. He would have to have fallen with some force, but he could have tripped and hurtled forwards, rather than toppling over.'

'And that injury killed him?'

Jonah looked thoughtful. 'The laceration is deep, but it wouldn't necessarily be severe enough to be fatal.'

'What are you saying? How did he die then, if not from a severed artery?'

'Blood loss,' the pathologist said. 'It's true the external carotid artery was severed but, had he received immediate medical attention, he might have survived. It's possible, anyway.'

'How immediate would the medical attention need to have been?'

'A matter of minutes.'

'So the death could have been the result of an accident.'

'Oh yes, it's certainly possible. Boys get drunk, they start fighting, in the scuffle a bottle is broken, someone grabs hold of it and another boy slips in his drunken state and falls over –'

They stood gazing down at the dead boy, silently considering the circumstances of his death.

'And don't forget we haven't got the tox report back yet,' Jonah added. 'Who knows what else was floating around in his blood stream, before he lost so much of it. I wouldn't be surprised to learn this incident was fuelled by more than alcohol. Not that it makes any difference.'

Geraldine nodded. The thought had occurred to her. Teenage boys, drinking and smoking cigarettes, were likely to have been using controlled drugs as well.

'We didn't find anything at the scene,' she said. 'But the other two boys might have got rid of the evidence, if there was any.'

'Well, I'll tidy him up,' Jonah said, suddenly brisk. 'I guess you'll be wanting to bring someone along for a viewing shortly?'

'Yes, he lived with his mother so we'll invite her to formally identify the body when you've finished with him. Will you be much longer?'

'No. I'll do something about his face, conceal those scratches and try to improve his skin, at least superficially. It'll be a challenge, but I'll make him look better dead than he did when he was alive.'

Geraldine shrugged. Daryl's bad skin was of no consequence now.

37

GERALDINE RANG THE BELL and waited. After some delay, the door was opened by a dowdy grey-haired woman who peered suspiciously at her, brushing hair off her face with the back of a hand. Geraldine wasn't sure whether the woman recognised her, although it was only a few days since they had last met. Geraldine had certainly not forgotten how Daryl's mother had hit him for getting in trouble with the police.

'Mrs Bowen, we met at the police station,' she said, holding up her identity card. 'Can I come in?'

'He's not here,' the woman replied. Her voice was hoarse from heavy smoking.

'I know –'

'I don't know where he is and I don't know when he'll be back.'

'Mrs Bowen, Daryl won't be coming back. May I come in?'

'What? You gone and locked him up?' She snorted and reached to close the door. 'Nothing to do with me what he gets up to. I done my best to be a good mother, but he was always trouble, that one.'

'Mrs Bowen, please, can we go inside? I have some bad news for you.'

At last the woman seemed to take in what Geraldine was hinting at.

'Has something happened to my Daryl?' she cried out, her irritation with her son forgotten. 'Where is he? What's happened?'

Geraldine despaired of persuading the woman to go inside

the house. Standing on the doorstep, she told Daryl's mother as gently as she could what had happened.

Mrs Bowen shook her head. 'What?' she said staring blankly at Geraldine as though she had been speaking a foreign language. 'What did you say? Where's Daryl?' Her eyes seemed to glow, too large for her narrow face.

All at once she broke down in sobs that shook her whole body. Lunging forward, she grasped Geraldine's shoulders and clung to her, weeping.

'My boy,' she sobbed, 'Daryl. He was my boy.' She sniffed and straightened up, wiping her nose on her sleeve. 'He wasn't always an angel, but he was my son.' She broke down in tears again. 'I want to see my son, I want to see my son.'

Gently Geraldine disengaged herself from the weeping woman and ushered her into the house.

'Let's put the kettle on and make some tea, shall we?'

The door opened on to a square living area with two doors leading off it. A shopping channel was playing on a television in the far corner of the room. Picking her way across the room between ragged magazines, a laundry basket with a broken handle, dirty cups and plates, empty bottles and other detritus of slovenly living, Geraldine pushed open the first door and found the kitchen. Having cleared away several dirty plates to reach the kettle, she emptied the stained sink of food-encrusted plates. There was no washing up liquid and the two mugs she had managed to find felt greasy after she washed them. There were no tea bags in view. Abandoning her attempt to make tea she returned to the living room. Mrs Bowen was slumped in a chair swigging from a bottle.

Seeing Geraldine, she put the beer down. 'I was thirsty,' she mumbled. 'It's for the shock.'

Geraldine cleared a pile of magazines from a chair and glanced at the screen where an energetic presenter was promoting a complicated kitchen appliance.

'Shall we mute the television?'

Mrs Bowen raised her eyebrows as if this was an outlandish suggestion. Without waiting for an answer, Geraldine made her way across to the corner and switched off the television.

'What happened to my boy?' Mrs Bowen asked in a hoarse whisper.

'We're trying to find out. We think he was in a fight.'

Mrs Bowen let out a sob and mumbled something about 'boys'.

'Who did it? Who was it?'

'He was with two other boys, Andrew Nelson and Billy Whitelow, who the other boys called Carver. Do you know them?'

Daryl's mother shook her head, muttering. 'That Nelson was always trouble.'

'We're going to need you to come and formally identify the body.'

Mrs Bowen raised her head, her expression suddenly hopeful. 'You mean to tell me you don't know it's him?' she said. Her voice hardened. 'You don't even know who it is, and you come here telling me my boy's been killed. There ought to be a law against people like you. What the fuck are you doing here? Get out of my house. Go on, get lost.' She sounded tipsy. 'My boy's all right. I'd know if anything had happened to him. He's my son. It's you lot that have scared him off, that's what it is. You been hounding him and he's run off, scared, poor lad. Why don't you get lost and leave us alone? We don't want you here.'

It took Geraldine a few minutes to persuade Mrs Bowen that it would be best if she accompanied her, if only to confirm that the body was not that of her son.

'At least you'll know then,' Geraldine said. 'Like this, you're going to be plagued with uncertainty.'

'It's you that's plaguing me,' Mrs Bowen replied, before following Geraldine out to the car.

They reached the mortuary where they were met by Avril,

the cheerful anatomical pathology technician, who led them to the visitors' room.

'I'll just check everything's ready for you,' she said. 'Please, make yourselves comfortable here for a few minutes. Help yourselves to tea or coffee.'

As she bustled away, Geraldine thought how well suited she was to her job. With her air of cheerful efficiency, there was something comforting about her presence. She returned about five minutes later and nodded at Geraldine. The body had been prepared for the viewing.

Mrs Bowen started when she saw her son's white face. His injured neck had been neatly patched up so that the damage was scarcely visible. Only the uneven surface of his skin indicated where broken glass had sliced through his neck. His lips were curved in a faint smile, and his eyes were closed, so that he could have been sleeping, were it not for his extreme pallor. True to his word, Jonah had succeeded in smoothing over all but the worst of Daryl's unsightly acne. The pathologist was right. In life Daryl's appearance had been marred by unsightly pimples; in death he resembled a marble cherub.

'Yes,' Mrs Bowen whispered. 'That's my boy.' She turned to Geraldine, her eyes filled with tears. 'What did they do to him? What did they do?'

She was shaking so badly, Geraldine was afraid she might collapse. Gently she led her back to the visitors' room and poured her a cup of tea.

'What is it with you people and tea?' Mrs Bowen asked, bursting into tears. 'Can't a person get a proper drink here? It's for my nerves,' she added plaintively. 'Who did that to him?' she asked, when she had recovered sufficiently to talk again. 'Who did that to my boy? Tell me, I want to know.'

'We're doing our best to find out.'

'You will tell me, won't you? I know it won't make any difference. Nothing's going to bring him back now, is it? But I want to know who did that to my boy.'

The words sounded like a threat.

'We'll keep you informed at all times,' Geraldine assured her cautiously.

Daryl's mother had a right to know who had killed her son, but Geraldine was concerned that her curiosity might lead to further tragedy.

'If your son was attacked, his killer will go down for murder,' she went on. 'Rest assured, whoever did this won't get away with it. Daryl's killer's going to be locked up for a very long time, hopefully for life.'

She hoped that wouldn't prove to be an empty promise.

'Prison's too good whoever did this,' Mrs Bowen said fiercely, speaking through clenched teeth. 'Just tell me who it was. I want to know. I'll make sure he doesn't live long enough to stand trial. Scum like him don't deserve to live. Let me know who it is, and I'll do us all a favour.'

'We'll keep you informed,' Geraldine repeated. 'But you have to leave us to take care of this now. There's no point in trying to take the law into your own hands.'

'Tell me who did it,' Mrs Bowen repeated, becoming hysterical.

'Is there a friend or a relative you can go to?' Geraldine asked.

'I don't need anyone else. I'll do the job myself. Finish off whoever did this. Who was it? Who was it?' Her voice rose in a screech.

'Come on,' Geraldine said gently. 'I'll take you home. Is there someone who can come and keep you company for a while?'

Mrs Bowen's fit of anger had faded as quickly as it had come. 'I only had Daryl,' she sobbed, rocking backwards and forwards in her chair. 'There was only ever Daryl. I never had anyone else. Only Daryl.'

'Come on,' Geraldine said, 'let's get you home.'

She led the crying woman to the car and drove her back

to her squalid home where she sat, dry-eyed and wretched, staring blankly into the distance.

'Are you going to be all right?' Geraldine asked, conscious that it was a crass question.

Mrs Bowen picked up the half-empty beer bottle she had been drinking from earlier.

'I'll be fine,' she mumbled. 'My boy will be back soon.' Tears trickled down wrinkled cheeks. 'He's not coming back, is he?' she whispered after a few minutes.

'No,' Geraldine replied gently. 'He's not coming back.'

38

THE POLICE STATION WAS buzzing the following morning. Usually a time when everyone settled down to plan their week's tasks, Geraldine's colleagues were gathered together in small groups discussing the news about the gang of muggers.

'It *must* have been an accident,' Geraldine heard Ariadne say. 'Why else would those other two boys have come forward to report the death?'

'It was an accident waiting to happen,' someone else agreed. 'Those kids were never going to live to a healthy old age. It's not going to end well for any of them.'

'Accident my arse,' another officer said.

There was a murmur of agreement.

'If one of the other boys *did* kill him, surely the only sensible thing the two of them could have done would be to call us and report it as an accident right away?' Geraldine said, standing up and joining the group. 'I mean, the body was bound to be discovered pretty quickly. Don't forget, the door had been kicked in and they hadn't had time to repair it. Without any transport, they couldn't hope to keep the body hidden for long, so what else could they do but report it? Unless they wanted to try their chances and run. But they'd have been on the run for the rest of their lives –'

'So you're saying the fact that they reported the death doesn't indicate they didn't kill him deliberately?' Eileen interrupted her.

The detective chief inspector had entered the room without Geraldine noticing her.

'My thoughts exactly,' Eileen said, and several other officers murmured in agreement. 'So I suggest we question these two delinquents, and keep on at them until one of them cracks and tells us the truth.'

'Innocent until proven guilty?' someone murmured.

'What if they stick to their story?' Ariadne asked.

'Then we keep a close eye on those two boys,' the detective chief inspector replied briskly. 'One false move and the borough intelligence boys will be down on them like a ton of bricks. A young boy died last night, and although we might not be able to nail his killers, we all know who's responsible. They might get away with mugging people, and even with killing their friend, but it won't be long before they find themselves behind bars, or my name's not Eileen Duncan. In the meantime, we'll be doing everything we can to get them to talk.'

'Why are we wasting time on this? The boy who was killed would've ended up knifed sooner or later anyway,' a constable muttered, 'if he hadn't ended up in prison costing us a bloody fortune.'

Without thinking, Geraldine turned on him. 'That's a terrible thing to say! We're talking about a human being here. He was a sixteen-year-old boy, barely more than a child!'

She was afraid she might have spoken out of turn, but before the constable could retort, Eileen addressed the man who had spoken so dismissively of Daryl.

'Don't ever let me hear you speak like that about a victim again. Everyone is treated equally here. Everyone. You can think what you like in private, but as a police officer on duty you speak respectfully of everyone. Is that understood?'

The constable opened his mouth, then closed it again and looked down at the floor.

'Now,' Eileen said, 'let's see if we can get those two wretched boys to talk.'

'Come on,' Geraldine muttered to Ian. 'Let's do what we can to nail them.'

Spurred on by an uneasy suspicion that earlier police intervention was partly responsible for Daryl's death, she strode towards the interview room where Billy Whitelow was waiting. Geraldine and Ian stared at the heavily built boy facing them. The lower part of his face was covered in stubble, and he glowered at them across the table.

'Your name is Billy Whitelow,' Ian said.

'My name's Carver,' he replied impassively.

'Very well, then, Carver, tell us again, in your own words, what happened last night.'

The boy glared at them in silence.

'You've been insisting Daryl's death was an accident,' Geraldine said. 'But if you really are innocent as you say, then what possible reason could you have for refusing to talk to us?'

'I don't have to say anything to these pigs, do I?'

The portly lawyer who had defended the boys before was back, seated beside the boy known as Carver, and looking half asleep.

Now he grunted. 'My client has already made a statement. He is under no obligation to repeat what he has already told you. My client is a very young man –'

'He's nineteen,' Ian cut in.

'And he doesn't wish to talk about this anymore. He's given his statement.'

'Why doesn't he want to talk to us, if he's got nothing to hide?' Geraldine asked.

'He's young –'

'Oh, change the record,' Ian muttered.

The lawyer gave him a dirty look. 'He's young,' the lawyer repeated, 'and he's traumatised by the death of his friend.'

'But why won't he speak to us?' Geraldine insisted. 'I still don't understand.'

'Is it that you're afraid you can't remember the story you and your accomplice fabricated?' Ian asked.

'Bollocks,' Carver said. 'You think you can scare me with your big words?'

'Why are you so reluctant to talk to us?' Ian pressed him.

'I'm shy,' Carver said.

And that was all they could get out of him, however hard they pressed him. It was frustrating, but they couldn't force him to talk to them. The boy who called himself Carver wasn't officially a suspect, as the lawyer kept reminding them.

The second boy, Andrew Nelson, was garrulous, but equally unhelpful.

'It was an accident,' he said. 'It was horrible, but it was Daryl's own stupid fault. He was pissed and he tripped and fell on the broken bottle I was holding.'

'So you were holding a broken bottle in your hand?' Ian asked quietly.

Nelson shrugged, looking slightly uncomfortable. 'It broke,' he said. 'It was glass, you know. It was a bottle. And it broke. Bottles do,' he added, sounding more confident. 'Daryl dropped it and it broke. Then he fell over and –' He shrugged.

'You just said Daryl dropped the bottle and it broke, so how did it end up in *your* hand?' Geraldine asked.

'I picked it up, didn't I? I wasn't going to leave it there. I was going to tidy the place up. Broken glass is dangerous. Only Daryl slipped –'

'So you were holding a broken bottle?' Ian repeated.

'Yeah, I was clearing up the mess. Carver should've been doing it. It's his place, but he was too busy laughing at Daryl.'

'Hardly,' Geraldine interjected. 'You were trespassing.'

'Yeah, well, whatever. Anyway, Daryl was so pissed he couldn't stand up straight. He tried to walk and fell over. He couldn't hold his booze and he had a tankful. It was a stupid thing to do, and look what happened to him as a result. He always was an idiot. That's why it happened. He had it coming.'

Geraldine sat forward slightly. 'What are you saying? What do you mean?'

'He brought it on himself. It was his own stupid fault.'

She could hardly breathe. 'How? What had he done to you? How did he bring it on himself?'

'He couldn't hold his drink, that's what. And look what happened to him. It served him right. He should never have drunk so much. He was just a kid. He couldn't hold his drink. I warned him. I kept telling him not to drink any more, but he wouldn't listen.'

'So, he tripped?' Ian asked. 'What happened then?'

'Yeah, he tripped. He was pissed and stumbling around, so we were laughing at him, and he got mad at us. Then he went for me –'

'So you were fighting?' Ian asked.

'No, I told you, we were both laughing at him and he got mad and went for me but he slipped and fell and – well, he never got up again. And then we saw the blood, and it was obvious he'd croaked.' He shrugged again. 'So that was it. We called your lot and… well, you know what happened after that. Daryl was dead, wasn't he?'

Geraldine stared at him, trying to discern any trace of emotion in his face, but he returned her gaze calmly.

'It's one of those things,' he went on. 'Like I said, it was his fault. He was the one who went for me. And now we're being harassed by you lot. That's hardly fair, is it? We just lost a good mate. We should be getting sympathy not hassle. How does that work? It's not like we're to blame for what happened to him. It's not like we treated him badly or anything. We took him in. We looked out for him.'

'Why did you keep knives?' Ian asked.

'Haven't you got knives at home? Haven't you got knives in your kitchen?'

'These weren't in a kitchen.'

'What did you have all those knives for, if you never

intended to use them?' Geraldine asked.

'We collected them,' Nelson replied.

'Why?'

'We liked collecting them. It's interesting, collecting things. Don't you collect things?'

'We're talking about dangerous weapons.'

Nelson shrugged. 'Whatever. It was just a collection.'

39

EXASPERATED, ZOE HUNG UP. Really, her mother was becoming even worse, constantly fussing. Zoe had thought she would be free from her parents' nagging and restrictions while she was away at university. That had been her main reason for choosing to study so far from home. Her phone rang again.

'We don't like to nag,' her mother said.

'Well, don't then.'

'But we keep hearing on the news about all these murders in York –'

'Two people, mum, and it's not as if they were anywhere near the university. People get killed all the time in London and you're happy to live there.'

'In a suburb, darling, a suburb,' her mother replied, as though that made any difference.

'Listen, mum, I've got to go. I'm meeting someone.'

That wasn't true, but she wanted to end the call.

Her mother sighed audibly down the phone. 'Well, just be careful. And call me this evening.'

Zoe rang off without answering. It hadn't been her choice to come to university at all. She was only doing it for her parents' sakes. Everything she did was to please them, and they still refused to let her get on with her life. With a sudden burst of irritation, she spun round and nearly barged into a tall woman in a long brown coat.

'Are you all right?' the woman asked her, in a low gentle voice.

Zoe scowled. 'I would be if my bloody parents would leave me alone.'

It was a stupid thing to say. Her problems with her parents had nothing to do with anyone else, but the woman smiled in sympathy.

'Parents can be a problem when they're intrusive,' she agreed, 'but I'm sure they have your best interests at heart.'

'No, they don't. They're only thinking of themselves and how they can impress their friends. They just want to be able to boast that I'm doing well. It's never been any different with them. They never listen to what I want.'

She knew she was speaking out of turn, venting to a complete stranger, but it was a relief to have someone to talk to, and the woman's interest seemed genuine. It was different with her tutors at university. She didn't like to discuss her parents with them. It felt too personal.

'Let's walk and talk,' the woman suggested. 'Where are you going?'

Zoe shrugged. 'Nowhere in particular,' she replied. 'I was just on my way home, actually, but I thought I'd go for a walk first.'

'I live not far from here,' the woman said, 'or we could go into town for a coffee, if you prefer.'

There was something slightly odd about the way she seemed to assume that Zoe would accompany her, when they had never met before.

'It might help to talk a bit more,' the woman added, seeing Zoe hesitate. 'I work as a counsellor and, while it's clear to me that you don't need any professional support, it can be useful to talk through your problems, and get it off your chest. Would you like to talk about it?'

Zoe nodded.

'I thought so.'

The woman seemed to know what she was talking about, and Zoe had nothing else to do. Besides, the woman worked as a counsellor. She would have been vetted to check she wasn't a weirdo.

'It's just my parents,' she muttered. 'They won't leave me alone.'

'Growing up is a process,' the woman said. 'Sometimes it helps to take a step back from the problem and gain some perspective on the situation.'

The woman began to bug Zoe. She didn't want to stand in the street listening to a stranger spouting homespun philosophy, and she didn't need any help growing up. She was eighteen and had left home. But she didn't want to be rude. The woman had been kind to her and, besides, it wasn't as if Zoe had anywhere pressing to go, or anyone else to talk to. Nevertheless, the woman was a stranger, and she was being over familiar.

'It's very nice of you to take an interest in me,' Zoe said. 'But I think I need to get going now.'

Zoe was flustered when the woman reached out and took her by the elbow. For the first time she noticed the woman was wearing very heavy make-up. Her cheeks were caked in some kind of powder, and her dark eyes were accentuated by stark black lines and thick mascara.

'Before you go, how about joining me for a coffee?'

There was a note of insistence in the woman's voice that made Zoe uncomfortable. No longer attempting to conceal her reluctance, she pulled her arm out of the woman's grasp and shook her head.

'No, I'm sorry, I just remembered I'm supposed to be meeting my friends. They'll be wondering where I am.'

She was about to turn away, but the woman seized her arm again in a surprisingly strong grip.

'I just want to help you,' she said. 'Trust me, I understand your situation. I've met so many young people struggling to adjust to adulthood. It takes time. Now, there's someone I want to introduce you to, someone who can help you.'

'What? What are you talking about? I don't need your help and I don't want to be introduced to anyone.'

The woman's features twisted in disappointment. 'You

think because you're young, and pretty, you can cope on your own. Well, you're wrong. Your looks aren't going to help you forever.'

'What are you talking about?'

Too startled to feel scared, Zoe struggled to free herself from the woman's grasp. Just as Zoe raised her voice, shouting at the woman to let go of her, a couple of young men came into view around the corner.

'Hey,' one of them called out as they approached. 'Are you all right?'

At the sound, the woman let go of Zoe's arm and strode away, leaving Zoe shaken and shocked.

'Are you all right?' the man repeated as he reached her.

'Yes, yes,' she snapped, almost shouting in her agitation. 'I'm fine thank you very much. I'm quite capable of looking after myself.'

'OK, keep your hair on, I was only asking,' the man replied, and he and his companion walked on, muttering insults at her.

Zoe made her way home, keeping to the main road as far as she could. Her legs were trembling. Now that it was over, she wasn't sure what had just happened. Either she had chanced to meet a lunatic or else she had overreacted to a friendly overture from a sympathetic stranger. Admittedly there had been no need for the woman to take her by the arm, but some people were more tactile than others. It was possible she had just wanted to be supportive. Yet she had talked about Zoe's looks fading, and her rambling had made no sense. So she must have been drunk, or drugged, or just plain crazy. On reflection, Zoe thought she had done well to get away from her. Zoe's big mistake had been in talking to the woman at all, and she should certainly never have confided in her, inviting her to share a kind of intimacy. Now she just wanted to forget about the embarrassing encounter.

Reaching her digs, she decided not to call her mother. She didn't need anyone keeping tabs on her. She could just imagine what her mother would say if she found out a weird stranger had tried to drag Zoe off the street. Still, her mother need never know about it, and in any case Zoe felt she had handled the situation well. No harm had come of the encounter and if she ever saw the counsellor again she would simply avoid talking to her. She felt an unfamiliar surge of confidence in her ability to take care of herself. So, in a way, the woman had helped her after all.

40

HAUNTED BY THE THOUGHT that Daryl had been killed as a direct consequence of informing on his associates, Geraldine confided her concern to Ian.

'If those two boys found out he was a grass, they would have turned on him. What if he was killed because he spoke to us?'

'That's pure speculation,' he replied. 'But even it's true, we're never going to get those two thugs to admit it, so you might as well put it out of your mind. They were violent kids, drinking and probably high as well. You can't think we're in any way responsible for what happened.'

'We have to try and find out the truth. If he was killed for betraying their trust, we can't just let them get away with it.'

'What exactly are you proposing to do?'

Briefly Geraldine outlined her idea and he listened, frowning.

'We'll do it all by the book,' she added quickly, 'but if we can persuade Carver to tell us the truth –'

'By lying to him?'

'No, that's not fair. I'm only suggesting we do everything possible to encourage them to tell us the truth. If they weren't lying to us, we wouldn't need to resort to these underhand tactics. They're the ones in the wrong here, not us, and remember Nelson's eighteen and Carver's nineteen. They're not minors. They could be lying and obstructing us in a murder enquiry. And one of them did it. So don't make out they're being abused in some way. We've treated both of them with kid gloves, and for all we know they deliberately murdered Daryl knowing they would get away with it as long as they both stuck to the same story. All I'm suggesting is that we introduce an element of doubt into their pact, and try to get at least one of them to tell us the truth.'

'But we'd be lying to them. Even if we got them to tell us what happened, it would never stand up in court if we got at the truth by tricking them into confessing. And in any case, we don't know the two boys lied to us, and we don't know Daryl was murdered,' he insisted.

'If they're telling us the truth, they'll stick to what they said. But we ought to do everything we can to find out.'

Ian shook his head. 'I'm sorry, Geraldine. We've followed procedure and got statements from them both, and there's an end of it. There's nothing more to be done.'

'So you won't come with me to speak to Carver?'

'No, and if I were you I'd forget about this, and I certainly wouldn't go and speak to him alone.' He paused, staring at her. 'If you go ahead, and something goes wrong, you do know I won't be able to protect you.'

'Like we failed to protect Daryl,' she muttered sourly.

'Geraldine,' Ian called out as she turned to leave his office, 'I'm warning you against this. It's not a good idea.'

She walked out without a backward glance. That evening she searched for Carver. Nelson was crafty, but Carver hadn't struck her as particularly smart. In one of the pubs he frequented she found him sitting alone at a table in the corner, his eyes flicking around nervously as though he was expecting someone.

'What the fuck do you want?'

'The truth,' Geraldine replied, pulling a stool over and joining him.

'Jesus, I already told you what happened. Now fuck off, will you? I'm waiting for someone.'

'It's lucky for us your friend is more helpful,' Geraldine fibbed.

Aware that she ought to feel guilty at the subterfuge, she

ignored her qualms and carried on. She had already scuppered her own career by impersonating her twin sister in a drugs deal. Although she had lost any hope of advancement, she didn't regret having saved her sister's life. Even if she now landed herself in trouble for lying to a potential witness, it didn't matter much because, whatever happened, her own career was going nowhere. There was a certain liberation in knowing that she had little left to lose. The worst that could happen to her was that she would have to leave her job altogether, and she didn't think that would happen. Now, with Daryl's death weighing on her conscience, she felt she owed it to him to take that risk.

'Nelson's told us what happened to Daryl,' she said softly.

And the lie was told.

'Then you know it was him holding the bottle.'

'That's not what Nelson told us, and that's not what happened, is it?' she replied, without taking her eyes off Carver. 'Nelson said it was you holding that bottle and he said you could have moved out of the way when Daryl fell.'

Carver's heavy brows lowered. 'Nelson's a filthy liar.'

'Or I am,' Geraldine thought.

But the memory of the sixteen-year-old boy in the mortuary spurred her on.

'Nelson said you struck Daryl, deliberately, with a broken bottle.'

'That's a lie!' Carver retorted, banging his fist on the table.

A couple sitting nearby looked round. The constable Geraldine had brought with her stirred, but she deterred him from approaching with a slight shake of her head, and he resumed his position at a table by the door.

'Why don't you come down to the police station and give us your statement? And this time stick to the truth. Or,' she went on seeing Carver hesitate, 'you can leave us to draw our own conclusions. But I have to warn you, Nelson was very detailed in his account of how you murdered Daryl.'

'Oh fuck him. All right, I'm coming.'

Once Carver had agreed to revise his statement he co-operated fully, and refused to wait for a lawyer to arrive.

'Let's get this done,' he said. 'I'm not letting that motherfucker stitch me up. Fucking hell, I thought he was my bro. I'll get him for this.'

'Like you got Daryl?'

'I told you, that wasn't me.'

Once he had finished giving his version of the circumstances surrounding Daryl's death, Geraldine had Carver locked in a cell. He was furious.

'Now, now,' the custody sergeant said, shaking his head at the angry youngster, 'there's no call for all this.'

'I haven't been charged with anything,' Carver fumed. 'You can't keep me here.'

'Well, I expect they'll let you go home in the morning then,' the sergeant replied cheerfully. 'After we set you up with a nice breakfast. That's something to look forward to.'

'I'm going home now,' Carver replied.

'Now come along, son,' the sergeant said. 'There's no need for all this. Come on, let's get you in handcuffs until we get you in the cell, just to make sure you don't do anything stupid. There we go.'

Geraldine left them to it. She had what she wanted from Carver. Accompanied by a constable, she went to look for Nelson and found him at home. When he resisted her request to accompany her to the police station, she handcuffed him and the constable assisted him to the waiting car. Unlike Carver, Nelson insisted on representation. It was growing late by the time the stout lawyer arrived and they took their seats in an interview room.

'Your friend Carver told us everything,' Geraldine said. 'He explained how you argued with Daryl –'

'He had it coming,' Nelson said as he had before, only this

time his expression was wary. 'He was –' He hesitated.

'Go on.'

'I'd like to confer with my client –'

'Your client is trying to talk to us. Are you sure you want to stop him?' Geraldine turned back to Nelson. 'Go on.'

'Daryl was trouble, right from the start. Carver and I, we got along just fine till he came along.' He paused and narrowed his eyes, calculating. 'Carver never blamed me for what happened. I don't believe it, not for a minute. You're lying. Like we both told you, what happened to Daryl was an accident, a tragic accident.' His voice sounded sad, but his expression remained wary.

'Carver told us you brought the bottle with you.' Geraldine stared evenly at the boy, trying to interpret his reaction. 'We can easily check that. All we have to do is track you on CCTV and find out whether you bought a bottle of vodka on your way to the lock up. Or perhaps one disappeared from a store you visited recently? You know it won't take us long to find out.'

Nelson leaned back in his chair, adopting a nonchalant posture.

'Sit up,' Geraldine snapped so fiercely he jolted upright in surprise. 'We know you went to the garage armed with a bottle that evening.'

'So I took a bottle with me. So what? I never said I didn't. I took it so we could have a drink. There's no law against three friends having a drink, is there? I shared what I had with my mates. You know we were all drinking together. Why would I want to shiv one of my mates?'

'If you're such good mates, why has Carver accused you of murdering Daryl?'

'He hasn't.'

Geraldine switched on the tape she had brought with her, set to the right place.

First, they heard her own voice. 'So Daryl's death wasn't an accident. Is that what you're telling us, Billy?'

'Oh Jesus, yes. I'm telling you, Nelson had a problem with Daryl. They was always at it, them two. It had nothing to do with me. It did my head in the way they was always at it.'

'At what?'

'You know, arguing.'

'Had they ever been in a fight before?'

'Sure they had. All the bloody time.'

'What happened on this occasion? Tell me in your own words.'

'Nelson went for him.'

'How exactly did Nelson go for Daryl?' Geraldine's voice enquired patiently.

'He bottled him.'

As he listened, Nelson's face turned pale, then flushed with fury.

'And you lied to cover it up?' Geraldine's recorded questions continued.

'Yeah, well, Nelson's my man. We go back a way.'

'Well, I'm not his man anymore!' Nelson burst out. He was trembling now with fury, or perhaps fear. 'The scumbag. He's a fucking snake. We had an agreement. Anyway, you can't prove it was me. As for Daryl, he deserved what he got, the snivelling piece of shit. Carver and me, we was fine until he came along. Served him right.'

The lawyer held up his pudgy hand. 'I need to speak to my client,' he said urgently.

'Wait. How did you find out?' Geraldine asked, speaking over the lawyer.

'What?'

'How did you find out he had spoken to us?'

'What you talking about? Who spoke to you?' He turned to the lawyer. 'What the fuck is going on here?'

Almost speechless with relief, Geraldine shook her head. 'It's nothing,' she muttered. 'Andrew Nelson, I'm arresting you on suspicion of murder –'

'What the fuck?' he cried out as she read him his rights. 'You can't do this. I never done it. I'm innocent. It was an accident.'

'That's for a jury to decide when you take your chances in court. And your friend will be charged along with you, as an accessory. Take him back to the cells.'

'Eileen wants to know how you managed to convince Billy to talk,' Ian said, pausing by her desk later that day.

'Did you tell her what I was planning to do?'

'I told her you can be very persuasive,' he replied, and smiled.

'I never actually lied to Carver,' she said, although he must have known that too was a lie. 'Anyway, let's hope they both go down for murder.'

'And now you know they never found out about Daryl's betrayal, and his co-operation with us had nothing at all to do with him being killed,' Ian said.

Geraldine nodded. Whether Carver or Nelson was convicted for murdering Daryl was out of her hands, but at least she had done everything in her power to ensure his killer was brought to trial.

'We did a good job,' she said.

'You did a good job,' he replied. 'I'm still not condoning what you did, mind.'

'You don't know what I did,' she said, although of course he did. 'You don't think the ends ever justify the means?'

'No.' He shook his head. 'And once you start making exceptions, it's a slippery slope. You're going to end up getting yourself in serious trouble if you bend the rules again.'

After he had gone, Geraldine thought about what Ian had said. He was right, of course. Even now she wasn't sure why she had been prepared to put her job itself at risk for the sake of one dead delinquent. Nothing she did could make any difference to Daryl now. She hoped it was more than just a sense of guilt that had driven her relentless pursuit of his killers. Someone had to pursue justice on behalf of the voiceless dead and, for better or worse, she had devoted her life to doing just that. But Ian was right. She wouldn't play such a dangerous game again.

41

Zoe stared at the other girl in dismay, wishing she had kept quiet about her unsettling experience. As soon as the words left her lips she regretted having mentioned it, but after a couple of beers she had blabbed and told Josie everything. Her new friend's reaction had been disappointing, to say the least.

'Now I'm confused,' Josie frowned, shaking her head so violently that her pink hair fluttered around in an untidy halo. 'First you tell me this woman assaulted you, and then you say she wanted to buy you a coffee?'

'Accosted me,' Zoe corrected her. 'She accosted me.' In her inebriated state, the word sounded unlikely. 'She accosted me,' she repeated as firmly as she could. 'She didn't assault me, she accosted me.'

'So? Jesus, you made it sound like she attacked you in the street.' Josie's eyes narrowed in suspicion. 'You said you were lucky to get away from her, like she was some violent maniac prowling the streets looking for victims to murder. And now you're saying all she did was offer to buy you a coffee?' Josie looked as though she was trying not to laugh. 'So you met a lonely old woman. So bloody what?' She muttered something about birds of a feather that Zoe didn't quite catch.

Zoe hesitated. Josie hung out with all the cool students, and was confident and independent, just how Zoe wanted to be. But the attempt to impress her had backfired, and Josie was dismissing her as an idiot.

'She grabbed my arm,' Zoe said, 'and I had to pull myself away. But it was more about what she said.'

'What? About you losing your looks when you get older? Well, won't we all, if we live that long?' Josie inhaled and blew out a cloud of white smoke.

'But she grabbed me.'

'So? Why are you telling me this, again?' Josie asked, in a bored tone. 'It's not as though you were grabbed by a fit bloke, is it? That might be worth talking about.'

'I just thought maybe we should warn the other girls to watch out for her. I mean, she's bonkers, and the next girl might not get away from her.'

'From some old woman?' Josie burst out laughing. 'Please, Zoe, get a grip. You'll be frightened by your own shadow next. I suppose you're scared of spiders.'

She wiggled her fingers at Zoe, holding her cigarette at the edge of her lips and screwing up one eye against the thread of smoke rising from the glowing tip.

'She was strong,' Zoe protested, 'and honestly, Josie, if those two guys hadn't come along –'

'What? You might have ended up – oh shock horror – going out for coffee with an old woman?' She laughed again.

'She wasn't that old.'

'Well, if you're that bothered, go to the police,' Josie said, and closed her eyes, muttering something about being a drama queen.

Zoe wondered whether it was worth going to the police to report what had happened. She suspected they would react just as Josie had, and dismiss her as a hysterical teenager, even though she was eighteen and had left home and was living independently. She probably wouldn't have bothered taking it any further had she not hoped that going to the police would persuade Josie to take her seriously.

The following day Zoe only had one lecture in the morning so, on a whim, she checked out the location of the police station and found it was just a short bus ride from her digs. Instead of going straight home from university, she caught a bus to

Fulford Road, and asked the driver to put her off at the right stop. A sign displayed on a brick post announced the location of the police headquarters where a large ugly square building was tucked away from the street along a road that ran through the police compound. She went into the door marked Visitors and hesitated for a second before marching up to the desk. A man in uniform nodded at her. He didn't smile, but he looked friendly.

'Yes, Miss?'

'I'd like to report –' she hesitated again.

Before entering the building, she had rehearsed what she was going to say, but now she was there, her mind went blank.

'Yes, Miss?'

'I want to report an assault,' she said.

The man nodded. 'Let me take down a few details, Miss, and then we can see if there's someone here you can talk to.'

Having made a note of her name and address, and written down her occupation as 'university student', he summoned a young female officer who led Zoe into a small interview room. They sat down, and the constable asked her to relate what had happened to her. The policewoman didn't show by so much as a movement of a muscle whether she thought Zoe was overreacting, as she asked her to describe the woman.

Zoe hesitated, flustered. She could hardly admit that she couldn't remember what the woman looked like.

'I think she was taller than me,' she said. 'And she had dark eyes.'

'Can you remember anything else about her?' the police woman asked, with exaggerated patience.

Her condescension stung Zoe. Embarrassed to admit she couldn't remember anything else about the woman, Zoe launched into a description of her aunt. It didn't really matter what she said, because no one was taking her seriously.

'Is that it then?' Zoe asked when her interlocutor thanked her politely for coming forward, and stood up.

The policewoman looked faintly surprised, or perhaps slightly amused. 'What more would you like us to do?'

Zoe shook her head. 'I don't know. Shouldn't I be given a crime number or something?'

'A crime number?'

'Yes, you know, a reference number for the crime.'

The other woman shook her head. 'You haven't reported a crime,' she replied quietly. 'Nothing happened.'

Losing her opportunity to impress Josie, Zoe grew desperate.

'But it could have,' she said. 'She wanted to take me home with her. She said she didn't live far from there. What if those two men hadn't come along, or – or what if this woman grabbed hold of someone less sensible than me, or – or a child?'

'I'll circulate her details to the local patrols,' the constable assured her, 'and we'll keep an eye out for anyone matching her description.'

Feeling despondent, Zoe allowed the constable to escort her out of the building. As she made her way back to the road and waited for the bus to take her back into town, she reflected on what had just happened. She couldn't decide whether to tell Josie about her visit to the police station or not. In a way, going to the police sounded quite serious but, if she was honest, nothing had happened, and the police weren't going to do anything. Josie would just dismiss her as an attention seeker. She had already accused her of being a drama queen. On balance, Zoe decided it might be as well to simply forget the whole thing. It was stupid, and she had wasted enough time on it. The woman who had accosted her in the street was odd. If Zoe saw her again, she would just walk the other way, fast.

That would have been the end of the matter if she hadn't seen a woman reading a paper on the bus. One of the headlines gave her an idea. The police might have dismissed her account as uninteresting, but there was something else she could do that might impress Josie. And as long as she didn't give her real name, there was no way her mother would ever find out what had happened to her. Smiling, she took out her phone and googled the contact details for the local paper.

42

AFTER HIS RECENT SUCCESS, he had been staying indoors most of the time, concerned to keep out of sight. To avoid temptation, whenever he left the house now he left his rucksack at home, along with his gloves and cape, and he was also careful not to carry a knife. In many ways it was frustrating, having to wait around like that, but he knew better than to rush blindly into his next kill, ignoring what was going on around him. The police presence on the streets had visibly increased, and he needed to wait until the fuss died down before going out to find another victim. Even on an ostensibly empty street a stray witness could appear at any moment, and now there was the added risk a police car might drive past. He had to be patient. There was no other option if he wanted to avoid detection.

None of this meant he intended to stop. On the contrary, he had every intention of pursuing his plans as vigorously as ever. Without the excitement of the kill his life felt empty, days stretching out in pointless tedium. He was just taking a break until the police turned their attention elsewhere. They couldn't keep on throwing money at an investigation that was never going to reach a satisfactory conclusion. Eventually they would realise they were never going to find him, at which point they would have to give up and move on. It couldn't happen soon enough as far as he was concerned. Unlike the movie stereotype of a serial killer, he wasn't seeking notoriety, and he had no wish to attract attention by taunting the police. He more closely resembled a hunted animal, hiding in the shadows while he stalked his prey. Recently he had blundered into attacking people who were likely to be missed, well-dressed people who looked as though they had jobs, and homes to go to. He wouldn't make that mistake again. The less anyone knew about his activities the better, because any attention increased the risk he would be tracked down. But there was little danger of that. He had taken steps to ensure he would never be found.

The media weren't helping, with their hysterical reports of his activities. Some of the articles he read were so far removed from the truth, he wondered whether they were writing about a different crime altogether. It both disturbed and amused him to think there could be another killer on the streets of York. On Sunday morning he read a brief report in the local paper about an attempted assault. Swallowing a growing sense of unease, he read it through several times. 'University student repels attacker', he read. 'A student at the York St John University foiled an attempted abduction on Thursday,' the article continued. 'Eighteen-year-old Jane Smith, a student of English, was accosted in the street in broad daylight by a woman claiming to work for the council. "She grabbed hold of me and wouldn't let go," Jane told our reporter. "I was terrified." The young girl managed to pull herself free and fled. No one was injured but the police are taking this account of an attempted abduction very seriously. Anyone who saw a grey-haired woman in a long brown coat near the university on Thursday should speak to the police.'

Whatever else happened, the girl had been foolish to disclose where she was studying. Now it would be easy to find out where she lived by looking for her at the university, and simply following her home. He was surprised the police had sanctioned her speaking to the press like that. But her indiscretion probably had nothing to do with the police. The girl had most likely gone to the papers herself, looking for attention. As a result of her stupidity, she might now find herself attracting exactly the kind of attention she had been hoping to avoid. He smiled at the irony of the situation. The girl should have kept her mouth shut and stayed out of the limelight. Attention of any kind was best kept to a minimum when you were avoiding people who wished to harm you. Now she really had put herself at risk because, if anyone attacked her now, the police would be looking for a grey-haired woman. He smiled at this unexpected stroke of luck, and his gaze flicked to his rucksack.

43

FINALLY GERALDINE'S PERSISTENCE WAS rewarded because the next morning, when she took the same detour on her way to work, the door was opened by a woman whose long dark hair hung nearly to her waist. She was tall and striking, and her heavily made-up dark eyes narrowed in suspicion when she saw Geraldine.

'Who are you?'

Geraldine introduced herself.

'What do you want?'

'Is your name Lindsey Curtis?'

The woman took a step back from the threshold and closed the door slightly.

'Can we go inside? I'd like to ask you a few questions.'

Geraldine could tell from the way the woman drew back further into the hallway that she didn't intend to invite her in.

'What's this about?'

Carefully Geraldine told her she had been recorded on CCTV leaving a crime scene, and the police wanted to ask her a few questions about what she had seen.

The woman scowled. 'What are you talking about? What crime scene am I supposed to have been at? What do you mean? Are you saying I've been accused of something I didn't do? I never committed a crime in my life. I've never stolen anything from anyone.'

Geraldine interrupted her tirade to explain that she wasn't under any suspicion, but the police were hoping she might be able to help by describing what she had witnessed. Still scowling, the woman shook her head. Before Geraldine could ask her anything else, she slammed the door. At least Geraldine had confirmed the woman was still alive. Thoughtfully she drove off to work and spent the remainder of the day preparing budget reports for Eileen.

Many of Geraldine's fellow officers congregated in the pub near the police station for a drink before setting off home after work. That evening she walked up the road with Ariadne, chatting about the case. Arriving at the pub, Geraldine's mood didn't improve on seeing Ian and Naomi sitting together, deep in conversation.

'You're both looking gloomy,' Ariadne commented as she and Geraldine joined them.

'We're just having a moan about the case,' Naomi said. 'It seems to have ground to a halt.'

'There's a lot of work going on in the background,' Geraldine said. 'These investigations take time, but as long as we put in enough hours, we'll get a result.'

'That's part of the problem,' Ian replied. 'We aren't putting in the hours. If we weren't understaffed we'd be so much further ahead.'

They discussed the recent budget cuts which were affecting police forces throughout the UK.

'And it doesn't help that the staff we *do* have are plagued by time wasters,' Geraldine said.

'Yes, there are always the nutters,' Ian agreed.

'And the lonely,' Ariadne added.

'A lot of people are lonely,' Geraldine said, carrying on quickly so her colleagues wouldn't think she might be talking about herself. 'Most of them don't call in and waste police time.'

'We spend so much time running around chasing false reports, apart from the admin involved in taking statements and creating records,' Ian complained. 'It's an absolute disgrace when we're already so understaffed. It's not as if the budget cuts are a secret. It's been in the news. You'd have to be a moron not to be aware of what's going on. If there were only a few it would be bad enough, but there are so many people messing us about, wasting our time.'

Naomi agreed with him.

'But there's nothing we can do about it,' he added with a shrug.

'No, there's nothing we can do,' Naomi echoed him.

Ian smiled at Naomi who looked down with a coy expression.

Listening to them, Geraldine could no longer contain her irritation. 'That's easy to say, but if *we* don't try and educate the public, who will? We can't just sit back and say there's nothing we can do. We need to do everything in our power to spread the message that unnecessary calls on police time have a negative effect on an already overstretched force.'

She stood up pushing her stool back so vigorously it toppled over and fell to the floor with a startling clatter. Feeling like a fool, she leaned down and righted it.

'Let me get you another drink,' Ian said with a grin.

Ignoring the offer, Geraldine said goodnight and hurriedly took leave of her colleagues. Back at home, she couldn't sleep so she took out her laptop. After rereading all the forensic reports, she wrote up her conversation with Lindsey. It didn't amount to much, but she logged it anyway. At least she had established that the woman still lived at that address, and that she wasn't keen to talk to the police. Almost as an afterthought, she added that the woman's neighbours had mentioned she only went out at night.

'I read your report on that woman with the long hair,' Ian said when he saw Geraldine the following morning. 'You were writing it at two in the morning. I hope you're not going to be distracted from your work here. We need you to be wide awake and focused. Remember you're part of a team, and we don't have unlimited time and resources. It's highly unlikely this woman witnessed a murder. She's had enough opportunity to come forward and talk to us if she does have anything to tell us.'

Geraldine shrugged off the implied criticism. 'Oh, you know me. I never go to sleep early anyway.'

'You reported this woman only appears to be seen at night. So what exactly are you suggesting?' he asked severely. 'Do you think she's a vampire?'

He laughed, and Geraldine joined in, relieved.

'Seriously,' he went on, 'she could be working night shifts at the hospital, or be a prostitute, or the neighbour might be mistaken.'

Geraldine nodded. 'I suppose so.'

'You don't sound convinced.'

'I just feel we may be missing something.'

Eileen wasn't impressed. 'What were you doing up so late, Geraldine, and what was all that about this woman we're trying to find going out at night?'

Quickly, Geraldine reiterated who the woman was, and how she might fit into the murder investigation.

'But she refused to speak to me,' Geraldine concluded.

Eileen looked irritated. 'So that's all been a waste of time.'

'Geraldine did all that chasing after work,' Ian said quickly.

Eileen grunted. 'Very well then.' She turned away from Geraldine. 'Now let's see. The important thing now is to track down the owner of the DNA found on the two victims.'

Eileen had instigated a search to request DNA samples from every blond blue-eyed adult male in York who had ever been questioned in connection with a violent incident without being charged.

'Unless someone comes up with a better lead, this seems to be the only way forward at the moment,' she said. 'We have the DNA, we need to get a conviction. The only thing missing now is a match. Somewhere out there is a killer whose DNA hasn't been entered on the database. But he must have a history of some kind.'

She sighed, no doubt thinking that the man they were looking for could easily evade them. He might already have left the area, or have been living elsewhere all along, only coming into the city to look for his victims before vanishing again. But if the strategy offered even a slim chance of finding the killer, it had to be relentlessly pursued.

'We're going to get him, however long it takes,' Eileen said.

'Perhaps he's descended from the Vikings,' someone muttered. 'They had fair hair, didn't they?'

No one answered. They all knew that looking for a blond man who might or might not be living in York was a massive undertaking with limited chance of success.

44

NEARLY A WEEK HAD passed since Zoe's encounter with the stranger, but she still hadn't completely recovered her equanimity, which was shaky at the best of times. She had hoped that reporting the incident to the police would be the end of it, but she remained scared to go out on her own. It was particularly galling as she had always promised herself she wouldn't grow up to be like her mother who was fearful of everything. Still, she had to get on with her life and travel to and from the university campus to attend lectures. Struggling to control her anxiety, she remained alert and kept to busy roads as far as possible. On the Tuesday after her unnerving encounter, it began to rain shortly after she left college. With very few pedestrians around, she found herself alone on an empty street. She glanced repeatedly to both sides, and over her shoulder, as she hurried on her way. The shower didn't last long, and she was reassured when a few people appeared on the pavement, and even more relieved when she bumped into Josie.

'So, what are you up to?' Josie asked.

Hopeful that Josie might agree to stick around for the evening, Zoe abandoned her intention of going home. But when she suggested seeing what was on at the cinema, Josie pulled a face.

'No point,' she replied. 'I'm skint. Hey, I don't suppose you could lend me twenty quid, just until next term?' She took Zoe by the arm. 'Then we could go and see a film together.'

Zoe cursed herself for having made the suggestion. She

wasn't exactly flush, and was going to have to eke out what she had left if she was going to last until the end of term. But she could hardly say she was broke when she had just suggested going to the cinema. Casting about for a way to change the subject, with a sudden flash of inspiration she jabbed Josie on the arm.

'Look!' she cried out.

'Ow, what the fuck?'

'Look there, across the road, in the brown coat. That's her.'

'Who?'

'It's the woman I was telling you about, the one who tried to abduct me. Come on, let's not lose her. I've been thinking about it,' she went on, taking Josie by the arm and urging her forward. 'Do you think she might have been planning to sell me as a sex slave?'

'Don't be stupid. And sex trafficking is no laughing matter,' Josie replied.

'I wasn't laughing,' Zoe said, deflated. 'This is serious. It wouldn't do any harm to find out a bit more about her, anyway.'

'How are you going to do that?'

'We could follow her, find out where she lives, and report her to the police.'

'Never mind the police, let's stalk her and find out what she's up to,' Josie said, the cinema, and the twenty quid loan, supplanted by the new distraction.

Zoe hesitated, but she didn't want Josie to start on about money again and, in any case, it might be fun to stalk a stranger. As long as she was with a friend, she didn't mind getting lost.

'Come on, then, let's get after her. Come on, Josie. We need to hurry.'

Josie glanced at her phone. 'I've got half an hour.'

'Have you got a deadline tomorrow?'

'God, no. I'm meeting a friend at eight.'

Zoe tried not to betray her disappointment on learning she was being used to fill in time while Josie was waiting for someone else. But in the meantime she had Josie to herself for half an hour. That gave her an opportunity to lure Josie away from whoever else she was meeting. So she didn't admit that the woman they were following was actually nothing like the woman who had accosted her in the street.

After about five minutes, Josie stopped. 'This is stupid,' she said. 'We're just following a stranger who could be going anywhere. She might not live in York. What are you going to do if she gets in a car and drives off? There's no point in wandering about like this. I'm going back.'

Zoe turned round with her and they retraced their footsteps in silence. When they reached a café near to Lendal Bridge, Josie suddenly darted forward and flung her arms around a girl Zoe had never seen before. While she was hesitating over whether to join them, they strode past her, arm in arm and laughing. Either Josie was ignoring her, or else she had forgotten about her. Either way, Zoe was mortified. If Josie looked back and saw her lingering on the pavement like an idiot, her humiliation would be complete, so she pushed open the door of the café and went inside. It was pleasant in there so she sat down to wait for a few minutes until she was confident Josie would be out of sight. While she was wondering how long to wait, a girl in a white apron approached her table. Zoe could hardly sit there without ordering anything so she asked for a cup of tea. It was the cheapest item on the menu. By the time she finished, she was sure Josie would be long gone. Leaving the café, she set off back to her digs.

It began to drizzle when she got off the bus so she hurried along empty streets, dodging puddles. As she was crossing her front yard, out of the corner of her eye she noticed a movement at the side of the house. Turning her head, she glimpsed a tall hooded figure stepping out of shadows. With a thrill of terror, she turned and sprinted for the corner of the street. As she ran, she conceived a vague plan of somehow finding her way to the police station. It was raining more heavily now, and the street was deserted. She kept going, panting with the exertion, and didn't slow down until she reached the main road. Reassured by cars driving past in both directions, she looked around. The street behind her was empty.

She hesitated to return home, but she couldn't stay out all night, and it would soon be growing dark. Fumbling in her bag, she found her phone and called her flatmate.

'Where are you?' she demanded.

'Zoe?'

'Yes, it's Zoe. Where are you?'

'I'm at college. Why? Has something happened?'

'What time are you coming home?'

'I don't know. Later. I'm going out with some friends.'

Zoe hesitated. 'Can I come with you?'

'What? Where are you?'

'I'm at home.'

'Well, no, not really then. We're leaving now.'

'Where are you going? I can join you there.'

'I don't know. We'll probably go back to someone's house. Look, I'll see you later. We can talk then. Only I've got to go now. Laters. Bye.'

Zoe tried to call her back but there was no answer. She made her way to the bus stop and waited for a bus to take her to the city centre. She would feel safer among other people while she decided what she was going to say to the police. But she was afraid they wouldn't believe her. In any case, there was nothing they could do, because nothing had happened. She might have been mistaken in thinking she had seen a figure lurking at the side of the house. Even to her it seemed pretty unlikely when she thought about it now. In any case, when she had plucked up enough courage to look over her shoulder, there hadn't been anyone there. She had been stupid to think someone had been following her.

Crossing the road, she made her way back to the flat. As she hurried along the street, she kept looking around. At the first sign of a tall figure in a hooded jacket, she would run. The streets were empty, and there was no one in her front yard. With a shudder of relief, she felt in her bag for her key. She had nearly reached the steps leading up to her front door when she heard a whisper of a breath behind her. She spun round, but she was too late. A hooded figure was blocking her path back to the street.

For an instant, anger overcame her fear. 'What are you doing here?' she demanded, trying to sound authoritative. 'If you don't leave at once, I'll call the police.'

To indicate how serious she was, she took her phone out of her bag. Before she could switch it on, the stranger lunged forward and swiped at it, knocking it out of her hand.

'What the…?' Zoe began.

In the middle of her sentence she broke off at the sight of a knife in front of her face. Jerking back, she tripped on the steps. The blade slashed at her throat and pain seared through her windpipe. She was dimly aware of a horrible rushing sound in her ears as she tried to speak, but she couldn't breathe.

45

SHE COULDN'T HAVE SAID why, but Geraldine was bothered by Lindsey's refusal to talk to her.

'I can't see why you've got a problem with it,' Ariadne said when Geraldine voiced her concern as they were leaving their desks at the end of the day. 'There's no point in taking it personally.'

Geraldine laughed to hide her irritation. 'I'm hardly taking it personally. But she might have something useful to tell us. Besides, don't you find it odd that she won't speak to us?'

'Not really. She's hardly the first person to feel uncomfortable talking to the police. We're not everyone's favourite. To some people we're no better than traffic wardens.'

'Well, I want to talk to her, and I'm not going to give up until I do. We know the house is rented from an ex-pat living in Spain, and our tenant paid up front for six months.'

Ariadne raised her eyebrows. 'You have gone into it.'

Geraldine wasn't sure whether Ariadne was impressed or amused by her tenacity.

'But if she won't talk to you, there's nothing you can do about it. You can't force her to answer our questions.'

'There never seems to be anything we can do.'

'But seriously, Geraldine, members of the public refuse to talk to us all the time. It's hardly unusual. I really can't see why you're obsessing over this woman. Why is she such a problem?'

Ian was passing through their office. Overhearing the end of their exchange, he halted, frowning. 'Did I hear you say there's a problem?' he asked. 'Anything I can help with?'

Naomi was walking behind him and she stopped as well.

'Geraldine's annoyed because a woman she's been looking for has finally turned up, and won't talk to her,' Ariadne replied.

'That sounds like a real problem,' Naomi replied lightly.

But Ian frowned. 'I don't follow you. What's going on?'

Although Geraldine was gratified that he was taking her concern seriously, she hesitated to repeat what was worrying her. She couldn't explain her conviction that Lindsey might have seen something significant.

'I can't say why,' she admitted, pulling a face. 'It's just a feeling I have.'

'A feeling?' Naomi repeated. 'What do you mean, a feeling?'

'Oh, I don't know. Don't take any notice of me. It's nothing.'

Ian grunted. 'It's not generally a good idea to ignore Geraldine's feelings.'

Geraldine was struck by the irony of his comment, given that he was oblivious of her growing affection for him, but she merely smiled.

'Come on,' Naomi interrupted him, 'let's go for that drink.'

Geraldine couldn't help noticing that Naomi had addressed her suggestion to Ian alone, as though she and Ian had already arranged to go to the pub together. Perhaps they had.

'Who else is coming?' he asked at once, as though he too had picked up on the way Naomi had appeared to exclude the others. 'We could discuss your thoughts over a drink, Geraldine.'

'Oh yes, do join us,' Naomi said.

'No, I'm off home,' Geraldine said. 'I've got some calls to make.'

That was true, although she could easily have gone for a drink first. As she walked to her car, she decided Ariadne was right. There was no reason to fret over Lindsey's refusal to talk to her. If Geraldine was honest, what had upset her had nothing to do with Lindsey; it was the proprietorial way Naomi had spoken to Ian. Geraldine knew there was no reason for her to feel jealous. It wasn't as though she and Ian had ever been anything other than colleagues. Any close friendship they had developed had existed only in her mind. It was just as well she had been shown how absurd she had been, in allowing herself to grow fond of him. It would have been mortifying to have revealed her feelings only to be rejected. Thinking about it on her way home, she wasn't even sure what her feelings towards him were any more.

Reaching home, she was too dispirited to cook properly, so she looked through her freezer and took out a prepared meal. Having eaten most of it, she poured herself a second glass of wine before phoning her twin. The conversation didn't start well.

'What do you want?' Helena asked.

Geraldine hesitated. There was so much she wanted from her twin. The last time they had met they had got on better than usual, and Geraldine had allowed herself to hope their relationship would steadily improve. But she suspected she might never be able to relax with her volatile twin, not knowing from one moment to the next how Helena was going to behave.

'I just wanted to see how you're doing,' she replied.

'I'm fine, thank you. How are you?'

The conversation was brief and stilted. Geraldine was pleased when she could extricate herself. Unlike Geraldine's twin, her adopted sister sounded really pleased to hear from her.

'It's lovely of you to call! I know how busy you always are.'

Geraldine muttered her excuses. Celia always made her feel guilty for having so little time to spare for her family.

'How are you? And when are you coming to see us? It's been ages!'

It was true, Geraldine hadn't been to visit Celia for a few months. Hearing the genuine excitement in her sister's voice, Geraldine felt a surge of gratitude. At least someone wanted to see her. She made a snap decision.

'I'm hoping to come over on Sunday, if you're around?'

Geraldine tried to dismiss her frustration about Lindsey but lying in bed that night, unable to sleep, she brooded over how she might persuade the woman to speak to her. In the end, she made up her mind to return to Lindsey's house the next day and simply insist on asking her a few questions.

Setting off early the following morning, Geraldine reached Gillygate at about seven. Lindsey was unlikely to have left the house so early, but when Geraldine rang the bell, there was no answer. She rang a second time, and knocked on the door, and rang the bell one last time, but there was no point in hanging on. She didn't mention her concerns to anyone. She would keep trying, but had to accept she might never find out whether Lindsey had seen anything that might help the investigation. Much as she hated leaving loose ends, sometimes it was unavoidable.

46

ON HER WAY OUT, Jenny grabbed a bag propped against the wall by the front door waiting to be thrown in the bin outside. Her flatmate had already gone out so if Jenny ignored it the rubbish would sit there for another day. It was typical of Zoe to forget her turn on the rota. It wasn't exactly a complicated schedule, and the bag was in the hall, so there was really no excuse for overlooking it. Irritated, she picked up the rubbish bag and stomped out of the house. Next time they saw each other, Jenny was going to complain that Zoe wasn't pulling her weight.

The bins stood in a row by the fence. As Jenny carried the bag of rubbish across the front yard, she was startled to see someone lying on the ground, half hidden by the bins. Assuming a homeless person or a drunk had fallen asleep there, she froze. The rubbish bag slid from her grasp and landed at her feet with a soft thud. Taking a step closer, she halted with a faint gasp. The figure on the ground looked very like her flatmate, with the same curly brown hair and red jacket. In fact, were it not for the fact that the woman was lying on the ground by the bins, fast asleep or unconscious, Jenny could easily have mistaken her for Zoe. She hesitated before taking a step closer. If it *was* Zoe, then something must be very wrong. She appeared to have collapsed in a sozzled heap. Even if she had lost her key, she was hardly likely to have fallen asleep out there when she could have rung the door bell, or phoned Jenny. Either she had been horribly drunk, or drugged, or else she had fallen ill and passed out.

'Zoe?' she called out. 'Zoe? Is that you? Are you all right? Wake up!'

She took a step closer until she could see part of the woman's face. One glance confirmed her fears. The figure *was* Zoe, and she wasn't moving. Trembling, Jenny pulled out her phone to call 999 and paused. It would be embarrassing to summon an ambulance only to discover that Zoe wasn't ill after all but had passed out after a drunken binge the night before. As she stood there, prevaricating, it began to rain. Still Zoe didn't stir. Jenny was already going to be late for college. With a burst of impatience, she hurried over to the body, and squatted down beside her prone flatmate.

'Zoe,' she called out, 'wake up! You're getting wet!'

Looking around, she noticed a dark pool beside Zoe's head. It could have been blood. Swallowing a sour taste in the back of her throat, she stood up. All her instincts urged her to get away from there as quickly as possible, but her legs were shaking so much she could barely stand, let alone walk. In any case, she couldn't just go and leave Zoe lying there in the rain.

Squatting down again, she reached out gingerly to take hold of Zoe's upper arm, and shook her. There was no response. Zoe's arm felt strangely hard. This must be what was called rigor mortis. Jenny had come across the term, and heard people talking about it on crime series on television. There could no longer be any doubt that Zoe was dead.

Jenny began to cry. 'Zoe, Zoe! Wake up, please!'

She had no idea how long she crouched there beside her flatmate's body before she pulled herself together. With a loud sniff, she straightened up and took her phone from her bag. The rain was heavier now so she took off her coat and laid it on top of Zoe. It was a pointless gesture. Rain mingled with her tears as she called 999.

Giving up on college for the day, Jenny waited for the emergency services to arrive. She was shivering with cold and shock by the time a police car drew up. A young policeman walked over and hesitated when he caught sight of Zoe's body.

'Are you Jenny?'

He was joined almost at once by a young female officer who took Jenny gently by the arm and urged her to stand up.

'I'm sorry you had to see this. Are you feeling all right?' she asked. 'Shall we go and get you a cup of tea and then you can tell us what happened here.'

Jenny tried to answer but broke down in tears. Sobbing hysterically, she allowed herself to be led to a police car.

'She's dead, isn't she?' she blurted out when she had recovered enough to try and talk. 'She's dead.'

Her sobbing had subsided, but she was still shaking so much that she could barely speak. All she could think of was Zoe's body, lying in the rain.

'She's getting wet.' She burst out crying again. 'She's getting wet.'

47

Eileen shook her head, her expression drawn. 'I know it's hard to believe there's been another victim, but we just have to maintain our efforts to find the killer.'

Geraldine wondered whether the detective chief inspector had been about to urge them to 'redouble' their efforts but had thought better of it. Everyone had been working hard. It wasn't for lack of trying that they hadn't yet succeeded in making an arrest.

'We don't know whether this latest death is connected to the other two,' a young constable piped up.

No one responded to the comment. They all understood this third death was connected to the other two under investigation. They were still waiting to hear the results of the post mortem but they had received results of forensic testing carried out on the body. It made no difference to the dead young girl, but her body bore traces of the DNA that had been found on both Grant and Felicity. A double murder was worrying enough. To be hunting for a serial killer was far worse. So far the papers and news channels had not reported any details of Zoe's death, but it wouldn't be long before they latched on to it and began hounding the police and winding up members of the public. Geraldine could just imagine the headlines: 'Serial Killer on the Loose', with an equally disturbing subheading: 'What Are the Police Doing?' At a time when the police desperately needed members of the public to supply them with information, they couldn't afford to let the media discourage people from coming forward, but there was little they could do to stop the negative reporting.

'All we're doing is trying to find out who killed them.'

Geraldine's colleagues all turned to look at her and she realised she had voiced her thoughts.

'Sorry, just thinking aloud,' she said.

Several of her colleagues smiled.

Eileen grunted. 'Let's run over what we already know about him. He's Caucasian, blond with blue eyes, and he seems to be killing in the centre of York. His first victim was a history teacher, male, thirty-two, the second one was another teacher, female, twenty-seven, and now this third one was a female student, eighteen years old.' As she mentioned Zoe's age, her voice seemed to harden. 'Is it a coincidence they were all involved in education in some capacity? Or that the victims are becoming progressively younger? Or is this just opportunistic indiscriminate killing?' She paused to allow the implications of her questions to sink in, before resuming briskly. 'So come on, let's get on with tracking him down. If there's anything else that connects these three victims, we need to know what it is. Were they ever in the same place at the same time? Do they have any associates in common? What's the link between them?'

Eileen strode back to her office to tussle with schedules and budgets, and no doubt prepare to fend off journalists. Geraldine didn't envy the detective chief inspector her workload. In the meantime, teams were set up to work with the borough intelligence unit looking into the victims' histories, and Geraldine's own task was waiting. Disconsolately she made her way to the car park. The latest victim was only eighteen. It was going to be hard speaking to the bereaved parents.

Jonah looked up without his customary grin when Geraldine entered the room.

'Another youngster,' he said, by way of a greeting.

'Eighteen. She was just finishing her first year at the university.'

'The same age as my daughter,' Jonah said.

They were silent for a moment, gazing at the body. Unclothed, with her hair scraped back off her face, she looked like a child.

'She was fit,' Jonah began and broke off with a scowl. He sighed and resumed. 'She was fit and healthy.'

Geraldine rarely saw Jonah looking downcast.

'What was the time of death?'

She already knew the answer, but hoped a specific question would draw him away from his internal musings. She was right. With a shiver, Jonah snapped back into his usual briskness.

'Right then. She was young – eighteen –but I'd have judged her to be around thirteen from her physical development. She was killed yesterday evening, somewhere around nine, but –'

'I know,' Geraldine interrupted him, 'the body was lying out in the rain overnight so it's impossible to be precise about the time.'

Jonah shrugged as if to say, if you know so much, why are you here questioning me.

'I'm sorry, I interrupted you.'

'She was killed by one slash that cut through her carotid artery.' Jonah paused and frowned. 'I would have thought the killer must have been splashed with her blood.'

'He left a trace of his own DNA in the brief struggle.'

Jonah nodded again. 'Yes, he seems a bit careless, doesn't he? Almost like he's leaving a calling card. Here I am, your blond blue-eyed killer, come and find me.'

Jonah's words were lighthearted, but he sounded angry. They had worked together on several cases, but Geraldine knew nothing about him beyond the fact that he was a pathologist. She had only just learned that he had a teenage daughter. It was easy to forget that outside the narrow context in which they met, he had a life she knew nothing about.

Zoe's parents were due to arrive to make a formal identification of the body but Geraldine hadn't been tasked with meeting them. Instead she went to speak to the dead girl's flatmate. Until now Jenny had been too distraught to give a coherent account of how she had found the body. Her mother had arrived to take her home, and Eileen wanted her to give a statement before she left York. She had agreed to speak to Geraldine in her flat.

Jenny was a slender girl with light ginger hair and hazel eyes bloodshot from crying. She was seated on a sofa in the living room with her mother at her side.

'I went to put the rubbish out,' Jenny said, before breaking down in tears.

'That's all right. Take your time,' Geraldine replied gently, inwardly fretting at the waste of time.

Her mother held her hand as, stammering and sobbing, Jenny described how she had found her flatmate lying by the rubbish bins.

'I didn't know it was her at first. And then I saw the blood. And then her face...'

'Jenny, I know this is difficult for you, but if you could answer a couple of questions, that might really help us,' Geraldine said.

'What do you want to know?'

'What time did you get home last night?'

Jenny glanced at her mother. 'I don't know.'

'Was it late?'

'No.' Jenny sniffed and made a visible effort to control her tears. 'It must have been about ten thirty or eleven. It wasn't late. I had an early lecture...'

'We think this happened around nine o'clock last night.'

Jenny let out a sob. 'She must have been there when I got back, lying by the bins. If I'd known... if I'd known...'

Geraldine leaned forward in her chair and spoke slowly, to emphasise the significance of her next question.

'Did you hear anything unusual, anything at all, outside your flat last night?'

'No,' Jenny shook her head, 'no, no, I didn't. I wish I had. I wish I'd known...'

She dropped her head in her hands and sobbed.

Her mother looked at Geraldine, with tears in her own eyes. 'I think Jenny's told you everything she can about her traumatic experience. Please, can you leave us in peace to come to terms with what happened?'

Geraldine sighed. There was nothing Jenny could tell her about the night her flatmate had been killed. All Geraldine could do was fish for information.

'Was there anyone you can think of who might have held a grudge against Zoe? Any violent boyfriends?'

Jenny shook her head. 'I don't know. I don't know.'

'Did she have any particular friends she might have confided in?'

'Josie.'

'Josie?'

Jenny nodded. 'Zoe had a friend called Josie. They were on the same course.'

Making a note of Josie's name, Geraldine left.

48

IT WAS FORTUNATE FOR Geraldine that all the students who had known Zoe had been called to a meeting on the campus that afternoon. She made her way to the packed lecture hall.

'Remember the college counselling service is open to all, students and staff,' a pastoral tutor was saying as Geraldine made her way to the podium. 'If you have been affected in any way by the loss of this popular member of our community, remember you are not alone, and please don't feel you have to deal with this by yourself. We are here to support you.'

There was more along those lines. Geraldine waited until he finished speaking before she approached and introduced herself.

The tutor invited her to join him on the dais. 'Would you like to say a few words?'

Geraldine hadn't been planning to talk to the assembled students, but she took advantage of the opportunity to urge anyone who had known Zoe to contact the police. When she finished, she asked the tutor to point Josie out. Then she waited outside. When the meeting was over the students filed out of the building. The atmosphere among them was subdued. Josie's pink hair was easy to spot, and Geraldine hurried after her. Josie was chatting to another girl and didn't hear Geraldine call her name, but her companion paused in her stride and looked around.

'Josie,' Geraldine repeated, drawing level with them. 'Might I have a quick word with you?'

The other girl sniggered. 'Ooh, the police are after you. What've you gone and done?'

'Shut up, you twat, this is about Zoe.'

Josie turned away from her crestfallen companion and smiled sadly at Geraldine. 'If there's anything I can do, I'd like to help, really I would. But I didn't know Zoe that well. I only really spoke to her for the first time this term, and now –' She broke off with a shrug, her features contorted in dismay.

'But you were friends with her?'

'Yes, that is, I knew her, but not very well. But we connected, you know. I like to think we would have been friends if only we'd had time to get to know each other better.'

'Can we go and sit down for a moment so we can talk?'

She led the girl over to a bench beside the path. Josie looked appropriately solemn, although Geraldine had the impression she was basking in the attention. Her eyes flicked up constantly to glance at the students filing past, as though checking that they had noticed she was engaged in a private conversation with the policewoman who had spoken to them en masse.

'I was wondering if she might have confided in you?'

'Confided? Yes. All the time. People seem to find me easy to talk to.'

Geraldine didn't comment on that, but pressed on with her questions.

'Did she mention anyone who might have had a grudge against her?'

'Not exactly, but…'

'But…?'

Josie looked unexpectedly uncomfortable. 'It sounds daft, but she was attacked on the street recently.'

Geraldine didn't even attempt to hide her surprise. 'Attacked? When was that?'

Josie shook her head, and her pink hair fluttered in the breeze. 'I don't know exactly.'

'Can you tell me what happened?'

Josie thought for a moment. 'It must have been about a week ago.'

'What happened?' Geraldine repeated, wondering whether the girl actually had anything useful to tell her or was just stringing her along.

'Well, I wasn't there, but she told me some old woman approached her on the street and wanted to buy her a coffee.' Josie gave a reluctant grin. 'You're thinking it sounds pretty lame, aren't you? Honestly, I don't blame you. I thought just the same. But the thing is, she seemed really spooked by it. I mean, I think she was actually scared. I told her to go to the police if she was really that worried. But I can't say I took it seriously. I mean, an old woman offering her a coffee. It's hardly the Yorkshire Ripper, is it?'

'What else did she say?'

Josie screwed up her eyes in an effort to recall what Zoe had told her. 'She said this old woman grabbed her by the arm and told her she was going to lose her looks, and she said – that is, Zoe said to me – we should warn the other girls because this woman was crazy. And she said she might not have got away at all if two guys hadn't come along and rescued her, because the old woman didn't want to let go of her and she was strong. I know it sounds daft, but that's what she told me. Anyway, she was so rattled, I told her to go to the police about it, but I don't know if she did. I figured that if she really was scared, she ought to do something about it. And if she was just making a drama out of nothing, then there was nothing more to say. What was I supposed to do about it? There was nothing I could do, was there?'

Beneath her bravado, Geraldine could see that Josie really was very upset. At any age it would be a terrible experience to lose a fellow student in such a sudden and violent manner, but she was young. Like Zoe, she was only about eighteen.

'You did the right thing,' Geraldine reassured her. 'There was nothing else you could have done.'

But it was an unsettling report all the same. On her return to the police station, Geraldine scanned the records for the past week and discovered that six days earlier Zoe had indeed turned up at the police station to report that she had been attacked on the street by a middle-aged woman. The details matched what Josie had said, and sounded equally unlikely. It was the kind of report that might be dismissed as an overreaction by a hysterical teenager. But a week after reporting the attack, Zoe had been murdered. It was hard to believe that could be coincidence.

'Are you suggesting a woman is working in tandem with the male killer we're looking for?' Eileen asked, when Geraldine told her what she had discovered. 'And why the hell didn't anyone else flag up that Zoe visited the police station just six days before she was killed?' She turned to Geraldine. 'Are you really the only person who came across this? It wasn't even down to you to check through recent reports. Who the hell did Zoe speak to when she came here last week?'

Geraldine muttered that it was only by chance she had come across Josie's name.

'If you hadn't pressed Zoe's flatmate for names, and followed up her mention of Josie, we might not have turned this up for another few weeks, if at all,' Eileen snapped. 'This is just the kind of thorough detective work that gets results.'

'Geraldine's certainly thorough,' Ariadne said.

'She doesn't let anything go,' Ian agreed.

Used to being respected as a successful inspector, Geraldine had struggled with working as an unknown sergeant. She was pleased to know that she was gradually reestablishing her reputation as a good detective. But her fleeting gratification was overwhelmed by distress over the death of another teenager, killed after appealing to the police for help. Along with her colleagues she had failed to protect first Daryl, and now Zoe, with the most terrible consequences imaginable for them both.

49

GERALDINE HADN'T BEEN TO visit Celia and her family for a couple of months, and was eager to see them again. The baby would have changed quite a lot since her last trip, and she couldn't wait to hold him again, and see with her own eyes how much he had grown. Hearing Celia talk about him wasn't the same at all. She was also keen to see her niece as often as she could while Chloe was still a child. In addition to her excitement at seeing her family, she was looking forward to getting away from York where the case was virtually at a standstill, with three murders and no leads to the killer. Everyone at the police station was pressing on in an atmosphere of sombre determination but they weren't making any progress, and she desperately needed a break from it all.

'Solid police work is what will get us a result in the end,' Eileen kept telling the team. 'There are no easy answers in our line of work. We just have to keep going and not leave anything to chance.' She carried on for a while along those lines.

Geraldine didn't interrupt the detective chief inspector to say that dogged police work was all very well, but what they could really do with was a stroke of luck. The way things were progressing, it seemed they would hear about another murder before they discovered the identity of the killer.

'We have his DNA,' Ariadne grumbled, voicing the general frustration. 'How long is it going to take us to find him?'

They all knew that the longer a case dragged on, the more difficult it was to resolve. While the traces grew cold with the passage of time, and potential witnesses forgot what they had seen, the police could do nothing but wait for the results of forensic examination of potential evidence found at the crime scenes. Meanwhile the killer could be anywhere by now.

The sun was shining and the traffic was relatively light, yet somehow Geraldine didn't experience her usual feeling of elation as she drove away from York. The investigation weighed too heavily on her conscience to be readily dismissed from her thoughts. Her whole purpose in working had always been to help and protect the public. Recently two young people had approached the police for help, and both were now dead. After what had happened, Geraldine couldn't help questioning the usefulness of her work. But without it her life would have no purpose at all. She put the radio on in an attempt to distract herself from her miserable thoughts, but it didn't help. Whatever music came on irritated her. After switching channels to hear a high-pitched woman's voice in the middle of a story about marital breakdown, she turned the radio off.

At last she arrived at her sister's house in Kent and was instantly cheered by the warm welcome she received. The baby was asleep, but Celia assured her that he would wake soon enough for a feed.

'And then he'll start crying, and then you'll complain about having to change his nappy, and then you'll want him to go to sleep again,' Geraldine's niece, Chloe, said. 'All mum wants him to do is sleep, sleep, sleep, and then when he does, she wants him to wake up for a feed.'

Geraldine used to be touched by Chloe's wildly excited reaction to her visits. As she approached her teens, Chloe was often out when Geraldine went round, so she was pleased to find her at home. Before she could question Chloe about school and life in general, the baby woke up. Celia was occupied attending to him, while Geraldine looked on and made appropriate comments about how well her nephew looked, and how contented he seemed.

'You should hear him crying,' Chloe told her cheerfully. 'He cries all night.'

Celia laughed. 'He does not cry all night.'

'But he does cry a lot, doesn't he?'

'He hardly cries at all.'

Chloe pouted. 'But he does cry.'

Geraldine smiled. 'Do you think you didn't cry when you were a few months old?'

'I was a good baby, wasn't I, Mummy?'

'Yes, you were, and so is your brother.'

'That's because they have such a caring mother,' Geraldine said.

Her brother-in-law, Sebastian, made lunch and they all sat down at the table together. With the baby sleeping again, and Chloe in a good mood, the atmosphere was cheerful, and Geraldine was really glad she had made the effort to drive there. It was just the respite she needed, spending time with family like this.

'So, how's school?' she asked when Sebastian joined them from the kitchen.

'It's OK.'

'What's your favourite subject these days?'

'Art,' Chloe responded promptly. 'It's amazeballs.'

'All she talks about is her art lessons,' Sebastian said stiffly.

'She likes her art teacher,' Celia explained. 'That'll soon change when she has a different teacher.'

'Miss Beech is so cool!' Chloe enthused. 'She's really really pretty, and she wears the coolest clothes, and she changes her hair every week.' She scowled. 'Mummy won't let me dye my hair. Mummy, can I, please?'

'No.'

'Absolutely not,' Sebastian chimed in.

Geraldine smiled. 'So what colour is Miss Beech's hair?'

'Last week was blue, wasn't it, Chloe?' Celia said.

Chloe nodded. 'It's only the front bit. That's all I want to do too. Just this little bit here. It's so cool! Why can't I, Mummy?'

'I don't think it's very good for your hair,' Geraldine said.

'Miss Beech does it.'

'Yes, but she's a grown up, and it's up to her. A child's hair is different to an adult's,' Celia said firmly.

'When she changes her hair, she changes the colour of her eyes as well!' Chloe said, opening her own eyes wide in admiration. 'It's so cool!'

'She wears coloured contact lenses,' Celia explained, laughing. Geraldine frowned. 'That's interesting. That's very interesting.'

But she wasn't thinking about the art teacher's eyes.

'Aunty, are you listening to me?' Chloe asked. 'Aunty?'

'Yes, yes, of course I'm listening.'

Geraldine turned to look at Chloe but her thoughts were, literally, miles away.

'I have to make a call,' she said suddenly, and stood up.

'Can't it wait? We're in the middle of lunch,' Celia protested.

'No one's allowed to get down when we're all eating,' Chloe said. 'It's bad manners.'

With a muttered apology, Geraldine hurried from the room.

'What do you mean, the killer might not have fair hair?' Eileen barked down the phone.

She reacted as though the suggestion was a direct attack on her approach to the case. Which, in a way, it was. At Eileen's instigation, a massive hunt had been initiated for a blue-eyed man with fair hair living in the York area. He might have changed his name from Jamie Drury, but he couldn't alter his DNA. Samples had been solicited, obtained, and processed, from thousands of men, without a match being found. The project continued, with Eileen insisting they wouldn't stop testing DNA of appropriate local residents until they found their man.

'That's the only thing we do know about the killer. His DNA clearly shows fair hair and blue eyes. The DNA samples can't be wrong.'

'I know,' Geraldine conceded. 'I'm not suggesting he's not naturally fair. What I'm saying is he might have dyed his hair to hide the fact that he's blond. We haven't been testing dark-haired men, have we?'

'And his eyes? Don't you think a man with dark hair and blue eyes might attract notice? We've been testing all men with blue eyes, regardless of their hair colour, and including men with no hair at all.'

'But what if he's not only dyed his hair black, or shaved his head, but has been wearing dark contact lenses to change the colour of his eyes. If he's done that, we wouldn't even approach him to request a DNA sample.'

Eileen was silent for a moment.

'What are the chances?' she asked at last.

Geraldine shrugged. 'Granted it's unlikely, I'm just saying it's possible, isn't it?'

Eileen sighed. 'We'll extend the programme,' she agreed heavily. 'It's possible he's changed more than his name.'

Although she had won the point, Geraldine rang off feeling as dejected as Eileen sounded.

'Is everything all right?' Celia asked as Geraldine took her seat at the table again.

'Everything's fine,' Geraldine lied. 'I'm sorry –'

Before she could say any more, the baby began to cry and the focus of everyone's attention shifted.

'Who would like seconds?' Sebastian asked.

Geraldine's bad manners were forgotten in the flurry of activity around the baby and lunch.

50

ON HER WAY HOME, Geraldine thought about Celia's happy family, and how different her sister's household was to that of old Mr Drury whose family had all died or deserted him. The contrast made his isolation seem even starker because, unlike Geraldine, he had never expected to live out his old age without the support of a partner or children. Whatever happened, she hoped tragedy would never tear Celia's family apart. Edward Drury's wife had killed herself out of guilt and grief, claiming she had raised a monster. As she drove, it struck Geraldine that perhaps Mrs Drury had not been referring to Peter the drug addict, who had ended up dying in prison. She might have been referring to Jamie, her other son. Had she stumbled on a dark truth about him that she had taken with her to her grave? With a sudden thrill, Geraldine called Ian and ran her idea past him.

'What if Jamie was the monster his mother was referring to? Remember the sister who died? What if Jamie was responsible for that and their mother found out? I mean,' she added, 'why would a mother call her son a monster, just because he was a drug addict?'

'Peter Drury wasn't just an addict,' Ian reminded her. 'He was sentenced for robbery with violence. He was a vicious criminal. Surely that's why she called him a monster?'

Neither of them broached the unspoken subtext in which Geraldine was defending drug users and Ian was distancing himself from the claim that addicts were necessarily malicious. He had to concede that Geraldine's theory was plausible, but they both knew they needed more information. Ending the call with Ian, Geraldine phoned old Mr Drury to question him about Jamie's possible role in his sister's death.

'I'm very sorry to trouble you, but I need to ask you a question.'

'Go ahead. Ask your question.'

'Who was looking after your daughter when she died?'

There was a slight pause before he answered. 'No one.'

'I mean, who was with her?'

There was another brief pause, barely a hesitation. 'My sons.'

'So Jamie and Peter would both have known what really happened that day when your daughter fell into the water?'

'I don't know what you're getting at,' Edward replied.

His voice had altered slightly. Geraldine wasn't sure if she only imagined that he was sounding defensive. She regretted having phoned him. She could have told a lot more from a face-to-face encounter, but it was too late now. She listened closely to what Edward was saying.

'I've already told you what happened. Do we really have to go over it all over again? She fell from the bridge into the weir. Even a strong swimmer wouldn't have been able to withstand the force of the water, and she was only a child. She didn't stand a chance.'

'And both your sons were with her at the time?'

'Yes. I told you that.'

There was no way of checking the details with Peter, but Geraldine determined to scan through all his records and find out whether he had ever talked about the tragic incident. In the meantime, there was nothing more to be learned from Edward. If Jamie had been responsible for his sister's death, Edward might want to defend him. It was also possible that the truth had been concealed from Edward. Thanking him, she hung up and drove on, replaying the conversation in her mind.

Her suspicion of the dead Jamie remained unsubstantiated. It made no difference now, since Jamie and both his siblings were dead, but she wanted to discover the truth. The only two people who might have known what had happened that day by the weir were both dead. But it was possible Peter might have talked to someone while he was in prison. The following day, she looked up Peter's records. Gazing at his mug shot, she thought there was something familiar about his face, but she couldn't place what it was. Puzzled, she contacted the prison where he had been incarcerated and the governor gave her the name and address of a man who had shared a cell with Peter.

'I think they became friends,' the governor said. 'If Peter confided in anyone, it would have been Brendan.'

That afternoon Geraldine went to see Peter's former cell mate. Elderly, and broken, he was living in a care home in Oxfordshire. Brendan was in his seventies, but he looked very frail and could have been mistaken for a man twenty years older.

'Yes, I remember Peter,' he wheezed, breaking off to cough. 'We shared a cell. Poor Peter. It was the drugs got to him, you know.'

Geraldine nodded. 'Yes, I heard. But it wasn't actually Peter I wanted to ask you about.' She hesitated. 'It's his family I'm interested in.'

'I never met them,' Brendan said.

'Did he ever talk about them?'

The old man sighed. 'There was a sister, if I remember rightly.'

'Yes, she drowned.'

The old man's eyes lit up in recognition. 'That's right. She died as a child, and then Peter started on the drugs. Ruined his life.'

It wasn't clear whether he was referring to the death of his sister, or the drugs, but Geraldine didn't interrupt him to find out.

'Poor Peter,' he repeated and coughed again.

'And he had a brother?' Geraldine prompted him when the coughing fit subsided.

'Oh yes,' the old man gave a lopsided grin.

'Were they close?'

'Close?' The old man cackled. 'Hardly. Peter told me he never wanted to see his brother again.'

'Why was that?'

Brendan shrugged his narrow shoulders. 'I don't know. I suppose it was the drugs talking.'

As Geraldine drove home, another possibility occurred to her. It was unlikely that Jamie had not died abroad after all, but it was possible. They had not yet tracked down a death certificate for him which meant there was a chance he was still alive and, if so, he might have returned to England. And if his sister had also not actually died, but had been fished out of the weir half dead, Jamie might have traced his sister who could now be calling herself Lindsey Curtis. That would explain why Lindsey had failed to come forward to give any information to the police; she knew her brother was a killer and was protecting him. It was such a long shot that Geraldine resolved to keep the possibility to herself and do a little ferreting around in her own time before sharing her idea with anyone else. But she experienced a visceral sense of excitement that she might have uncovered information that would lead them to the killer.

On Monday, Geraldine went into work early and hurried through her morning tasks, eager to spend some time on her own research, but that only confirmed that the Drurys' daughter had indeed died when she was just ten years old. The death had been recorded, certified by a local GP. Edward Drury had told her the truth when he had said his daughter had drowned. So, the unformulated suspicion Geraldine had barely dared admit even to herself turned out to be a false start. There was no way Jamie Drury's sister could have survived and now be calling herself Lindsey Curtis. It had been a far-fetched idea really but, unlike in fiction, truth could be unbelievable, and Geraldine was not one to leave any possibility unexplored. And all the time, the suspicion that she had missed something about Lindsey kept niggling at her.

Putting her disappointment behind her, Geraldine wondered whether Lindsey Curtis had somehow been involved in the recent murders all the same. The CCTV film indicated she had been walking along High Ousegate at the time of Grant's murder, and she could have been the figure that followed Felicity down the steps to the river just before the second murder. Despite Eileen's dismissal of the idea, Geraldine still wondered whether Lindsey might be involved in some way. She had definitely been very quick to shut the door on Geraldine.

She ran her idea past Ian.

'It would explain why she refused to talk to me. Is there any way we can get a warrant to search the house?'

Ian frowned. 'This all sounds extremely fanciful and it would be tricky to initiate a search without any grounds other than your suspicion. I don't think we can force our way in with nothing to back up what is nothing more than a vague hunch.'

'I realise that if I'm wrong, we'd be in hot water.'

'*You'd* be in hot water, going out on a limb like that,' Ian replied.

'But what if I'm right?'

'Then it's equally risky because we could end up merely alerting the suspect before we're ready. If she is involved in some way – which seems highly unlikely – the last thing we want is for her to do a runner. It is just a suspicion, isn't it? You could be wrong.'

Geraldine nodded. 'Yes, it's just a suspicion.'

Seeing her anxious expression, Ian frowned. 'There is another way of looking into this. I'm only suggesting this because your instincts have been right so often before. I honestly don't believe you're right about this, but if you insist on looking into it, here's what you might do.'

As he outlined his plan, Geraldine nodded. 'That's just what I was thinking,' she said, and smiled.

51

THE STREET WAS DESERTED early the next morning and Geraldine hoped to complete her mission and be gone before anyone else was stirring. The sun had not yet risen and there was a fresh damp feeling in the air, adding to her sense of optimism. Having sworn Geraldine to secrecy about his complicity in her enquiry, Ian had persuaded a young forensic scientist he knew to help her.

'I can't thank you enough,' she greeted the young man who met her outside the police station.

He climbed into the car beside her.

'I owe Ian a favour,' he said. 'He explained you might be on to something but your boss isn't convinced and won't release the funds for this. Anyway, here's hoping you're right. And if I can help you put this killer behind bars, that's all the thanks I'll need. '

Geraldine nodded. She hoped his trust wouldn't turn out to be misplaced.

'That's the house,' she murmured, although no one could hear them from outside the car. 'See what you can get for us, and be as quick as you can. We want to be away before we're spotted.'

Her companion nodded. 'I'll do my best,' he replied earnestly, 'but you know that trying to collect DNA samples from an external surface is going to be a hit and miss affair at the best of times.'

'I'm sure you'll get something.'

'The problem is it will have been exposed to variations in

temperature and God only knows what bacteria and mould in the atmosphere besides. It would be much easier if we could get inside the house.'

Geraldine hesitated. 'Like I said, it's only an idea. But without any evidence that's all it is. I'm hoping you can find something, and then we'll be in there like a shot. So come on, let's get on with it before anyone comes.'

Closing the car doors as quietly as they could, they stole through the gate and up the path to the front door. Fortunately there were no security lights to trigger and they reached the entrance without hindrance. Geraldine stopped and held up one hand, but there was no sound from inside the house. She nodded at the forensic scientist who pulled out a small torch. Under its powerful narrow beam of light he studied the door and frame carefully while Geraldine watched with growing impatience.

At last the officer appeared satisfied. Handing the torch to Geraldine, he indicated where to direct the light before he pulled on gloves and a head covering. Moistening a swab with distilled water, he dabbed it gently on the wood and placed it straight in a swab box which he dropped into a paper bag. He changed his gloves before repeating the process, until he had used multiple pairs of gloves and dropped swab after swab into separate boxes which he placed in different paper bags. He seemed to be fiddling around with different swabs and boxes and bags for hours. At last he straightened up and took a step back before removing his mask and head covering.

Without a word, they hurried quietly back down the path just as the sun was rising.

'Phew!' the forensic scientist said as they climbed back into the car and pulled away from the kerb. 'That was tricky.'

'Did you get anything you can use?'

'Who knows? But with the new hi-tech forensics it's possible to sometimes get a complete DNA sample from smudged or partial fingerprints and even from surfaces where no prints are visible. So you might be lucky. I'll get these straight back to the lab anyway, and have them tested.'

'You'll let me know straightaway if you find a match for the sample found on the murder victims?'

'Of course.' The forensic scientist broke into a smile. 'So does this mean you think we might have found your murderer?'

'Like you said, we might be lucky.'

They drove back to the police station in silence after that. The scientist took his swabs straight to the forensic lab, and for the rest of the morning Geraldine was forced to wait impatiently for the results. Aware that she had nothing more than an impression to go on, she hadn't mentioned her theory to the detective chief inspector. At last the results came back. A trace of DNA matching that found on both murder victims had been identified on the door frame of the house now occupied by long-haired Lindsey. Clutching the results, Geraldine ran to tell Ian and together they went to see Eileen.

'Can't this wait?' she asked when they opened the door. 'I'm due at a meeting and can't be late.'

'No,' Ian replied promptly. 'It can't wait. We think Geraldine's found out where the killer lives.'

Eileen had half risen to her feet. She sat down again abruptly. 'Say that again, slowly.'

Geraldine gave Eileen the address. 'It's where Lindsey Curtis lives, but something didn't quite add up, which is why I wanted to test her door frame, just in case we found a match.'

'The killer's DNA was all over it,' Ian said.

Eileen frowned. 'Hers was the only name on the tenancy agreement, if I remember correctly?'

'We've established the killer went there, so even though he's not actually living there she must know him,' Ian said.

'She's been living there for three months and it's unlikely the DNA traces would have survived on an external surface for more than a few weeks,' Geraldine added.

'Obviously she's not the killer,' Ian said, 'but if she knows him she might be able to help us to trace where he's hiding out. He could even be in the house with her right now.'

'Let's bring her in and find out,' Eileen snapped. 'And while we're at it, we'll search the house. Good work, both of you.'

'This was all Geraldine's doing,' Ian said quickly. 'I can't claim any responsibility for it.'

'Yes, well, let's find this killer and then we can spend time arguing about who takes the credit for his arrest.'

Ian and Geraldine exchanged a quick glance. Obviously Eileen would claim the kudos for the success of the investigation she was leading, but that no longer mattered to Geraldine. Her days of caring about making a name for herself were over. She had no reputation left to protect.

Geraldine and Ian went to see Lindsey, but once again there was no one there. Worried she might have done a runner, they sent out an alert to all stations, ports and airports, as well as circulating her details to police stations nationwide. The best image they could find on the CCTV footage had been enhanced as far as possible, but it was blurred, making it difficult to broadcast. Her house was put under surveillance and around midday, a message came in that a woman had been seen entering the property. Geraldine and Ian went straight there, taking a search team with them. On the way, they agreed that Ian would wait in the car outside, with the team on alert, while Geraldine went to speak to Lindsey. There was no point in alarming her unduly, and a chance that Geraldine might learn more from her by questioning her gently. With a surge of excitement, Geraldine approached the front door. Even though there was no reason to suppose Lindsey knew where Jamie was hiding out, Geraldine couldn't help feeling she was moving closer to the killer.

52

FOR A LONG TIME, Lindsey didn't come to the door. Geraldine rang the bell repeatedly, and rapped on the door with her knuckles, and eventually a voice called out, asking who was there. When Geraldine introduced herself, there was a long pause before Lindsey answered.

'I don't open the door to strangers so you can go away, whoever you are.'

'Lindsey, this is the police. We just want to speak to you for a moment. Please open the door.'

'What do you want?'

'Lindsey, something's happened that you need to be aware of,' Geraldine replied, being as circumspect as she could.

'Go away.'

'Lindsey, we're not going anywhere until you've answered a few questions we have. Please, listen to me. We're here to protect you –'

'I don't need your protection. I can look after myself. Go away.'

'Lindsey, please can you open the door so we can talk?'

'You can talk to me like this.'

The door opened on the chain just enough to allow Geraldine to make out a sliver of a figure inside. Peering into the poorly lit hall, she could see one side of a pale face with a dark eye staring back at her.

'What do you want? Go away and leave me alone.'

Carefully Geraldine explained that the police were looking for Jamie Drury.

'Who's he?'

'You might know him under a different name, but we know he's been in this house recently.'

'Well he hasn't. No one called Jamie has been here. Not while I've been living here anyway. There hasn't been anyone else here.'

Lindsey tried to shut the door but Geraldine had slipped one foot in the gap to prevent it from closing.

'We think this man we're looking for can help us with our enquiries into a case concerning a very serious crime. This is really important, Lindsey. Is there anyone in the house apart from you?'

It was hardly possible to be more vague, but Lindsey didn't question Geraldine about the nature of the crime she was investigating. And she was adamant there was no one else in the house.

'There may have been someone else in the house before me, but not while I was living here, and I don't know anyone called Jamie, so you can go away and leave me alone.'

Lindsey jogged the door in an attempt to close it. Geraldine hesitated. This was not going well.

'Lindsey, I need you to let me in,' she said. 'Or if you prefer, you can come along to the police station to answer some questions.'

'Go away,' Lindsey replied, refusing to be cowed by a threatened visit to the police station. 'Just go away and leave me alone. You've got no right to pester me like this.'

'Is someone in there with you?'

'No, I told you, there's no one else here.'

'Then will you allow us to come in and take a look around?'

'No, you can't come in. I told you there's no one here.'

It was time to be firm. 'Lindsey, there's a team of police officers outside the house, front and back, waiting to come in and conduct a search, with or without your consent. If we need to get a search warrant we will, with the evidence we have –'

'What evidence? What are you talking about? I told you

there's no one here. You're just trying to intimidate me. It won't work.'

The door jiggled again. Geraldine explained about the DNA found on the door frame.

'We believe it belongs to a man we'd like to speak to, a man called Jamie Drury, so I'm sorry, but we do need to come in and look around. This is a murder investigation and if you refuse permission you will be prosecuted for obstructing the police. We're obtaining a warrant to search the premises.'

'I told you, there's no one called Jamie here now.'

'But there might be something in the house that will help us to find him. We do need to take a look. Lindsey, I really don't understand why you're so determined to stop us coming in. I've told you why this is so serious.'

'Wait a minute.'

Lindsey shut the door. Even though she knew officers were watching the back door, Geraldine was growing anxious by the time the front door opened a few moments later and Lindsey stood aside to let her in. Geraldine entered, followed by the search team.

Geraldine turned to Lindsey. 'I'd like to ask you a few questions.'

As Lindsey ducked her head, Geraldine caught a glimpse of eyes nearly as dark as her own. Circled by stark black lines, they looked like holes cut into her long pale face.

'I let you in. Now leave me alone. I don't know anything about the man you're looking for.'

Her tone was so irate Geraldine didn't feel inclined to insist. Instead she watched Lindsey enter the front room and close the door behind her. She hadn't been able to prevent Geraldine from entering her house; shutting her out of the front room was a petty triumph. If there were any clues to Jamie's whereabouts in the house, the highly trained search team would find them. There was nothing Geraldine could do to help, but out of curiosity she had a quick look around the house. She could see no sign of a man's presence there. Downstairs, apart from the front room where Lindsey was ensconced with the television blaring, there was a kitchenette that looked out on to a narrow strip of overgrown garden, and another room set up with a small square dining table and four chairs, that looked unused. The search team went through all of the rooms, including the front room where Lindsey was sitting. There was only one laptop in the house which was taken straight to the police station for a technology expert to investigate, while a team conducted a meticulous physical search of the property.

Upstairs, apart from a bathroom crammed with bottles and tubes of ointments and lotions and cosmetics, there was a box room with a small bed that appeared to have been slept in, and a larger bedroom that was apparently used as a dressing room. Clothes were strewn all over the bed: brightly coloured dresses and skirts, sequinned gowns and velvet capes, and frocks decorated with beads and sparkles. Geraldine picked up a flouncy pale pink chiffon dress dotted with tiny pink pearls. Somehow she couldn't imagine the tall angular-faced woman downstairs wearing something so flimsy and delicate. The search was fruitless. Not only was there no one else hidden in the house or garden, but there was no sign of anyone else having been there.

Feeling deflated, Geraldine returned to the car where Ian was waiting for her and they drove back to the police station in silence. There was nothing more they could do but scour the country for Jamie. It was likely to be a long drawn-out manhunt. In the meantime, they would put Lindsey under twenty-four hour surveillance.

53

HAVING DISCOVERED THE KILLER'S DNA on the door frame of Lindsey's house, they seemed to be closing in on the man who had killed Grant, Felicity and Zoe. Yet even though Jamie had now become a suspect, despite all their efforts they could find nothing to link him to his victims, and his motive for the murders remained as much of a mystery as his whereabouts. They weren't even sure he was still alive. His father had reported that he was dead but, without firm evidence, they were proceeding on the assumption that he was still alive and had returned to the UK, if he had even gone abroad in the first place. Certainly they had found no record of him ever having left the country and had only his father's word for that. He could have been mistaken, or lying to mislead them in an attempt to protect his only surviving child. Speaking briskly, Eileen said they would be able to question him about his motives once they had him in custody but, before that, they had to find him. It was proving more of a challenge than anyone had anticipated. They had all assumed that establishing the killer's identity would be the difficult part. Now they knew who to look for, the suspect seemed to have vanished without trace.

Lindsey's landlord was contacted as a matter of urgency, and details obtained for his previous tenants dating back ten years. None of them was called Jamie Drury. All were traced and local officers were promptly dispatched to question them and obtain DNA samples from the males. None of the samples matched that of the elusive killer, and no one admitted to having known a man called Jamie while they were living there. Yet the fact remained that his DNA had been present on Lindsey's door frame. While the hunt continued, the surveillance team remained in place watching Lindsey's house, and there was still no sign of Jamie.

'Needle and haystack,' Ian muttered.

This wasn't the first time they had been in this position, but they usually at least had an idea of who they were looking for, and what he or she might look like. All that happened on the following day was that a couple of Lindsey's neighbours called to say they had noticed a car parked in their street with someone sitting inside it.

'So much for discreet surveillance,' Eileen grumbled. 'And you've come up with nothing at all that might help us to find him?'

'Nothing at all,' Ian confirmed.

He looked crestfallen. Having organised the physical search, he had led the team with serious hopes of discovering a lead to the killer's whereabouts.

'What about the laptop?' Eileen barked, turning to the officer who had been in charge of that part of the search.

He too shook his head. 'It belonged to Lindsey,' he replied. 'Most of the searches relate to female fashion. Apart from looking on the internet, there's no visible presence on social media outlets at all, and she doesn't appear to have an email account. She didn't make any online purchases and the laptop's hardly been used. There are no contacts listed, and basically it doesn't help us in any way.'

Such a disappointment was hardly out of the ordinary in a murder enquiry, yet Ian looked devastated. No one else appeared to register quite how wretched he looked, but Geraldine knew him well enough to realise that something was amiss. She tackled him about it after work, hurrying to catch up with him as he walked to the car park at the end of the day.

'Is everything all right?'

He paused and hesitated before turning to face her, his expression rigid. 'All right? I wouldn't say everything was all right, no.'

'I mean apart from the fact that we don't seem to be getting anywhere with the case. I wouldn't have asked,' she added quickly, 'only you seem so down.'

'Is it that obvious?'

'Only to someone who knows you as well as I do.'

Ian's face contorted for an instant, as though he was struggling to keep his emotions in check.

'Bev called.'

'What did she want?'

'She wants me to take her back. She said she's prepared to give our marriage a second chance.'

'A second chance?' Geraldine echoed stupidly. 'What about the man she ran off with? The baby's father?'

'They split up. I don't know why. All she said was that it didn't work out between them.'

Geraldine felt a fleeting pang of sympathy for Ian's ex-wife, but her main concern was for him.

'Do you want her back?'

'After the way she behaved?'

'What do you want to happen with her?'

'What do I want?' he repeated. 'I don't want anything from her. She left me. Why would I take her back?'

Geraldine shrugged. 'You loved her once, enough to want to ask her to marry you.'

'And in a way I suppose my feelings for her haven't changed. But even if I do still love her, how can I ever trust her again?'

His last sentence sounded like a cry for help. Geraldine wished there was something she could say that would make him feel better. She spent so much of her working life offering words of comfort to the bereaved, complete strangers with whom she shared nothing more than a bond of common humanity. Now, witnessing the sorrow of a friend she loved more than anyone else she knew, she struggled to find the right words.

'Relationships take constant work –' she began.

Ian interrupted her. 'Spare me your platitudes.'

Geraldine hesitated, trying to think of something to say that would help him.

'It's hard,' was all she could come up with.

It sounded pathetic.

She tried again. 'I wish there was something I could do…'

'Well, there isn't. There's nothing anyone can do to make this situation any better.'

'Ian,' she spoke firmly. 'You know I'll help you if I can, but you need to decide what you want to do.'

'I know what I want. I want my wife back, but not the woman who cheated on me for God knows how long. Can you turn the clock back? I want the woman I married, the woman who –'

'Ian, she's asking you to take her back. If you can forgive her, maybe you *can* go back. She's offering you that chance. But you need to be sure that's really what you want.'

'I don't want her back.' He spoke very slowly, as though the words were being torn out of him against his will. 'I thought she was happily settled in a new life with a man who could make her happy, a man who could give her the life she wanted. Yes, it was hard to accept that I wasn't that man. I could never be who she wanted me to be, not unless I gave up being who I am. But I was resigned to losing her. Only now she's not happy and I don't know what to do.' He turned to look at Geraldine. 'What do you think? Do you think I should take her back?'

'You're the only one who can make that decision.'

He shook his head.

'You can only try again if you really want to. You were happy together once –'

'Were we?' he interrupted her again. 'Were we ever happy together?'

Geraldine remembered how he used to grumble that his wife

constantly complained that he was married to his job. Living with a police officer didn't suit everyone.

'The trouble is, she's on her own now and I don't know what to do. Help me out, here, Geraldine. I feel as though I'm drowning.'

'You can't take her back just because you feel sorry for her,' Geraldine said quietly. 'That's not a good idea. What if you meet someone else?'

'What if I already have?' he replied so softly she nearly missed his words.

Geraldine remembered how Naomi followed Ian around and nodded.

'Well,' she said briskly, 'it's up to you. I'm off home. See you tomorrow.'

Afraid her dismay might show in her face, she turned and hurried to her car.

54

THE NEXT MORNING THEY received a message to say that Lindsey had left the house. A constable had followed her to Sainsbury's and was waiting outside the store for her to come out. Geraldine drove straight there. Instructing the constable to stay at the exit in case Lindsey left before Geraldine found her, she went into the store. If the constable hadn't warned her that Lindsey was wearing a blue head scarf, Geraldine might have missed her. As it was, she spotted her, partly because she was so tall. She watched her as far as the tills and then slipped outside to wait for her. Despite Lindsey's protestations to the contrary, if there was still the faintest chance she might be going to see Jamie they had to keep tailing her. When Lindsey left the store on foot Geraldine decided to follow her, even though there didn't seem to be much point. With just one carrier bag that looked half empty, Lindsey set off in the direction of her home but instead of going straight there she walked down into town. Geraldine hung back before following her.

If Lindsey had glanced back even once, she might have spotted Geraldine behind her, but she never looked round. That alone suggested she was innocent of any wrongdoing. Nevertheless, Geraldine followed her all the way to a lingerie store. After half an hour Lindsey emerged from the shop and went home. Leaving a constable watching the house, Geraldine went back to the shop Lindsey had visited. A neatly dressed middle-aged shop assistant approached her.

'I'm not here to make a purchase,' Geraldine said, gazing

around at the elegant lacy lingerie. 'Although it all looks very nice,' she added politely.

'What can I help you with then?'

'A lady left here a short while ago. She's tall, with very long dark hair, and she was wearing a long coat.'

'Oh yes, I know who you mean. How can I help you?'

'Is she a regular customer?'

'Regular?'

'Has she been in here before?'

The woman screwed up her face. 'I really couldn't say.'

Geraldine paused. She wasn't quite sure what she was doing there. The shop assistant wasn't going to be able to tell her anything about Lindsey but, before she could leave, the woman detained her.

'Can I interest you in our sale items?'

'Thank you, but no. I'm not looking to make a purchase today.'

A young girl standing behind the counter had overheard their exchange.

'I've seen her in here before,' she called out as Geraldine walked towards the door.

Geraldine looked round. 'Are you sure?'

The older woman frowned but the girl nodded. 'She's hardly the sort of person you can forget, is she?'

Geraldine considered. 'Do you mean because she's tall?'

The girl paused, considering. 'It's more because of her make-up. I notice these things because we have to be careful when customers are trying things on.'

The older woman nodded. 'Yes, that's true. But who are you and what exactly are you doing here?'

Geraldine identified herself and explained that the woman she was enquiring about might be able to assist the police with an investigation.

'Well, there is something else,' the young assistant said.

'Go on.'

'I don't know. She's –' The girl paused, seemingly uncertain whether to continue. 'She's very particular about trying on bras,' she said at last.

'Particular in what way?'

'She refuses to be measured.'

'Is that unusual?'

'It's not unheard of, but slightly unusual, yes, I'd say so. I mean, why wouldn't you want a bra that fits well? But then, some women are very shy about being fitted.'

The older woman interrupted sharply. 'Our customers' preferences are not something we talk about.' She lowered her voice. 'She may have had a mastectomy. Women can be embarrassed about things like that, although I don't know why they would mind in here. We're very discreet and it's not something to be ashamed of. But in any case –'

Geraldine took a step towards the other two women. 'Did she ever mention a man called Jamie?'

The shop assistants looked at one another.

'No,' the older woman replied.

'Or say anything about a man she was living with?'

'No,' the woman said, more firmly. 'We don't gossip here.'

'She never said anything to me apart from asking about our stock,' the younger woman confirmed.

Geraldine thanked them and left. There had been no real point in her questioning the women in the shop, but she wanted to speak to everyone who had been in contact with Lindsey, in case they could pass on any information. So far no one had given her anything.

Checking with the surveillance team, Geraldine found out that Lindsey was still at home. There was no sign of Jamie. Having wasted the best part of the day on a pointless chase, Geraldine went back to the office.

'You'd think she'd want to help us,' Ariadne said. 'What if he turns up again. She could be in danger. She could be next.'

'I don't think she ever met him, and there's no reason why

he would return to that house. It was a false lead,' Ian replied.

'Let's hope so for her sake.'

'Well, we're keeping a watch on the house, but we can't keep that up forever,' Geraldine added.

'Let's hope we find him soon. If we don't, you're right, Lindsey might end up as his next victim,' Ian said.

'Anyone could,' Geraldine agreed miserably. 'He doesn't seem to have been very choosy about who he's killed so far.'

The media had already picked up on the fact that a serial killer had claimed three victims in the past month. It was difficult for the police to continue sending out positive messages to reassure the public when they were being criticised for incompetence. What made the situation worse was that the reporters were right. The police had found nothing to connect the three victims, and they had no idea where the killer was. For all they knew, he might be preparing to claim his next victim while they were casting around helplessly for a lead.

That evening Geraldine and Ariadne had arranged to go out for a curry. The investigation was wearing everyone down and they were both subdued. By tacit agreement they did their best to avoid talking about work, turning instead to personal matters.

'How come you're still single?' Geraldine enquired, 'If you don't mind my asking.'

'No, that's fine,' Ariadne responded with an easy smile. 'I guess I've just never met the right man. I mean, I've had boyfriends, quite a few actually, back in the day.' She laughed.

Geraldine could believe that. With lively dark eyes and clear skin, Ariadne seemed to glow with health and a quiet confidence that made her very attractive.

'Back in the day?' Geraldine echoed, with a smile.

'Maybe that was part of the problem,' Ariadne added. 'I was spoilt for choice really, so I couldn't decide who to settle for.'

'It does sound as though you haven't met the right man yet. If you had, you wouldn't be talking about settling for someone, as though you had to choose the least bad option.'

'Yet?' Ariadne repeated. 'I'll be thirty-eight soon.'

'So?'

'So I need to get a move on if I'm going to have a family.'

'Meeting someone doesn't mean you have to have children.'

Ariadne laughed. 'If you had a Greek mother, you wouldn't say that.'

It was a relief to sit and chat for a while as though they hadn't a care in the world, but it wasn't long before they were drawn back to the case.

'I just can't help thinking he might still be around here in York somewhere,' Geraldine said. 'It doesn't seem possible he would have escaped attention if he'd travelled anywhere in the country.'

'Unless he's gone off the beaten track where no one can possibly see him.'

Geraldine frowned. 'We're missing something.'

'What do you mean?'

'If you were a man and you wanted to hide, where would you go to be sure no one would ever find you?'

'I don't know,' Ariadne replied with a half-smile. 'If I knew that, I might be able to find him.'

'Exactly,' Geraldine said. 'We're missing something.'

'I don't know what you mean.'

Geraldine sighed. She couldn't explain her feeling that they were overlooking an obvious lead.

55

EVERYWHERE HE LOOKED, HE came across accounts of himself. The media had discovered where he grew up, and where he went to school, and seemed to take great delight in describing his victims' injuries in minute detail. If he hadn't known better, he would have thought the violence of his attacks on them had been exaggerated. Journalists often embellished the truth in an attempt to sell more papers. But every gruesome detail they reported was true. He knew that better than anyone.

A reporter had taken the trouble to visit the Yorkshire village where he had been born and brought up, and had taken photos of his old school, and the village church. Jamie had never met the local vicar, but that didn't deter a journalist from questioning him and reporting the whole ensuing dull conversation. The landlord of the village pub claimed to remember Jamie drinking there regularly as a young man, even though Jamie could count on the fingers of one hand the number of times he had set foot in there. Another journalist had spoken to his junior school teacher, who remembered him as a 'troubled child'.

They had tracked down his father who had refused to answer any questions. That was typical. His father had never been willing to open his mouth to anyone. He had admitted to a reporter only that he had spoken to the police and told them everything he knew about his son. As if that was going to help them. Jamie laughed. His father had thought he was dead. That wasn't going to help anyone.

The local news was full of articles about him and his exploits.

He could hardly turn the television on without seeing artists' impressions of his face, or out-of-date images that reporters had dredged up from somewhere. One of his parents' neighbours had been quoted in several papers, talking about how she had always suspected there was something psychologically wrong with him. In reality, the old bitch had barely even spoken to him. He didn't care about their tittle tattle. People could make up as many insulting stories about him as they liked. If it brightened up their pathetic and boring lives, good luck to them. Far from finding the lies galling, he was amused.

'He never actually attacked anyone physically,' a former classmate at school was quoted as saying, on one of the news channels, 'but there were certainly times when he made us all feel very uncomfortable. That's why we stopped having anything to do with him. Everyone used to avoid him when he lived around here. But I don't think any of us had any idea what he was capable of. Now he's left the neighbourhood I feel a lot safer, and I'll feel even better when they put him behind bars, where he belongs. If he ever shows his face around here again, they'll lock him up in prison, which is where he deserves to be. He's worse than an animal.'

There was a lot more along those lines, most of it from people claiming to have known what he was really like before he moved to York, which was all lies because no one had really known him back then. For three days, the phone had hardly stopped ringing, with reporters calling to find out if he had returned to the house in York that he had rented for a while. Lindsey had steadfastly refused to meet any of them in person. After a while she had tired of the constant barrage of questions and refused to talk to them anymore, until they had more or less given up phoning her.

'I've told you I don't know anyone called Jamie,' she had insisted.

That wasn't entirely true, but in the end the reporters had believed her.

Only one journalist had persisted in trying to contact her. Desperate for a scoop, he had even followed her when she left the house, and tried to question her as she walked to the shops. She was wearing dark glasses in an attempt to hide her identity so only someone who had seen her leaving the house would have known who she was. She had been forced to threaten to complain to his editor, and report him to the police, before he finally left her alone.

But for all their pestering, no one from the police or the media had picked up any information about where he was hiding. He had never for one moment feared that they would. Lindsey was the only person who had any idea where he was, and she was never going to give him away. All he had to do was stay off the radar and wait for the hunt to die down. The police were tenacious bastards, but even they would be forced to give up in the end. Once that happened, the coast would be clear for him to reappear. He would have to change his name, but that wasn't difficult. He'd done it before. In the meantime, he intended to remain out of sight. As long as Lindsey kept her mouth shut, that wouldn't be a problem. And he knew she wouldn't blab.

The police were never going to find him because he had the perfect hiding place. Thinking about the police running around, asking questions, checking details, and holding earnest meetings about where to look for him, made him laugh. The situation was priceless. He had outsmarted everyone. Most amusing of all were the bold statements the police persisted in issuing. 'We are following several leads,' they said, and, 'A man is helping us with our enquiries'. He could have revealed that those claims were no more than wishful thinking. They had even announced that they expected to make an arrest soon, implying they knew where he was. Each expression of confidence only served to further expose their ignorance of his identity. The truth was they were as close to making an arrest as they were to landing on the moon.

He did his best to remain composed, but couldn't stop laughter bubbling up from somewhere deep inside his chest. It spread across his shoulders and up into his throat until his whole body shook with it. Finally, unable to control himself, he had to sit down because he was laughing so hard. He laughed until his eyes watered and his stomach hurt and he was gasping for breath. The police had not only got hold of the wrong end of the stick, they were grasping at the wrong stick.

56

ON HER WAY HOME after the meal that evening, Geraldine decided to make one last attempt to speak to Lindsey on the off chance that she would see sense and agree to share some information that might help them. Even if she knew nothing about Jamie herself, it was just possible she had seen a testimonial from the previous tenant, or found a business card he had left behind. Any small snippet of intelligence might provide them with a much needed lead.

Once again, no one answered when she rang the bell, so after standing on the doorstep for about five minutes, she went home. There was nothing more she could do but wait, along with the rest of the team investigating the recent murders. The surveillance on Lindsey had stopped now that the house had been searched. It certainly appeared that Jamie was still alive and had been to the house in the past few weeks, before the DNA on the door frame had time to deteriorate in the rain and air, but they had no idea where he was now. It also appeared that Edward Drury had lied about Jamie having died overseas, but there was nothing they could do about it. He remained adamant that he believed his son was dead. In the meantime, a nationwide hunt for Jamie had been put in place and the local police could only press on with their DNA testing, sit it out, and hope to find their suspect soon.

Geraldine had a missed call from Celia that evening. By the time she reached home she thought it was too late to phone her back, but Celia called again, agog with the news she had seen about the hunt for the killer.

'That's the case you're working on, isn't it?'

Geraldine admitted it was. 'But the investigation has moved way beyond York,' she added. 'We don't even know if he's still in the area. He could be anywhere.'

'What? You mean he could be here?'

Geraldine laughed. 'Don't worry. I don't think he would have gone all the way to Kent.'

'But he could have. You just told me you don't know where he is. You said he could be anywhere.'

'Don't start imagining things. He couldn't have travelled all that way without being spotted. The chances are he's almost certainly hiding out somewhere near York. Don't forget we've got the whole of the police force out looking for him. The further he travels, the more he exposes himself to being spotted, and that makes him very vulnerable.'

'I don't think *he's* the vulnerable one,' Celia muttered.

'Well, you really don't need to worry. He was operating in York and he can't go far from here without being caught. You're perfectly safe.'

'What about you? I don't understand why you keep on with your job. You're getting too old for all that action and danger and stupid heroics. Why on earth you don't apply for a move to a desk job? Really, I mean it. You could quite easily get another promotion after all your hard work and dedication. What more do they want?'

Geraldine felt uncomfortable at being reminded that her sister still didn't know she had been demoted as a consequence of her action to protect her identical twin. In fact, she hadn't even mentioned to Celia that she had discovered the existence of her birth twin. At first she had been reluctant to risk upsetting Celia while she was pregnant but it was hard to see how she could share the news now, after so much time had passed since she had first learned of Helena's existence. So she continued to hide the truth.

'He could be anywhere,' Celia pointed out. 'You said so

yourself. And you should know. You're on the team who are supposed to be finding him.'

It took Geraldine a while to convince her sister that neither of them was about to be murdered in their beds. She rang off feeling emotionally drained. But Celia was right. As long as Jamie remained at large, he would continue to pose a threat to the public.

The following morning she called on Lindsey again on her way into work and this time the door opened, on the chain.

'Oh, it's you,' Lindsey said.

'Can I come in?'

'Clearly you won't stop pestering me until you do,' Lindsey replied, pushing the door closed so she could remove the chain.

Geraldine entered the dimly lit hall. She was fairly tall, but Lindsey towered over her.

'I wanted to ask whether you've remembered finding anything one of the previous tenants left behind when you moved in. Anything at all.'

'Wouldn't the landlord have found it, if anything was left behind when someone moved out? Shouldn't you be asking him?'

'I meant a phone number or an address –' Geraldine said.

She felt foolish. Clues like that might figure in films and old-fashioned TV cop shows, but they never turned up in real life.

'No, I've already told you I didn't find anything. He must have taken everything with him when he went, and he's not coming back, so there's no point in you pestering me anymore.'

The words gave Geraldine a cold shiver. With a shock, she wondered whether her suspicions had been right. It might have been a slip of the tongue, but Lindsey had just told her Jamie wasn't going to return to the house, and she could only be sure of that if she was still in touch with him.

'How do you know?' Geraldine took a step towards the other woman, who was standing in shadow. 'How can you be so sure he's not coming back?'

She stared closely at Lindsey, who appeared uncomfortable under the scrutiny and turned away. When she looked back, her hair had fallen over her face, partly obscuring it. But she was too late. Geraldine had just realised why the photograph of Jamie's brother had looked familiar. Lindsey resembled Peter so closely, Geraldine suspected her theory had been right all along. Somehow Peter's sister and brother had both survived. Now calling herself Lindsey, the sister was protecting Jamie. The two of them might even be accomplices.

'I know you want to find this man,' Lindsey said, glaring at her from the shadows, 'but you know it has got nothing to do with me.'

'Well, never mind, it doesn't matter,' Geraldine lied. 'We just thought you might be able to pass on some information that could help us, that's all.'

'What information?'

Lindsey took a step forward into the light. In that instant, gazing into the other woman's unblinking black eyes, Geraldine understood.

'I can see this is wasting time for us both,' Geraldine said. 'You clearly don't know where Jamie is, so I'm sorry to have bothered you again, and now I'll leave you in peace.'

Lindsey's expression darkened and Geraldine saw that Lindsey knew she had glimpsed the truth. As Geraldine backed away, Lindsey stepped forward and grabbed her by both arms in a tight grip. For all her training, Geraldine couldn't break free.

'Lindsey,' Geraldine said, as calmly as she could, 'or should I call you Jamie?'

Her captor's grip tightened until it felt as though Geraldine's arms had been trapped in a metal vice.

'There's no point in trying to detain me,' Geraldine continued speaking in an even tone, although inwardly she was terrified. 'My colleagues know where I am and they'll be here any minute now. They're on their way already.'

If no one turned up, Jamie would realise that was a lie. Hopefully by then the police would have tracked Geraldine through her phone, and found her car parked outside in the street. Jamie's painted lips twisted in a snarl exposing a smear of red lipstick on his teeth, and close up Geraldine could see the rim of his contact lenses.

'You're not going to get away this time,' Jamie growled, no longer attempting to disguise his masculine voice. 'You've pestered me for long enough. It stops right now.'

'Think about what you're doing. You can't possibly get away with this.'

Jamie smiled. 'I already have. They're never going to find out what happened to you. And they won't ever know it was me, because it's Jamie's DNA they'll find on your body, and I'm Lindsey.' He laughed. 'That's been your problem all along. A complete lack of imagination. You're the only one to guess my secret, and you're not going to be telling anyone.'

'You can't kill a police officer here, in this house,' Geraldine protested, trying to control her panic. 'The forensic team are bound to find out what happened. They'll know I was here.'

'Your DNA is already all over the house. No one will ever know you came back here.'

'With my car outside and my phone in my pocket?'

'Do you think I'm an idiot? Do you really think I'm going to leave your car outside, and not get rid of your phone when I move your car? You think you're so clever, but you're the one who's been outmanoeuvred. And they haven't caught me yet, have they?'

'You haven't attacked a police officer until now,' Geraldine replied.

Seizing the opportunity while Jamie hesitated, Geraldine wrenched her arms free from her captor's grasp and darted out of reach, but Jamie dashed after her and caught her from behind as they reached the bottom of the stairs. With Jamie's arm around her neck Geraldine struggled for breath, and a wave of weariness sapped the energy from her limbs. It seemed to start at her feet which she could no longer control, and sweep upwards and into her brain. As her legs gave way, she heard Jamie berating her for causing him so much trouble.

'You won't get away with it this time,' Geraldine gasped.

She tried to continue, but she could barely breathe. She felt her windpipe being crushed as Jamie replied.

'Watch me! Oh no, of course you won't be able to, will you, because you'll be dead.'

His laughter echoed in her head as she lost consciousness.

57

'WHERE'S GERALDINE?' EILEEN DEMANDED, glaring at Ian. 'You know her better than anyone,' she added in a milder tone. 'Has she gone off on one of her harebrained schemes?'

'I've worked with her before,' he replied slowly, wondering what Geraldine had got herself into now. 'But I've no idea where she is right now. I didn't even know she'd gone out.'

Eileen scowled. 'It seems she never turned up here this morning. What's she playing at?'

Ian shook his head. 'I don't know where she is.'

'Get hold of her, Ian, and tell her I want her in my office, now.'

'I don't understand,' he replied. 'Geraldine would never fail to turn up. It's just not something she would do. She lives for her work –'

'And yet we're at work, and she's not here, and no word of explanation.'

'Something must be wrong,' Ian replied, frowning.

'Well, send a constable round to her flat,' Eileen said. 'Only she's not answering her phone and it would appear she's still asleep, at eleven in the morning –'

'That's not possible.'

'Perhaps she's not well then. Whatever's going on, I need to know, now.'

'OK, I'll look into it.'

Leaving Eileen's office, Ian tried Geraldine's phone but it went straight to voicemail. Leaving a message, he ran out to his car and set off for her flat. On the face of it, that was hardly a task for an inspector, but he didn't care. He knew Geraldine, and if she hadn't turned up for work, there was a reason. He put his foot down.

There was no response when he rang Geraldine's bell. He banged on the door but still there was no answer. He tried her phone again, but it went to voicemail. With no way of knowing whether she had gone out, or was inside and unconscious, he hammered on the door but all was silent. Carefully he fiddled with the security lock on her door and eventually it opened. He ran inside and searched the flat. There was no sign of Geraldine. He couldn't find her iPad, which suggested she was out working, so he tried her phone one last time. Still there was no answer. With growing anxiety, he returned to the police station. He didn't know what else to do.

'No sign of her at all?' the detective chief inspector said, when Ian told her what had happened.

'She wasn't there.'

'Well, I need to see her when she turns up,' Eileen replied. 'If she's still not back in tomorrow, we'll initiate a thorough search. Wherever she is, she has no business going off like that without letting anyone know where she's gone.'

Ian didn't tell Eileen that he wasn't prepared to wait that long. He knew Geraldine would never disappear without a word. Apart from anything else, she would realise he would worry about her. As he began checking through the drawers of her desk, he saw Ariadne gaping at him.

'What are you doing? Are you looking through her –'

'Do you have any idea where she's gone?' Ian interrupted her.

'No. Where?'

'That's what I'm trying to find out.'

'You're saying you want to know where she is?'

'Yes, exactly. So do you know where she's gone or don't you?'

Ariadne sounded annoyed. 'Why don't you call her and ask?'

There was nothing to be gained from concealing the truth. If Ian was overreacting, he would deal with the flak once Geraldine reappeared. He didn't care that he might be scoffed at for fussing; he couldn't bear to contemplate how he would feel if Geraldine had met with an accident and he had done nothing to help her.

'I don't know where she is,' he admitted. 'She seems to have disappeared.'

Ariadne's eyes widened. 'She can't have disappeared,' she said. 'Do you think she's ill?'

Quickly Ian told her that Geraldine's flat was empty and she wasn't answering her phone. They stared at one another in dismay. Ariadne might not have known Geraldine very long, but she knew her well enough to realise that something was seriously amiss.

Ian went through all of Geraldine's records, searching for clues to where she might have gone. Meanwhile, Ariadne contacted Geraldine's sister and twin to find out when they had last seen her. She was careful to avoid letting slip that Geraldine was missing. All the same, Celia was instantly concerned.

'What's happened to her? Something's happened, hasn't it?'

It had clearly been a mistake to make the call, and it required all of Ariadne's ingenuity to reassure Celia that Geraldine was fine. She didn't actually know that was true, but until they knew what had happened, there was no need to worry her sister. After Celia's reaction, Ariadne was reluctant to disturb Helena as well. She checked with Ian before she called Geraldine's twin, but he was adamant they had to try everything. Ariadne worded her enquiry as carefully as she could.

'Geraldine?' Helena replied. 'I haven't heard from her for a while.'

'Has she been in touch with you at all in the past day or two?'

'No. But don't worry, she'll be OK,' Helena replied carelessly. 'Don't tell me my responsible sister has gone AWOL?'

'We just need to find her. Do you have any idea where she might be?' Ariadne asked.

It was difficult to persuade Helena to take her enquiry seriously, while avoiding worrying her.

'I told you, I've no idea where she is. She never tells me anything. And if she did tell me what she was up to, why would I tell you?'

Having set up a search for Geraldine's car, Ian returned to his desk and tried to focus on his own work, but he couldn't think about anything else. Before long, a report came in that a patrol car had spotted Geraldine's vehicle parked in a side street near the hospital. What was of particular concern was that the car had been easily located because Geraldine's phone was in the glove compartment. Ian wasn't sure whether to feel relieved that the hospital had no record of Geraldine turning up there.

'I wonder if she was going to try and see Lindsey again,' Ian said. 'She did seem convinced that Lindsey knew more than she was letting on.'

'But why wouldn't she have recorded the visit?' Ariadne asked.

'I don't know.'

'Maybe she forgot.'

'Geraldine never forgets anything. And she's too experienced to have done anything that might put her at risk without calling for backup first,' he added, speaking more to himself than to Ariadne.

'Well, it's hardly risky if that's where she's gone, because Lindsey didn't even know the killer,' Ariadne replied.

With no other ideas, and nothing to lose, Ian decided to speak to Lindsey. Taking Ariadne with him, he drove straight there. Neither of them spoke as they sat side by side in the car, or when they approached the front door. No one answered when Ian rang the bell and knocked, so he walked along the front of the house, peering in through the windows. There was no sign of movement inside the house. All they could do was wait for Lindsey to return home, so they agreed to go back to the car and watch the house. Meanwhile, time was passing and there was no word from Geraldine.

Having spent most of the day looking for Geraldine, Ian offered to drive Ariadne back to the police station to pick up her car so she could go home.

'I'll stay here,' she replied tersely.

Her response told him she was as concerned about Geraldine as he was. He desperately wanted someone to tell him he was worrying unnecessarily, but he knew that Geraldine would never have disappeared like that if there was nothing wrong. He rang the bell one last time. As he was about to turn and walk down the path back to the car, the front door swung open and Ian was surprised to see a woman's face, heavily made up, peering out at him. Black eyes glittered at him, cold with suspicion.

'What do you want?'

Ian held up his identity card and introduced himself. The woman shook her head. She was tall and striking, with long dark hair and strong features.

'Oh for goodness sake, there's already been a whole team of police officers here, searching the house. What are you after now? Listen, Inspector, of course I'd help you if I could, but I really don't think there's anything more I can tell you. What is it you wanted to know anyway?'

Her assurances of interest were encouraging. So often members of the public reacted with varying degrees of hostility on seeing Ian's identity card. He had expected her to slam the door in his face.

He answered her question with one of his own. 'Is one of my colleagues here, by any chance?'

'What's this about? I told you –'

'We're looking for a colleague of ours,' Ariadne interrupted her. 'I don't suppose you've seen her? She's got short black hair –'

'What makes you think I would have seen her?'

'We know she wanted to speak to you, and we thought she might have come here. We were hoping you might be able to tell us where she's gone.' Ariadne forced a smile.

Lindsey frowned. 'Why don't you phone her?'

'We can't get hold of her,' Ariadne replied.

'Do you mean she's disappeared?'

'No,' Ian replied quickly. 'But we don't know where she is right now.'

'What's all this got to do with me?'

'We're speaking to everyone she's been in contact with recently,' Ian said. 'This is just routine.'

That was partly true. They had already called Geraldine's sister and her twin, and Lindsey wasn't the only other person they wanted to speak to. But it was hardly a routine enquiry.

'You live here, don't you? And we were under the impression she was coming to see you. So we thought you might know where she is.'

'I'm sorry, but no one's been here from the police since all that fuss last week when your officers were crawling all over the house looking for God knows what. But if this colleague of yours turns up I'll tell her you were looking for her, shall I?'

'Please tell her to call us the minute she appears,' Ian said.

The woman nodded, then turned and went inside, closing the door behind her.

'You don't think Geraldine could be in there, do you?' Ian asked softly, turning to Ariadne.

She shrugged. There was nothing to suggest that was the case. They needed something more than vague supposition before they could go storming into the house again.

58

GERALDINE LAY IN DARKNESS, aching and confused, and the memory of Jamie's assault came back to her in shreds, like snatches of a dream. Finally her mind cleared but when she tried to stand up she had to acknowledge this was no nightmare she could wake from. Her ankles were tied together and so were her wrists. Every time she moved, an agonising pain stabbed at her neck and spread across her shoulders. Knowing she had been trapped by a serial killer, her mind seemed frozen in terror. All she could picture was his eyes, inhuman behind their dark lenses. But she wasn't dead. Fighting her fear, she clung to that thought. She wasn't dead. Jamie must be keeping her alive for a purpose. Perhaps he was planning to use her as a hostage, or else he intended to exact some terrible revenge on her for bringing the police into his house. Whatever his reasons for preserving her life, she had to escape before he returned.

Attempting to rotate her head gently to loosen the stiffness, she cried out in pain, and realised she must have been lying unconscious in one position for hours. Any movement was painful. Afraid she might seize up completely if she remained immobile for much longer she forced herself to push her head from side to side, gently at first, but with increasing force. Having loosened her neck muscles until she could move her shoulders and upper arms, she rotated her ankles for a while before finally struggling to her feet. Once she was standing up, she began thinking more clearly. Jamie wouldn't be expecting a counter attack, which gave Geraldine a chance to take him by surprise. But to catch him off guard, she had to be ready to pounce as soon as the door opened. With both her wrists and ankles bound, that was going to be difficult, if not impossible. For a long time she stood leaning against the wall, swinging her head around until she felt dizzy, and stamping her feet gently to stop them from going numb.

Finally she thought she heard footsteps. Shuffling over to the door and pressing her ear against it, she heard the footsteps grow fainter and guessed Jamie was going downstairs. Afraid he was going to go away and leave her there, she banged on the door with her elbow.

'Come back!' she shouted. 'Open this door! We need to talk! I can help you!'

The footsteps didn't return. Controlling her panic, Geraldine told herself that she wasn't alone. By now her absence must have been noticed, and her colleagues would be searching for her. Ian knew she had been investigating Lindsey. It was only a matter of time before the police turned up at the house. But Janie might return before that and, when he did, she would have to be ready. She breathed slowly to conserve her energy, and tried to work out a plan. But with her wrists and ankles tied together, it was going to be impossible to resist an attack. Defeated, she slumped back on the floor, listening to her sister's voice inside her head: 'I don't understand why you keep on with that job. You're getting too old for all that action and danger and stupid heroics.'

Celia was right. It was time to give up her job. Facing a choice between carrying on as she was or leaving the force, right now she wasn't sure she even wanted to continue. But there was no point in worrying about a future that might never happen. With an effort, she turned her attention back to her immediate situation. It wasn't easy feeling her way around in the darkness but she pressed her arm against the wall and shuffled forwards until she found the door. Taking up a position behind it she waited, still working to loosen the bonds on her wrists. She was thankful that Jamie hadn't found the handcuffs in her bag. As it was, he had merely tied her wrists together with something like a scarf that was gradually working loose.

She twisted her hands with dogged determination, ignoring the smarting in her wrists until at last she was able to pull one hand free. For a moment she stood, slumped against the wall, rubbing her chafed wrists. Reaching out, she felt for the door handle and wasn't surprised to find it locked. She couldn't afford to stand around waiting and doing nothing. She set to work on her ankles and before long she was free of her shackles. If she could only subdue him, Jamie would soon be behind bars where he belonged. Of course there was a risk involved in attacking him, but she wasn't afraid. Admittedly he was strong, but she had trained for years to deal with a situation like this.

It wasn't just that she thought she would be able to overpower her captor. If she failed to control the situation and was injured or killed in the struggle, she would still have won. Having assaulted a police officer, Jamie would never kill anyone else. Frantically she flexed and relaxed her hands, and rotated her feet, to restore her mobility. Without her handcuffs, she had to find another way of securing Jamie once she had subdued him. Looking around quickly, she selected a chain belt from a pile of clothes on the bed, and leaned back against the wall behind the door, listening out for his return.

The danger that threatened her kept her alert for the sounds of his approach, but he must have been walking silently because she heard nothing until the door handle turned. If he had flung the door open she might have been taken by surprise. As it was, the door seemed to open in slow motion as she tensed to pounce, clutching the belt.

Jamie took a step into the room.

Under other circumstances, Geraldine might have been tempted to grab her adversary by the hair, but he was wearing a wig. His head turned, searching for her. Before he could look over his shoulder, Geraldine sprang. Her forearm was round his neck before he had a chance to react. His arms flailed helplessly, but he put up little resistance. This time it was her grip that proved too strong to resist. She was tempted to squeeze so hard that he couldn't breathe. In addition to stopping his killing, she could so easily end his life. It was only what he had planned for her, and perhaps many others.

No one would call her to account for murder. This was justifiable self defence. Only she would know it had been an execution. A feeling of power coursed through her, like a bolt of electricity. She drew in a deep shuddering breath as she twisted his arm up behind his back. It was time to relax her hold on his throat and allow him to breathe, but her arm seemed to act outside of her control. Tears coursed down her cheeks as she listened to his gasps grow faint, and watched his arms become limp, but she didn't loosen her grip.

59

IAN AND ARIADNE WALKED back to the car in silence. He had been so sure they were going to find Geraldine at Lindsey's house that, although he should have been relieved, he felt curiously deflated. He had intended to chastise her for going off like that without having first logged her decision, and had even prepared what he was going to say when he saw her. Expecting her to request permission for her actions like any normal officer was clearly out of the question where Geraldine was concerned. She was in danger of becoming a complete maverick, and difficult to work with as a result. It might be just about possible for her independent activity to be overlooked when her instincts led her to discover a new lead, but running around off the radar, worrying everyone and wasting her colleagues' time for no good reason was unacceptable. Unless he kept a very close eye on her in future, she was going to end up in serious trouble.

He should have known better than to have been so generous with his praise when Eileen had asked him about Geraldine. When he had worked with her before, she had been heading for promotion. Only now did he realise that an officer who had been demoted had thrown away any hope of advancement, and was in a very different place to someone who was keen to further their career. There was no longer any reason for her to exercise restraint.

Feeling thoroughly irritated, he pulled away from the kerb and put his foot down. Geraldine wasn't going to enjoy being castigated by him, but he was her superior officer and responsible for her safety. The fact that she had been his inspector when he had still been a sergeant was beside the point. He was the inspector now, and he had to conduct himself accordingly. As soon as Geraldine returned to the police station, he was going to give her a dressing down, friend or no friend.

Ariadne broke the silence. 'I wonder what her car was doing so near the hospital?' she asked. 'We know she hadn't been to the mortuary. And in any case, she would have left it in the hospital car park if she was going there. So where *was* she going and why has she left her car there for so long?'

'What the hell is she playing at?' Ian burst out, giving up any attempt to conceal his irritation. 'You work with her, don't you? Didn't she say anything at all to you that might help us work out where she's gone?'

'All she said was, "If you were a man and you wanted to hide, where would you go to be sure no one would ever find you?" Something along those lines anyway. I had the impression she thought she was on to something, but I don't remember her saying anything else.'

'What do you suppose she meant by that?' Ian asked. 'If you were a man…'

'If you were a man and you wanted to hide, where might you go to be sure no one would ever find you?' Ariadne repeated.

'If you were a man?' Ian frowned. 'As opposed to what?'

He braked suddenly and turned to give Ariadne a hard stare. 'Lindsey doesn't have fair hair and blue eyes, does she?'

Ariadne frowned. 'No, dark eyes and dark hair.'

'But she could be wearing a wig.'

'And dark contact lenses,' Ariadne added slowly, catching his drift. 'Lindsey's tall, isn't she? For a woman.'

As Ian spun the wheel, Ariadne was on her phone.

'We need to know if she drove her car there herself,' Ian heard her say. 'There's no time to explain. Just see if you can find any record of it. And we need backup urgently.' She gave Lindsey's address. Ringing off she turned to Ian. 'Should I tell

Eileen what's going on? I've asked for backup.'

Ian grunted. If they were wrong, he was going to look like a fool for overreacting to a colleague being out of contact for a day, but he didn't care.

'Call her now. Tell her we have a potential hostage situation.'

'Do you really think it's that serious?'

'I'm looking at best case scenario.'

Once Ariadne had spoken to Eileen and explained what was going on, they drove the rest of the way without speaking. Daylight was already beginning to fade by the time they drew up outside Lindsey's house. As they stepped on to the pavement they heard sirens, and seconds later several police cars raced into the street. Before Ian had even reached the gate, Eileen leapt out of a police vehicle and snapped at him to move back. By now more officers had arrived. They moved swiftly into place, while a cordon was set up to stop members of the public approaching. A helicopter roared overhead and circled, sweeping the street with a bright light. Within minutes the house was surrounded. The helicopter wheeled away and a voice rang out through a megaphone, speaking with a reassuring air of calm authority. Ian felt as though the whole of his life hung on the outcome of that one moment. Past and future faded into insignificance. All that mattered was to save Geraldine's life.

'Jamie, we know you're in there,' the negotiator called out. 'Please, come out and talk to us.' There was a brief pause. 'We just want to talk to you. Come out now, please.'

The officers waited silently. It seemed to Ian that time itself had stopped while they waited for a response from inside the house. Just when it seemed certain that Jamie wasn't willing to cooperate, the front door opened. A lone figure emerged and hobbled slowly down the path. Ian struggled to restrain himself from running forward as they watched Geraldine halt at the gate and gaze around with a bewildered expression.

'What's happening?' she cried out. 'What are you all doing here?'

'Looking for you,' Ian replied, stepping forward.

'How did you know I was here?'

'Where's Jamie?' Eileen asked.

Geraldine gave a lopsided smile. 'He's upstairs.'

At a nod from Eileen, two uniformed officers dashed past Geraldine and ran into the house.

'There's no need to rush,' Geraldine called after them. 'He's not going anywhere.'

As she walked out into the street, in the light from a street lamp Ian saw that her neck was bruised, and she had red marks on the backs of her hands where something had rubbed her skin raw.

'You look as though someone tried to throttle you,' he said, joining her.

Geraldine raised her hands and pulled back her sleeves to show weals on her wrists.

'Throttled and tied up,' she said calmly.

'Are you all right?' he asked.

Looking closely at her, he could see her bottom lip tremble very slightly. Before she could answer, he heard a disturbance and turned to see Jamie being dragged from the house. His long wig was askew and his heavy eye make-up was smudged.

'This is an outrage!' he shouted. 'This is harassment! I'll sue you for this! Police brutality! Help!'

Still protesting, he was led to a police car and driven away. The other police vehicles followed and the roar of the helicopter faded as it flew off.

'I'm okay,' Geraldine said. 'In fact, better than okay.' She held up her arms again to display her discoloured wrists. 'There's no way he's walking away from all this now.'

She smiled, and Ian resisted the urge to hug her.

'We nailed him from his DNA. We didn't need you to get injured to secure a conviction.'

His words sounded far more churlish than he had intended,

but before he could say anything else, Eileen joined them. She was beaming.

'Are you all right, Geraldine?'

'Of course,' Geraldine answered, returning the detective chief inspector's smile. 'We've got him, haven't we?'

'*You* got him,' Eileen corrected her quietly.

They both knew that Eileen would reprimand her for going to see Jamie on her own, even though Geraldine had believed she was going to see Lindsey. They knew too that Eileen would take the credit for the success of the investigation. But in that moment, Eileen and Geraldine were just two women sharing their relief that they had been instrumental in apprehending a brutal killer.

60

WHEN THEY ARRIVED BACK at the police station, Eileen wasn't nearly as irate as Geraldine had expected.

'Well at least you're safe,' the detective chief inspector said. 'But what were you thinking of, going there on your own like that? With all your experience, you should have known better.'

Geraldine smarted at the criticism, not least because it was unjust. Her defence that Lindsey had never been a suspect fell on deaf ears.

'Well, I can't have officers gallivanting around on their own without telling anyone where they're going.'

That wasn't strictly true either, because Geraldine had made no secret of the fact that she had been trying to speak to Lindsey. Not only that, but she had left her car right outside the house so her colleagues would know where she was. Geraldine could hardly be blamed for failing to predict that Jamie would move her car. Still, now that they had apprehended the killer, Eileen seemed fairly relaxed about Geraldine's conduct, so she accepted the detective chief inspector's admonishment with good grace.

Jamie's wig and contact lenses had been removed when he was taken into custody, revealing his short and spiky fair hair. Stripped of his veil of dark hair the heavy black make-up around his pale blue eyes looked absurd. Geraldine stared at him across the interview table with a mixture of compassion and disgust. With blotchy make-up and bright red lipstick, he wouldn't have looked out of place in a troupe of circus clowns. Yet he remained defiant.

'Tell us what happened,' Geraldine said. 'You can speak freely here.'

Jamie's thin lawyer stirred in his seat. Poker-faced, he listened to the interview in silence. They all knew that whatever anyone said, none of it could make any difference to the outcome. Jamie's defence was immaterial. The evidence placing him at the crime scenes was indisputable, as was his attempted murder of Geraldine. But even with her sitting opposite him, he tried to bluff his way out of his predicament.

'I don't know what I'm doing here,' he blustered. 'It's not illegal for a man to dress how he likes. This is bigotry and harassment. You'll lose your jobs for this, if there's any justice in the —'

Geraldine cut him short. 'There is justice, of a kind, and it's going to put you behind bars for the rest of your life.'

Jamie's laughter sounded forced. 'Only in your dreams.'

'We know you attacked my colleague here.' As he spoke, Ian placed three photographs on the table in front of Jamie. 'And you also killed these three people.'

Geraldine listed the names for the tape.

Jamie shrugged. 'I don't know who those people are.'

He sounded bored, but his eyes darted restlessly around the room while his fingers on one hand tapped the back of his other hand in a silent tattoo. It gave Geraldine a flicker of satisfaction to know he was afraid.

'But you do recognise them as the victims of your attacks?' Ian asked.

'Whose attacks? You're putting words in my mouth.' He glanced at his lawyer. 'I don't know what you're talking about.'

Ian continued speaking in an even tone. 'I'm talking about the three people you killed.'

'Prove it! You're not going to pin this on me. You haven't got a shred of evidence.'

'The evidence is clear,' Ian said.

'What evidence? You're faking it. You'll never get away with this.'

'We found traces of your DNA on all three of the victims,' Ian told him.

After his vehement protestations of innocence, Jamie's capitulation was abrupt and unequivocal.

'Oh all right then, yes, it was me. You got me. Well done. I did it. It was me all along. Oh shut up,' he added, turning to his lawyer who had begun agitating for a break. 'Yes, I killed them. All of them. And I nearly got away with it too. My only mistake was not finishing you off when I had the chance,' he added, nodding at Geraldine.

'Did you know who they were when you stabbed them?' Geraldine asked.

'No. Does that matter?'

'Why would you kill people you didn't know?' she asked.

Jamie half turned in his seat to stare directly at her, his gaze unblinking, until his black pupils seemed to bore into her skull. 'Haven't you ever felt the urge to kill someone? Your arms round their neck, squeezing until they were gasping for breath? You understand what that feels like, don't you, Sergeant? Don't you?'

'I've never felt that without good reason.'

'Good reason?' Jamie repeated, picking up on her muttered comment. 'Good reason? There's always a good reason to kill someone.'

His eyes hadn't shifted from Geraldine. Holding her gaze, he seemed to be speaking to her alone.

'What reason can there be, other than self-defence?' she asked, beginning to feel uncomfortable.

'Oh, self-defence,' Jamie replied airily. 'Yes, there's always that excuse.'

'But you weren't acting in self-defence,' Ian said.

'Me? No, certainly not!' Jamie said. 'I was just doing what

felt right. I wanted to kill them. You know what I mean, don't you, Sergeant?'

As he threw his head back and laughed, Geraldine looked away from the bruising on his neck where she had almost throttled him to death.

'That's enough!' Ian cut in roughly. 'You're here to answer questions, not to ask them.'

'You said killing people felt right, but you haven't said why,' Geraldine went on, as though she and Jamie were the only people in the room. 'What drove you to do it, Jamie? Were you angry that you weren't allowed to live as a woman?'

'What?' Jamie's painted eyebrows shot up in genuine surprise. 'Bloody hell, I don't want to be a woman. No, all this,' he raised his hands and gestured at his clothes, 'it's only a disguise – a brilliant disguise, you have to agree. But you're right to say I was angry, because I was, and with good reason.'

'What "good reason" could there possibly be?' Geraldine asked.

'You wouldn't understand.'

'That's no answer. You don't know what we might understand.'

Jamie looked morose. 'How could you possibly understand? I was a child,' he replied, his voice rising in sudden fury, 'a child. And then she came along and straightaway she was the centre of everyone's attention. I might as well have ceased to exist.'

'I take it you're talking about your sister? The one who fell into the weir?' Geraldine asked. 'Her death wasn't an accident, was it? You pushed her into the water, knowing she couldn't swim.'

At her side she was aware that Ian had turned to look at her in surprise.

'Someone had to get rid of her,' Jamie murmured.

'So you killed your own sister because of what? Jealousy? Resentment? But that didn't help, did it?' Geraldine went on. 'Because the feelings wouldn't go away. Even after she died, you always knew your parents had loved her more than you. Your brother shunned you, because he knew what you had done. Perhaps he felt guilty because he was unable to save her when you pushed her into the weir. He couldn't live with that knowledge, so he turned to drugs. You destroyed his life along with your own, and your parents, when you murdered your sister. How did any of them deserve that?'

'I said you wouldn't understand,' Jamie told her.

Geraldine stared helplessly at him, lost for words.

'What about the others?' Ian asked. 'Grant and Felicity? You know they were both teachers, innocent people doing a decent job in society —'

'Innocent?' Jamie sneered, his black rimmed eyes swivelling round to gaze at Geraldine. 'Innocent? No one is innocent.'

'And the student. Why did you kill them? You didn't even know them, did you?'

Jamie let out a sigh. 'When they pulled my sister from the water, she didn't look any different. I mean, she was pale, and we knew she was dead because they told us she wasn't breathing, and she wasn't moving, but she didn't look any different. She was just dead.' He sounded almost offended.

'You were disappointed, weren't you? You wanted to see her blood, to know she was really gone from your life?'

Jamie's eyes lit up at the mention of blood. 'Yes, I wanted to see her life bleeding from her. I wanted to watch her die. Have you ever watched someone bleed to death, knowing you made that happen? No, I don't suppose you have.'

'Why did you do it?' Ian asked. 'They were strangers. They hadn't done anything to you.'

'It wasn't about your victims, was it?' Geraldine answered for Jamie. 'This was all about you and how killing them made you feel.'

Jamie nodded.

'How did you feel?' she asked. 'When you were killing your victims?'

'Watching them bleed to death was –' He paused, searching for words to describe the sensation, 'It was glorious!'

'You're sick,' Ian muttered.

'My client is clearly mentally disturbed,' the lawyer agreed, speaking for the first time in a while. 'He's not responsible for his actions.'

'That may be your defence in court,' Ian agreed, 'but you and I both know he's not some poor damaged victim, he's evil.'

'With at least three carefully planned murders on record,' Geraldine added. 'You're not going to get much sympathy out of any sane jury.'

There was nothing more to say, and Jamie was led back to his cell.

'It's just as well your little escapade ended in an arrest,' Ian said to Geraldine later, 'or you might have landed yourself in serious trouble. You certainly made me look a fool,' he added, but she could see he was trying not to smile.

'I still don't understand what you were doing, making such a huge fuss, calling out so much back up. What did you think was going on?' she asked.

'I thought you were trapped in there with Jamie.'

'I was. So what? Do you really think I'd still be in this job if I couldn't take care of myself?'

'What was I supposed to do when we couldn't get hold of you? I thought I was saving you.' Ian gave an embarrassed laugh.

'Actually, you did save me,' she replied softly.

'Well, you seemed to have the situation under control.'

'I'm not talking about that. I'm talking about a different sort of risk I faced.'

'What do you mean?'

Geraldine frowned. 'I was on the point of doing something I would have regretted for the rest of my life. But then I heard the sirens outside and it brought me back to who I am and what we're doing this for.'

'I'm not sure I follow you.'

'It's complicated.' She hesitated. 'You have to understand, he was threatening to kill me, and I really believe he would have done it. But the point is, I wanted to kill him. In that moment, I could so easily have strangled him. Even after I'd overpowered him and was no longer in any immediate danger, I don't know that I would have resisted the temptation to finish him off.'

Ian burst out laughing. 'Is that all? Bloody hell, woman, I have those moments all the time. We all do. I felt like killing *you* when we didn't know where you were.'

'I'm serious, Ian. This isn't a laughing matter. I was ready to kill him. I nearly did. What you're talking about is completely different. You knew you weren't really going to kill me. Or were you?' she added with a smile.

'Geraldine, you must know by now that you're the last person I'd ever want to hurt.'

'I'm serious, Ian. I nearly murdered a man. This wasn't just a thought, Ian, I had my arm round his throat and knew he couldn't breathe and I couldn't stop crushing his windpipe. It was like my muscles were acting without my control. I'm serious, Ian, I really think I was going to kill him. Then I heard the sirens and that's what stopped me. If you hadn't turned up when you did –'

She broke off, registering what Ian had said. But as she was wondering whether it was more than just a figure of speech, he turned and walked away.

61

THE KILLER WAS BEHIND bars but the atmosphere at the police station was far from jubilant. It was difficult to feel pleased when innocent people had been killed at the hands of a madman.

'l can't help feeling sorry for him in a way,' Ariadne said. 'I know he's a danger, but he's hardly responsible for his actions and he's going to be locked up for the rest of his life –'

'I certainly hope so,' Eileen interrupted her.

'What a sad existence.'

'It's going to be even sadder now,' Ian said with grim satisfaction.

'But is that really justice?' Ariadne asked. 'To punish someone who didn't seem capable of knowing that what he was doing was wrong?'

'No, it's not,' Geraldine responded so firmly that her colleagues all turned to look at her.

They had gathered in the pub for a drink to mark the close of the investigation, but it didn't feel much like a celebration.

'I know he'll be getting a psychiatric assessment, and they'll no doubt conclude what we could have told them, that he's insane, but what happened is an indictment of us all as a society. How was someone like Jamie left to his own devices and allowed to roam the streets without any help or supervision?' Geraldine asked. 'He's the one who'll serve a punishment, but we're all responsible. He should have been placed in a secure institution *before* he started killing people. What he needed was appropriate supervision, not complete freedom followed by a prison sentence.'

'He'll hardly be going to a normal prison if he's assessed as seriously disturbed,' Ariadne pointed out. 'He'll be placed in a psychiatric unit.'

'He's not that crazy,' Ian replied. 'He was clever enough to think of disguising his identity. That took some planning. If you ask me, he should be locked in a cell for life. But instead, he'll be placed in a secure mental institution where he'll receive any amount of cripplingly expensive treatment and care.'

Geraldine interrupted his diatribe. 'That's out of our control. What I'm asking is why three people had to be killed before that treatment was offered to him? Don't forget, he'd already killed his sister when he was a child, and we may well find out he killed other people before Grant, while he was travelling around the Australian outback, and Thailand, and goodness knows where else. He has a history of killing, going back over twenty years.'

'If that's true, and we don't know if it is,' Ian said, 'then I wonder what made him decide to come back here?'

'Perhaps because he thought of a way to disguise his identity,' Geraldine suggested.

'He might have been homesick,' Ariadne added.

'We'll probably never get to the truth of it, but my question is,' Geraldine said, 'what are we doing, as a society, to prevent these patterns of behaviour from continuing for so long?'

'Society,' Eileen said dismissively. 'Who is this society you're talking about? Who takes responsibility for the chronically sick? And the elderly? And the physically disabled? Social workers are so overworked it's criminal, and we're the ones who are left to pick up the pieces of these broken lives, to protect the public from them, because no one else is willing to do it.'

'But what can we do?' Geraldine asked.

'We can do our job,' Eileen replied. 'We can't change the world, Geraldine, but we can do everything in our power to protect the innocent. And that's what we do. Thanks to us, there's one less psychopath at liberty.' She raised her glass with a smile. 'So he won't be running around killing anyone else. Good work, everyone.'

The conversation moved on.

'Are you sure you're all right now?' Eileen asked Geraldine after a few moments. 'You had quite an ordeal.'

'Geraldine's tough,' Ian answered for her.

Geraldine just smiled.

Ian caught up with her when she was walking back to the car park.

'I was a bit flippant back there,' he said, taking her arm. '*Are* you all right, really?'

'Me? Oh, I'm fine. It's all part of the job. But what about you?'

'Me?' He sounded surprised.

'Have you decided what to do about Bev?'

He took a deep breath. 'I told her I want a divorce.'

'How did she take it?'

He paused, considering. 'Do you know, I'm not really sure. For all those years we were together, I've actually no idea what goes through her mind. She's gone back to live with her parents, so she's not on her own, and I dare say she'll meet someone else. Someone who's not a policeman, so he can give her the time and attention she wants. But as for her and me, it's over. And I can honestly say I'm not as sorry as I should be. If anything, it's a relief.'

Geraldine smiled. 'Then it was the right thing to do.'

'Do you really think so?'

'It's nothing to do with me, but yes, I do. You're better off on your own than trapped in a bad relationship.'

'What about starting a good one?'

'You mean Naomi?'

'What?'

Ian halted abruptly. 'What has she got to do with any of this?'

Geraldine stopped too. 'I thought – I thought –' she

stammered. 'Oh, nothing. I just thought maybe you and Naomi – I mean, you always seem to be together.'

'Yes, because I'm mentoring her. But that's all it is. We work together. It's nothing more than that.'

Geraldine didn't say that she was almost certain Naomi would like something more than that from her relationship with Ian.

'Well, I misunderstood,' she said. 'It's hardly surprising. She's young and pretty and smart.'

Ian shook his head. 'There's no way I'd look at another woman while –'

'I'm sorry, it's going to take you time to recover from your marriage.'

Ian hesitated. 'Geraldine, you know you've helped me through all this, probably more than you'll ever know –'

Geraldine interrupted him, with a faintly embarrassed laugh. 'There's no call for you to say that. And anyway, you've helped me far more than I've helped you.'

'How have I helped you?'

It was Geraldine's turn to hesitate. She had always believed Ian had been instrumental in securing her a post in York when she had been demoted and forced to leave the Met. Now she wondered whether he had actually played any part in her move after all.

'You've been a good friend to me,' she replied vaguely and paused, uncertain what to say next.

'I hope we'll always be friends.' He hesitated again. 'Actually, that's not exactly what I meant to say. Geraldine – I think I must be over Bev because – well, the fact is I've fallen for someone else. The trouble is, I'm not sure if she feels the same way.'

Afraid her face would betray her dismay, Geraldine looked away. She had been struggling to dismiss her own feelings for Ian. Now that he had found someone else, the time had come to put an end to her foolish fantasy once and for all.

'Perhaps you should ask her if she feels the same way?' she said. 'But be careful not to rush into anything on the rebound.'

She wasn't ready to hear about Ian's new love interest. Glancing around, she caught sight of Ariadne entering the car park and hailed her.

'Are you going somewhere to eat?' Ariadne called out, waving back.

Geraldine was hungry. Listening to Ian talk about his prospects with a potential girlfriend would have to wait.

'I'm starving,' she called back, hurrying to join Ariadne. 'Where shall we go?'

Acknowledgements

I would like to thank Dr Leonard Russell for his medical advice, and all my contacts in York for their help.

My thanks also go to Ion Mills, Claire Watts, Clare Quinlivan, Clare Holloway, Katherine Sunderland, and all the dedicated team at No Exit Press for their continued support, and continuing belief in Geraldine Steel. I could not ask for a stronger or kinder team of experts to help with Geraldine Steel.

Finally I would like to pay tribute to my brilliant editor, Keshini Naidoo, without whom Geraldine and I would not have survived. We have come a long way together and are not done yet!

A LETTER FROM LEIGH

Dear Reader,

I hope you enjoyed reading this book in my Geraldine Steel series. Readers are the key to the writing process, so I'm thrilled that you've joined me on my writing journey.

You might not want to meet some of my characters on a dark night – I know I wouldn't! – but hopefully you want to read about Geraldine's other investigations. Her work is always her priority because she cares deeply about justice, but she also has her own life. Many readers care about what happens to her. I hope you join them, and become a fan of Geraldine Steel, and her colleague Ian Peterson.

If you follow me on Facebook or Twitter, you'll know that I love to hear from readers. I always respond to comments from fans, and hope you will follow me on **@LeighRussell** and **fb.me/leigh.russell.50** or drop me an email via my website **leighrussell.co.uk**.

That way you can be sure to get news of the latest offers on my books. You might also like to sign up for my newsletter on **leighrussell.co.uk/news** to make sure you're one of the first to know when a new book is coming out. We'll be running competitions, and I'll also notify you of any events where I'll be appearing.

Finally, if you enjoyed this story, I'd be really grateful if you would post a brief review on Amazon or Goodreads. A few sentences to say you enjoyed the book would be wonderful. And of course it would be brilliant if you would consider recommending my books to anyone who is a fan of crime fiction.

I hope to meet you at a literary festival or a book signing soon!

Thank you again for choosing to read my book.

With very best wishes,

Leigh Russell

noexit.co.uk/leighrussell